Vail Pass

BY MARC LE VARN

ISBN 1-889707-24-4

Cover Design by Tara Stevens-Adams

Typesetting & Book Design by Cristin Wade

Printed in the United States

Vail Pass

Prelude:

Exodus

Every fall I am sure there are a thousand lost souls like me who make the drive over Vail Pass. Our Volkswagen Vans, Ford Escorts, and ancient Country Squire wagons bear license plates from far off and exotic locales such as New Jersey, Ohio, Dade County, Florida, and so on. Dressed in our college sweatshirts, with our possessions crammed into the backseats like gypsies, we arrive. We carry orange sleeping bags, ten pairs of blue jeans in various stages of decay, and doff baseball caps turned backwards on our heads, which make us resemble ducks whose bills have mutated and sprouted out the back of our skulls. Incurably romantic, each of us have migrated here for want of a better place or situation. We are the college educated children of the middle class, and our self pity is palpable.

Our un-insured jalopies are full of the essential items a twenty something year old ne'er do well requires. I have recently taken inventory of my worldly goods and find that I am the lucky owner of six and a half pair of Nike sneakers, some of which date back to a time when I had given up the practice of wearing socks. These I have lowered into the stream which runs by my campsite in an attempt to kill several of the local trout population. Though some environmental groups would surely protest that this method of fishing is akin to the use of dynamite, I absolve myself of all wrongdoing with the simple excuse of abject poverty. Sharing my campground with me is a family of six from Missouri who arrived last night by Winnebago and glared suspiciously at my Volkswagen Mini Bus. They have regarded me as some sort of lesser criminal, as surely all young men without jobs, a clue, or money must be...

October 21, 1991. Kelley Sapp paused for a moment before putting down his pen. Posed on a stool sized rock with his chin resting on his palm, a model for most young men his age. His t-shirt was white and grimy, and matched well with the green army shorts that covered his muscled thighs. His build was muscular, but not the meaty kind built in gyms with heavy

1

weights. Balanced atop of his broad shoulders sat the head of a classical Greek sculpture, except for the nose which was hooked and semitic. When not covered by the green baseball cap he favored, his black hair was thick and curly like wool. And when Kelley flapped his arm to shake out the cramp in his writing hand he resembled a swan much more than a duck.

Kelley was thinking. Completely unaware of the external world dancing about his heavy pate, he would have laughed had he been able to step outside of himself, The Thinker; Rodin's model. Who knows what silly problems cause the face to freeze with the spinning of internal cogs and wheels. Given to romantic notions, Kelley had moved to Vail on a whim. Living in a campground now, low on cash and more than desperate, he had grown wary of adults who asked him what his plans were. Almost two years ago he had graduated from the University of Massachusetts; and now he found his memories going sour, his world curdling.

The Volkswagen behind him contained all his possessions: a stereo, a CD collection containing all the hits of the Butthole Surfers, an old sleeping bag, un-washed clothes stuffed into industrial Hefty bags, ancient Kastle skis, museum quality Dolomite ski boots, and the library of paperbacks he had collected in school. These items, the van, and two and a half pounds of wild marijuana were all he owned.

He proofed the letter while shaking his wrist, finding himself both pleased and displeased with the cynical tone. The letter was for Z, who had spurned him. He hoped it would make him seem worldly and wise. The truth of his situation was far more simple. Kelley Sapp was drowning in the great ocean of his freedom.

He did not know what he was doing. He had no friends in the area. His parents were rightfully concerned that their son was spinning his wheels in a vacuum of indecision. Life had always been a large question mark for Kelley. He was against Republicans in principle, politics in general, Deadheads, patriotism, realistic novels, Hollywood, and people who believed in "The American Way". He did not want to go to war, but was fascinated with revolution, which would give him an excuse to carry a gun and shoot all the neo-fascists who wanted Kelley to knuckle under to what he so originally defined as The System. He tapped into his thoughts and continued translating them onto paper.

With so many of us drifting into town every day the search for housing resembles the situation in Mexico City. The vacation homes of the rich and powerful sit in un-used splendor while we grovel about in the trailer park for a moldy corner of a sofa. My fellow cast-offs scour the local real estate listings religiously, resembling so many sperm swimming toward the single egg in a blind, desperate gamble for fertilization. Rather than join them, I have come up with my own vagrant cast into the wind. Each day I shave and go about knocking on doors as if I was Avon calling. Today is day

2

number three. I have given myself five days to succeed, after which I will reconsider my life.'

Kelley Sapp's Volkswagen rumbled down the highway like an ancient albino rhino through the veldt, his window open and hair bouncing. Kelley cruised alongside cars and pulled an imaginary lever in the ceiling while honking his horn. Delighted children pressed their faces to the glass and waved to him.

Ahead, the outer limits of the Vail area sprouted condominiums. The condos filled the walls of the narrow valley. Each unit resembled the other as if they were inbred cousins. He exited at the suburb of Avon, thinking that surely this must be the pre-fab capital of the Western Hemisphere. His daily search began at the Silver Aspen Condominiums, a complex containing over six-hundred identical gray units.

Steadily, a stream of cars flowed in and out of the parking lots surrounding the unit blocks. The day was like summer, except for the light, which shimmered in a weak amber tone. He watched the people in their cars and kicked down the knot in his stomach. The romance of his move to Vail was now a memory, leaving only an incredible sense of loneliness in its wake.

He wandered around the Silver Aspen Condominiums, knocking on doors for over an hour. A knawing angst filled his stomach. For days he had been unable to pass anything but semi-liquid stool. He attributed this to his diet which consisted of nothing but the spiciest burritos available at Circle K. The stress he felt seemed unbearable. Kelley's whole life lay open in front of him and he had no idea where to begin. Up until this point every step had been pre-ordained. He had gone to school, high school, and college. He had wound his way to the end of the path with a blithe ignorance that left him stunned and disappointed when he at last held his diploma and stood with his parents for the obligatory photograph. Since graduation he was in a hazy dream remembering what he had been, and how certain life had seemed.

What had he done in the two years since graduation? Waited tables and tended bar. What had been the real education? What had been real? Kelley could discuss Mark Rothko and William Carlos Williams for hours. He had lost his first job in New York because of a customer's complaint that, "No waiter should be allowed to leave my water glass empty and lecture me on Nietzsche!" And he had been happy to lose the job. He had been happy to lose others. And he had moved to Vail with a most positive attitude.

Musing grandly about conversations he knew would never arise in this place, Kelley knocked at another door. Who here in Vail could discuss Langston Hughes as well as he? Futurist painting? Who had read all of Pynchon? "Rose is a rose": words were all he knew. And he knew more than most.

He had not been paying very much attention to the door of 201-B.

3

It was a pleasant surprise for him to discover an attractive young lady in the open doorway.

"Hi, I'm Kelley," he introduced himself. Christ that was stupid. His face froze in a plastic smile of idiocy. What now? Should he parlay this brilliant opening into a frank discussion of Walt Whitman's homosexuality. *"I celebrate myself, Kelley Sapp, and what I assume is a load of crap because you have a place to live and I don't."*

With a pleasant and reflexive smile the young lady regarded Kelley with the nascent curiosity young members of the opposite sex find unavoidable. Her appearance was similar to many other young women who flit with the change in seasons from one sporting life to another. Her hair matched the molting leaves of the fall aspens, now nearly barren on the hillsides. With the fall chill she had donned heavy twill hiking shorts and an aubergine fleece top. An enchanting ewe halfway into her winter coat, the swell of her breasts pressed against the fleece in a natural show of attractiveness. Toasted skin covered her striated legs making them glow with warmth despite their muscularity. Though she was Kelley's age crows feet tickled the corners of each eye; bearing witness to the hours she spent in direct sunlight.

"I know you," she said mistakenly, "didn't I lose my ring in your car?"

"No, I don't think so," Kelley stumbled out of his dead smile. He thanked Christ she had spoken. Unconsciously, he turned that corner and began comparing her with Z. This woman's hair was white blond, amber at the roots, and hung to her hips in a long, straight cascade that accentuated her curvaceous body the way a ruler would a ribbon. He liked her.

Here, Kelley thought, was the opposite of Z. He recalled Z's plastic devices, her studded dog collar and black lipstick, her daily changes in hair color. Everything about Z's appearance had been carefully planned to produce one reaction: shock. Z had been the woman only an anarchist could love. In front of Kelley stood all that was not Z.

His up-and-down had not gone un-noticed.

"I'm Kellie Kay, and my boyfriend would tell you that my purpose on Earth is to tantalize and send raving the race of man. Which is a quote from somewhere." Kellie Kay said this in an undeniably sarcastic tone while rolling her eyes back into her skull.

"Excuse me for being so flippant," she mock apologized to Kelley, "but my boyfriend and I were having an argument. You see, I don't think my purpose on Earth centers around men at all. If anything, men center their lives around me. I can do very nicely on my own. Hello honey."

She turned her cold attention to a young man with light blond hair that squeezed into the doorway to peer at Kelley. He did so with the eyes of a fish, expressing no interest in Kelley, simply observation.

"It's involuntary on her part," the boyfriend spoke in a deadpan, "she can't help tantalizing men and sending them raving. Which is a quote from Pynchon's _V_. Have you read Pynchon?"

"No," Kelley lied by instinct.

"Kris Blaze," he introduced himself in the same monotone, before adding, "I suppose you're here about the room. Kellie, I've got hot wax on my skis, could you show him it? Pepper sent you, right?"

"Uh, no. I was actually looking for C-building. I'm supposed to look at an apartment there. But, would you mind if I had a look, just as long as I'm here?"

"Come in," said Kellie Kay, "Please come in. It's such a small room, but I hope you'll like it." She stepped out of the doorway and invited him inside. Kris impassively shrugged his shoulders before disappearing back into the kitchen.

"He's a bore," Kellie whispered as they walked inside.

The room she showed him was standard. Bare plaster walls and an off-feces colored carpet. It reminded Kelley vaguely of a cheap hotel in any part of the country. It had a bed. It was wonderful and he knew it.

During the summer Kris and Kellie shared it as a study. Since Kris was a professional skier on the Pro Mogul Tour he would be gone for a great deal of the winter. Kellie Kay was a raft guide in the summer and ski instructor in the winter. With Kris gone so much and her fairly permanent they were renting it out.

"Three fifty a month," Kellie ran her fingers through her hair, "and we split utilities. I'll leave you to look at it."

Kelley watched her bare feet do a small tattoo across the living room before she disappeared into a large pink floor pillow that dangled her naked legs like the tantalizing bottom half to some pink confection.

Two hours later, with his worldly possessions safely claiming all the floor space, Kelley internally composed a hyperbolic addendum to Z's letter. Life had tossed a chunk of blind luck at Kelley's feet. That was the way of it he supposed.

"I have found an apartment with a budding tri-athlete named Kellie Kay. Every morning before breakfast she jogs three miles and does one hundred chin ups. During the day she works as a raft guide and saves her money for the all female ascent of K-2 that she and two friends are planning. Her boyfriend is a former NCAA champion in gymnastics and keeps a trampoline in their bedroom. The low plaster ceiling is dented and fractured from Kris's repeated mis-judgments and consequent collisions. This has caused considerable strife between us and the upstairs neighbors who own a waterbed. Any night now I expect we could all perish in a flood. Unless, of course, we die in a fire first. Fire?"

Smoke was coming from the kitchen. On the cheap white dining table, an iron was burning its way through the paint and into the oak. Against

5

the table was a pair of skis which had been getting a coat of wax.

"Kris, your skis," Kelley yelled.

"Shit!" Kris ran from the bathroom, book in hand.

"Moron!" Kellie yelled at Kris.

Kelley, Kellie, and Kris circled the smoldering table. A large, semi triangular impression of an iron was branded into the paint.

"I'll buy a new one," Kris seemed apologetic.

"With what?" Kellie brushed him off. "Just get some newspapers and do it someplace else next time."

They locked eyes for a second before Kris blinked and turned away.

"I've gotta train at the gym," he announced in his even tone before walking out the door as if nothing had happened. Kelley watched him go, the most unconcerned man in the world. Or was he naive? Kelley couldn't decide.

When he looked back at Kellie Kay, he was surprised to find her close to tears. "I have a question," she sniffed. "Do you find me attractive?"

"I suppose, yes. I find you very attractive."

"Really?"

"Yes."

"How can you be sure?"

Kelley watched Kellie's sadness fade into thought.

"How can you be sure that I'm attractive? You may think I'm attractive. But is that a certain indicator that I am?"

"I suppose not."

"In other words, even though you may think I'm attractive, I might not be?"

"If you believe in abstract ideals."

"Such as?"

"Such as beauty, for example." The quixotic Kellie Kay faded. Outside the sun was shining. How could he be sure it was the sun that shined? Maybe it is really the earth that shines. How can you be sure, Kelley pondered hypothetically?

"The ancient Greeks," he continued, "believed in abstract forms. Beauty, for example, had an absolute, idealized model. This idealized form floated in the heavens, and *was* beauty. All other forms of beauty, including yours, would be thought of in terms of how they related to the ideal of beauty sort of like God, the perfect being. If you are Christian, you believe in a perfect God. You try to measure up to God's perfect standard, even though it's impossible."

"But how do you know I'm attractive!?"

"I don't!"

Kellie's barometric face took a precipitous drop.

"Really?"

"I can only think that you're attractive."

"How awful! You think I'm attractive, but you don't know for certain if I am."

"No. I know you are attractive."

"But you just said you didn't."

"I know that what I think is correct. I am self-validating, and need no other confirmation of my opinions. Because I think you are attractive, you are. But that is me. In my world, you are attractive."

"But that's only your point of view."

"That's all we have."

"Well I don't care what just *you* think. Christ, I ask for a simple pacification of my insecurities and you give me a philosophical treatise on how you may think I'm beautiful, but the rest of the world might not. That is not reassuring, believe me. Have you ever had a girlfriend?"

"Yes, of course."

"Well, you must have driven her absolutely out of her skull."

"No. She drove me out of my skull."

"You must have driven her crazy too. I don't believe you couldn't have."

"What makes you think I'm so horrible?"

"You talk in circles."

"Do you think I'm attractive?" Kelley asked.

"Yes."

"And...?"

"That's my opinion."

"Right, precisely my point in the first place."

"Do you want to sleep with me?"

"Yes," Kelley wondered what his reply would lead to.

"You're typical," was all Kellie said.

"C'mon you would have been upset if I'd said no."

"That's not true at all. You don't understand women."

"I think you're right."

"Well just don't try anything."

"Ok."

"All right."

Kelley and Kellie went furiously into their opposite bedrooms.

An hour later the old sleeping bag was rolled out on the bed in Kelley's room. Kelley twisted himself a big joint, lit up, and took in his new abode. The simplicity of four walls, two windows, a floor and a ceiling amazed him. He remembered what it had felt like in school when he would return to his dorm room after a long day. The tiny room would be the same as he had left it in the morning. It contained none of the memories he held.

7

The feeling of a journey completed, victories and defeats, toil with books and work, would come to him as he walked across the finish line that was the threshold. Still damp towel on the bed, papers on the floor, poster on wall, everything waiting for him to return. The silence of the sameness had echoed and made him deaf, forcing him to stand still and take it all in. Where he had been, what he had done, since he had last left.

It was with that same feeling that Kelley surveyed his new *casa*. The long drive across the country, the stress of uncertainty and not knowing, all stopped here with this room. The end of the journey was here in this room. Nights spent at rest stops in Nebraska. Meals eaten at Bob's Big Boy near Grinell. The field of wild hemp he had found and gathered near Iowa City. The pot barely got him stoned. He sucked on the joint. It gave him more of a headache than anything. Four walls, two windows, a floor and a ceiling, the journey completed. He stood silent. Two small windows admitted a dusty sunlight that played with the twisted cords of hemp smoke. He waited until the room began to resonate with sameness, echoing itself, transforming into a place, a landmark in his life. This was his room, where he lived. From now on it would wait for him, and for whatever adventures he encountered between the time he woke until the time he returned to its embrace.

Ahh, Z. I have found a place to live with a girl you would hate. I love you and miss you very much.

Sincerely,

Kelley Sapp

Chapter 1:

Genesis

The Vail Valley is expanding. Balloonlike, the legend of its name has floated to all corners of the world. In Lebanon, where skiers swish between the cypress, the name drifts on air currents come down from the high cliffs of Chamonix. In guttural German and romantic Italian, the name passes into Arabic before continuing down. A zephyr above India, Brahmans poke their delicate noses into the air and sniff the prayer of a million skiers from between mooing cows. Down, down, the name whistles. Boomeranging, it lodges in an Aussie. "What the hell, mate? Finish that pint of Swan and we're off!" Could the Kiwis be far behind their cousins? A breeze ruffles the fine wool of the Merino sheep, and the shepherds drop their shears.

In Mexico, Peru, Bolivia, and Venezuela, the lily-white descendants of Cortez set sail for Eldorado. Borne aloft in aluminum cigars. Shimmering golden in the Rockies. The name resonates and echoes with the throb of a million jets. Vail. Home to those who seek, if only for a week. It answers their prayers for comfort, adventure, vacation. So many more, from so many places. Tokyo, New York, Los Angeles. In the Bronx, B-Boys wear ski parkas and knit wool caps. Stone cold lamping under the streetlight, they hang. While on Park, next to Madison, the people pack. Short, easy, euphonious: Vail.

In the beginning was the Gondola and two chairlifts. Two hotels soon followed, and the name was born on the site of a former sheep ranch. Nestled like a warm hollow beneath the thirteen thousand foot peaks of the Gore range, the Vail Valley extends over twenty miles east to west. Low, humpbacked mountain ridges frame the narrow valley along both sides. Construction has been crawling down this narrow path for three decades. A new ski area in the town of Avon is a mere ten miles west of Vail. Hotels and over one hundred and thirty restaurants crowd the cramped valley floor. Bulldozers and backhoes inch westward in a wake of condominiums and trailer parks.

We are headed to the western edge of the construction frontier, to a place where a new development is popping out of the sagebrush. Early in the spring of 1989, on top of a hummocky little mountain twenty five miles west of Vail, shipments of the most exotic building materials available began arriving. Eighteen wheel trucks spent half a day each crawling up the switchbacking little dirt lane that led to the construction site. A parade watched by elk, hare, hawk, and deer, the procession wound like a circus train with loads displayed on flatbed trucks like animals. Thirty tons of Manchurian slate, hauled from China, creaked up first. Destined for roofing, the slate had begun its odyssey six months ago on the backs of mules. One container ship later, and a thousand miles spent baking on American Highways, the slate arrived.

Next came the trees. Six majestic Douglas Firs, one to each truck, jackknifed around the switchbacks. Stripped of their bark, creosoted, preserved, and mummified. The corpse trees had been mined illegally from the last great stands of old growth timber in Oregon. Transformed into beams and supports for the new lodge. They stood as naked masts, stripped of their foliage and branches.

Stained glass windows, purchased from decaying gothic cathedrals in South America, were hauled up whole in their leaden frames. Twenty eight marble bathtubs, hand carved into swans with dragon feet by artisans in Carrara, began the bestiary. The stuffed heads of water buffalo, elk, emu, grizzly, moose, and antelope followed. And on one smaller truck, bound with ropes and tackle, a full grown polar bear stiffly rode.

Construction continued for over a year. Great cement trucks mixed vats of stucco for the walls. Brass bedframes and miles of pipe later, it was over. There stood a castle. Like the bastard child of some mad Bavarian Prince, the Snowy Mountains Guest Lodge reposed with all the grandeur of a fairy tale. Turreted towers thrust skyward toward the clouds. High stucco walls shaded a lovely tint of periwinkle matched the deep blue of the mountain sky. On clear days, when viewed from afar, the lodge would melt back into a shimmer of camouflage.

Finding the Snowy Mountains Guest Lodge could be a particularly disconcerting task. On opening day directions to the party were: 'Take a left off the highway. Drive for three miles past the Tailing Ponds. At the dirt road turn right. Drive for three miles. After the decaying barn, stop. Look! To your left is a narrow dirt road. Follow this for four miles. At the broken aspen tree turn left again. Follow for two miles. When you round the corner watch out for the cliff and stay to the inside. The Lodge will be immediately to your right. Please RSVP.

And once inside the Snowy Mountains Guest Lodge, logic dissipates in a consistently hazy cloud of paradox. Everyone is always lost inside

10

the Snowy Mountains Guest Lodge. Vacationers stumble about like blind mice in vain attempts to find their rooms. Employees disappear for hours at a time with no clear recollection of where they have been or what they have done. Clocks and watches lose hours and minutes in a disjointed frenzy of clacking jewels and short circuited chips. Only the walls mark the time. With the steady regularity of calm snowfall, the interior stucco flakes like sand in an hourglass. Everything reeked with the moldy stench of decay. Despite this, the lodge continued to operate and function. Restaurant Au Naturel gained a national reputation. Life continued as if nothing were amiss. And when Kelley Sapp applied for a job as a waiter in the restaurant he considered it a lucky stroke that he was hired.

The snow had been falling for twenty four hours when Kelley Sapp pulled his V.W. into the employee parking lot for his third day of work. The early morning sky hung shroud-like and peppered with dandruff snowflakes. Opium quiet drifted through Kelley's ears as he padded through a carpet of white toward the shadowed lodge. He felt as if he were in a dream. Four hours prior to his early morning sojourn, he had stood exhausted, drinking a beer, in almost the exact same spot he stood in now. Dinner service at *Au Naturel* had lasted until an early hour. Two tables of rich Mexicans, who had arrived late and catatonic from the nearly impassable road, stayed at their tables until two in the morning. Clucking like chickens, they ordered more and more wine until they passed out at the tables and were sent home to Vail, stacked like cordwood, in eight cabs. With hallucinatory *deja vu* Kelley regarded the presence of the lodge.

At one point long ago in restaurant time, meaning close to sixteen hours in the past, there had been a chain smoking, neurotic flatulent man named Pickle. It was Pickle who had been scheduled to work this morning's breakfast shift. In fact, Pickle worked every breakfast shift at the lodge. Pickle belonged to that strange fraternity in life that adheres to the art of knocking little white spheroids around great expanses of watered and cut grass. He hated snow with as much vigor as he detested low tar cigarettes. Consequently, he worked all winter, night and day, to support his summer golf habit. Fueled on a diet of nicotine, caffeine, and potato chips, he propelled himself about the Snowy Mountains Guest Lodge in the manner of a jet. Leaving no doubt as to where he had been, and striking fear into the hearts of those who saw him approaching, Pickle's baby dill body and sweet gherkin head were known and avoided by all. His skin was the pallor of decaying green leaves, and his knobby head completely bald. In summertime, his scalp metamorphosed into a pimple and his epidermis took on the color of caramelized mint jelly.

In summary, he was the court dwarf, the humpback of the Snowy

11

Mountains Guest Lodge, hobgoblin, and general poltergeist of the castle. Pickle's effigy, if carved in high relief and hung from the stucco parapets, would have carried with it the same aura of a gargoyle.

In Europe he would have been tolerated for the sake of tradition. But when Pickle let loose in the kitchen during the previous breakfast shift the pilot lights in the stainless steel stoves flared like roman candles and the whole lodge was evacuated into the ankle deep snow that covered the parking lot. Whether or not a momentary disturbance in the gas lines had occurred was immaterial. Chef Christian LeForrestier had had enough. He took Pickle in his delicate French beak and, in the manner of a griffin, tossed him out the employee entrance. Fired. Kaput. No more Pickle.

What now for Kelley Sapp? Poor Kelley Sapp, he with the least seniority; Kelley Sapp, the only one scheduled to be off the next day. Sloth, the alcoholic Maitre D', had called Kelley into his office a mere five hours ago.

"Uh, Kelley," he had begun while pouring himself a healthy slug of Puligny-Montrachet, "would you mind picking up Pickle's breakfast shift in the morning?"

Kelley Sapp ambled up the driveway in tired swerves. His head tilted toward the ground, he shielded his eyes from the falling snow with an open palm. He passed into the shelter provided by a looming stucco tower and relaxed his arm. The lights outside the foyer glowed like oil lanterns underneath the carriageway. In their yellow haze, poised one on top of the other, sat three vanilla ice cream snowballs. Imperfectly round gnomons, they formed a snowman. Black eyes peeked out at Kelley and a disarmingly simple mouth of red yarn was folded into a smile underneath the eyes. The nose was indeed a carrot, and mawkish stick arms pointed out at odd angles from "Frosty's" middle lump.

Kelley Sapp began to ponder the possibilities. He broke into a trot and set course for Frosty.

Inside the Snowy Mountains Guest Lodge twenty eight rooms slept and snored in unison. The guests would soon wake and shake their eyes before tossing back the sheets with a puff of blue dust.

They would want coffee, hot chocolate, warm croissants, seven grain whole wheat bread, oleo, honey, butter, bagels, and granola. Some would want eggs and omelettes, French toast and other such warm breakfast goodies that get the engine going on cold winter mornings. But they would not be able to get these hot items. There was hot chocolate, coffee, frozen bagels and such; but no eggs. The Snowy Mountains Guest Lodge offered a complimentary European Breakfast Buffet for its guests. Translation: no waffles, bacon, omelettes, sausage, hash browns, pancakes, grits, French toast with powdered sugar and maple syrup, none; and especially, no eggs. Neither poached, scrambled, over easy, over hard, sunnyside up, soft boiled, hard boiled, deviled, or any other way: no eggs! There's the buffet: go and stuff your face.

Kelley accelerated, churning his feet in the manner of a cartoon character. He kicked up a trail of dusty snow and homed in on Frosty's head. Die, he murmured, die you miserably happy piece of marshmallow fluff.

He would smash its head! Ahh! The injustice. Kelley Sapp was not merely angry with his job. He wished to express a far greater displeasure with the world as a whole and rumbled forward with every intention of committing an act of violence.

When he extended his leg for the kick and slipped, the whole world turned upside down. Frosty leered above him. In the snow, Kelley rubbed his ass.

"Oh screw you, Frosty," Kelley swore. He collected his feet and let the stormclouds gather over his head. When he pushed Frosty's head off with both hands it tumbled to the snow and broke open like a fractured lump of sugar.

And so it was that on the third day of his employment at the Snowy Mountains Guest Lodge, Kelley Sapp set rolling the chain of events that he could in no way have foreseen. With gloating happiness, he turned away from the deceased Frosty and bounced in through the main doors to the lobby. It had been three weeks since he had moved in with Kellie Kay. Today was opening day for Vail Mountain, and the season was upon him now. He had a job, a ski pass, a place to live, and had decided that he was in love with Kellie Kay. Of course love is a very difficult thing to identify. Various vague thoughts milled through his head before the door shut, sealing Kelley away from the outside world and its concerns. He was at work now. Morgue-like silence filled the air.

At the front desk sat Friday, the night auditor. Feet set between the brass service bell and antique telephone, he reclined back in the chair with a lolling head that sent snores up toward the ceiling. Flecks of powder blue stucco lay scattered like confetti all over the desk and stuck in Friday's short afro like pilled fabric. The quiet of a church hung in the air. Only the ticking of the grand cuckoo clock filled the lobby.

Kelley studied Friday. It was the same guy that had told him that odd story.

A week ago they had met, when Kelley had been sitting in the lobby directly beneath a giant elk head while filling out his application. Friday had walked behind him and begun to read Kelley's vital statistics out loud.

13

"Go away," Kelley had said, before twisting around to see who was behind him. There stood Friday, the only black man Kelley had spotted since coming to Vail. A thirtyish man, with ink-black skin and the shoulders of an aesthete, Friday wore a blue blazer with brass buttons, a red tie, and a little brass nametag that read, 'Friday.'

Ignoring Kelley, he commented in a loud voice, "Nice tie." Kelley had tugged at his matching crimson rope.

"You'll probably get hired," Friday continued. "Not many people around here bother to dress up. Since we'll be working together I thought I should introduce myself. Friday. I usually work the dead shift."

They had shaken hands amiably before Friday leaned back over Kelley's shoulder and again began reading Kelley's application out loud. "Graduated Acton High School, Acton Massachusetts, 1986. Graduated U. Mass. With a degree in what field, may I ask?"

"Twentieth century art history."

"And now you want to be a waiter. Excellent!" Friday had exclaimed. "But, before you start work here there are a few things you should know first. Number one, if you don't have housing yet they won't hire you. Number two, if you break your leg skiing you will lose your job. Number three is the polar bear."

The lobby of the Snowy Mountains Guest Lodge resembled the nave of a church. Delicate blue walls arched toward the cathedral ceiling, their surface crowded with the mounted heads of grazing animals arranged as saints around the rose windows that lit the ship's interior with lavender sun. Four Louis XVI couches were the pews before the altar of the fireplace. And like a white Templar guardian of the lobby, the stuffed polar bear resided in frozen attack next to the Steinway. The Snowy Mountains Guest Lodge lobby charted a course for comfort and escape. Masts made of Douglas Fir shot upward to invisible sails. A veritable Noah's ark for the rich and famous, only the polar bear showed signs of malice.

"Has his eye out for a seal?" Kelley had commented.

"It seems quite ferocious, doesn't it?" Friday had leaned over and began whispering his story into Kelley's ear. They both locked heavy gazes onto the enigma that was the bear. "I was at the Denver Zoo the day it died. Well, it didn't actually die that day: it was infected. I had just come from the monkey house and was deeply engrossed in my copy of Darwin's Origin of Species while I was walking toward the polar bear compound. It was a warm day in June, probably two years ago, and I was involved in a particularly interesting passage that compared the skulls of *Homo sapiens* with earlier forms of man when I bumped into the skinhead. He was dressed in the usual manner for a member of that sub-order, meaning naked pate, black leather, white skin, and a single furrowed eyebrow and sloping forehead that had me going back and forth between an illustration of *Homo erectus* and the real thing that I had in front of me.

'I say, the monkey house is back that way,' I told him, trying to be of some assistance.

'Bugger off and go back to the jungle, spear chucker,' he said to me.

"Well, oooga booga to him too, I thought. But I was somewhat perplexed since the Zoo is not within the normal range of the skinheads' habitat. And there, in front of me, occupying the viewing area of the polar compound, was a veritable herd of neo-Nazis holding quart beers in brown paper bags, pawing at the concrete, and looking very territorial. I quickly retreated behind the penguin display and covertly began to watch what was undoubtedly a strange tribal ritual, rich in hidden codes and messages.

"With an expectant air the group milled about for a while quaffing beer until the male polar bear emerged from his cave and lumbered over toward the pool for a swim. All the skinheads formed rank at the sight of him and shouted, 'Sieg Heil', saluting somewhat drunkenly the polar bear. I must say in defense of the polar bear that he seemed completely unfazed by all of the attention he was receiving. But the poor dear had his own problems, which I will get back to later.

"After a bit of speech-making about Aryan supremacy, the wrath of God, and Amerika, all of which seemed to have nothing to do with polar bears, a pale sickly skinhead was elevated above the rest of the herd where he stood swaying while his friends spontaneously burst into a spirited rendition of 'Deutschland Uber Alles.' He swayed on the shoulders of his companions, singing along with them in a horrid scratchy voice, then dove headfirst over the fence and into the little polar bear pool for a visit. Of course, he was completely devoured within a matter of minutes. The whole thing reminded me of Wagner, what with all that singing and blond hair and blood."

"What on earth did he do that for?" Kelley had asked.

Friday had explained that the skinhead the bear ate had been infected with the AIDS virus. Troubled by the controversial nature of his disease he had decided to commit suicide by diving into the polar bear compound and thereby sacrificing himself to the revered symbol of the white bear; which the skinheads, for reasons that seemed clear enough to them, took to be a symbol of Aryan supremacy. Zoo officials, Friday explained, had kept most specifics as quiet as possible.

"But the saddest thing of all," Friday had continued, "was that the poor polar bear had recently been under a great deal of stress. I told you that he had his own troubles, and here's where they come into play. It turns out that the male polar bear had recently been introduced to a new mate who had grown up in an Arctic three-ring circus. This young female polar bear had fallen in love with the lead act of the circus at a very early and impressionable age. As a result of her infantile obsession, she would not have sex with

15

the male polar bear unless he first barked like a seal and clapped his paws together at the same time. Of course, the male polar bear had absolutely no way of understanding this and was horribly confused by the fact that daily Zoo officials were taking him over to the seal exhibit in the hopes that he might catch a clue.

Friday had gestured over toward the stuffed bear, which now stood in a shaft of sacramental light. "All this confusion gave him a bleeding stomach ulcer. The first tests for HIV came back positive on the very day he learned to bark," Friday had concluded sadly.

Kelley's confusion was matched only by the cloak of depressive amazement that swept over him in a tube of blue. The walls parted like smoke and opened onto corridors that led to tiny garrets where mad poets and dreamers cradled their heads against windows in foetal supplication. The cackle of their fractured dreams echoed in a chorus of empty bottles that dropped longingly to the basement where they smashed in soft pops. Their deaths echoed and grew until, with maddening ferocity, they struck Kelley headlong between his eyes. So this was the imperfect world - an apartment with Sybil and a job in the land of abortioned lives. Is everyone crazy?

"What's the point?" Kelley had asked.

"The point, my young neophyte friend, is on the very tip of your tongue. You ask what is obvious. Is it not fitting that in the magnificent Snowy Mountains Guest Lodge there is a ferocious polar bear which, to the uninformed observer, would appear to have led an adventurous life out on the Arctic pack ice? I ask you to consider what the polar bear seems to be and compare it with the pathetic life it actually led, and the miserable manner in which it died. Could this be a metaphor for the very lodge in which we now sit? I ask you to contemplate the idea that things are not what they seem to be, especially in the case of those of us who work in the hotel. But now I see Sloth coming over to interview you and will depart without further ado. Farewell, Kelley. And if we should happen to meet again, you will be one of us. Friday bowed his head and withdrew.

There was a moment when Kelley could have run. The door stood open, unfiltered blue sky and sun streamed into the lobby. The songs of birds chirruped and life crept in among the blue walls. A shudder convulsed the span of Douglas Firs and a fresh rain of stucco floated from above in downy blue flakes, smothering the light. *Sleep now Kelley.* The dance of red and blue prisms cartwheeled from the windows. *Sleep and stay with us.* The door closed. Kelley Sapp sighed and waited, and waited...

Au Naturel, the restaurant in the Snowy Mountains Guest Lodge, had been designed in the manner of a tunnel. Abstract frescoes of bleeding reds and blues covered the windowless walls. Rough-hewn oaken ribs ran in symmetrical spaces down the entire length of the dining room. It had been remarked by more than one dazed customer that the decor made one feel as though he were sitting in the belly of a whale. The damp air did nothing to alleviate this impression and the vomit of color on the walls lent credence to the hypothesis that it was, indeed, a very sick whale.

Pressed against the edge of the dining room stood the buffet table. Carved from black wood, the table dated from the Middle Ages. A brass tag attached to it read:

> The Table of Lumsden of Strathdrummond
> Circa 1166 A.D.
> Lord of a vast stretch of barren moorland,
> legend has it that in a fit of rage,
> Lumsden of Strathdrummond
> one day hurled this table from the top
> window of the castle tower.
> Landing in the moat, the table was preserved
> in the cold peaty water until the great drought
> of 1968. Lumsden was supposedly a practitioner
> of the Black Arts.

The thermos jug slipped and fell to the cold flagstones. It exploded with a crack, and drenched Kelley's hose with droplets of steaming java. Dressed in his work uniform, Kelley resembled the liveried manservant of a European noble. He bent over in puzzlement. How could the pot have fallen? He was sure he had placed it far away from the edge. "Damn this stupid uniform," he thought as he attempted to rub the coffee stains out of the white hose. He imagined he resembled an extra for a Shakespeare production. But this was real. It was his job, and he could find no room for humorous thoughts concerning the immediate indignity.

When the alarm rang on Friday's watch he was not surprised to find it was running a half hour late. On his way to grab some breakfast in the kitchen, he strode into the dining room, whistling a warning to all ghosts and hobgoblins that he would be swinging 'round the corner soon. A recent convert to all things supernatural, Friday was not surprised to see Kelley sweeping up the remnants of the coffeepot. He paused his whistling, and as a teacher, said to Kelley, "You must put a napkin under the warm pots. She doesn't like heat. You should have seen it the day they tried to put a fondue on her. Cheese was everywhere. The whole floor was a congealed mess of fontina. There, there, baby," Friday petted the table, "Kelley didn't know you're so particular."

Kelley picked up the dustpan and together with Friday strode into the gloomy confines of the kitchen. "Is everything around here just a bit, I don't know, odd?" Kelley swung his arms, gesturing about the kitchen. During the past two nights at work he had not voiced his suspicion that things were out of the ordinary. With the revelation of the sensitive table, he glanced all about, confirming the queerness that surrounded him. Large cast

17

iron pots, straight out of <u>Macbeth</u>, hung from chains over gas burners. The brick walls were coated with a thick tar-like mold. Though the floor wasn't dirt, it was anyone's guess what it could be. Bits of tile poked out near the ancient wooden tub the dishwashers used, as if the kitchen were built over an archaeological site. Wafting from the dark corners, where bits of anonymous nests and decaying organic material lay heaped and composting, came the undeniable odor of a swamp.

"It's all authentic," Friday explained. "We have a special permit from the county for a historical and working rendition of a medieval castle's kitchen. Except for some of the modern appliances like stoves and sinks, everything is as it would have been back then." In a low voice, he added, "I don't think it's very sanitary. But, it was the owner's, Mr. Posthelwait, idea. He spent over four million dollars on the reconstruction. Even had an old castle carted in, smashed it, and put the rubble underneath this one for a foundation. Every once in a great while someone gets quite ill in the dining room, but we haven't had a fatality yet, thank goodness."

Bowl of granola and banana in hand, Friday followed Kelley back into the dining room. Being careful, now, to place authentically coarse linen napkins under the coffee pots, Kelley resumed the task of setting the buffet. Wicker baskets full of golden croissants were piled next to the whole grained breads and bowls of fresh cut fruit. Friday leaned back in his chair, gazing up at the frescoed ceiling, and hummed. He rocked his head back and forth, and Kelley imagined he must be quite mad. Despite this feeling, he was careful to place a thick pad between the table and toaster. Guests began arriving. They lined up at the buffet and shuffled along with their padded feet. If asked, Kelley was sure each one would admit to a night of insomniac sleep.

"It was so strange," he heard one woman murmuring to another, "I got up to go to the bathroom and couldn't find the door. When I tried to find the light, I stumbled about so loudly that Reginald picked up the flashlight he keeps by the bed and turned it on. I was standing on the open balcony with five hundred feet between myself and the ground..."

Friday's humming grew into a drone. The guests ate in drugged silence. They finished their plates and marched off with hypnotic stares. From the bowels of the kitchen came the tinkerbel chime of the room service bell. Kelley groaned and marched through the kitchen doors with a stack of used plates. After dumping the plates in the wooden tub, he yanked on the chain attached to the bell. Three hundred feet above him the yank registered on a corpulent hand and the ringing ceased. Kelley grabbed the tube and put the earphone to his head.

Three hundred feet above Kelley, Graham Tunniwinkle, of New York City, shouted his breakfast order into the brass horn that was attached to the authentic medieval voice tube. Beside him sat his wife, the lovely Mrs.

Tunniwinkle, and his precious son, Graham Jr.. The Tunniwinkles' favorite meal of the day was breakfast. Unlike anyone else in the hotel, they had enjoyed a restful night's sleep and were ready to devour large helpings of their favorite breakfast food: eggs.

At the other end of the voice tube, Kelley Sapp readied his pen for the order.

In a faint whisper, Mr. Tunniwinkle began. "Room 27 here. Coffee, orange juice." Kelley dutifully scribbled down the order. The Tunniwinkles paused. Unbeknownst to Kelley, a heated discussion was underway in room twenty seven. "Graham!" Mrs. Tunniwinkle rolled her sulfurous eyes, "you know I can only eat my eggs scrambled dry."

"Well why don't we just get a dozen scrambled dry then, and a dozen sunnyside up."

"Daddy," young Graham Jr. protested, "I like mine poached, with asparagus and hollandaise. You promised! You promised!"

"Ok. Three dozen it is then," Graham Tunniwinkle Sr. capitulated. He patted Graham Jr. on the head and pinched a roll of his wife's delicately layered stomach. Mrs. Tunniwinkle giggled, and Graham Jr. jumped up on the bed, where he began bouncing like a spongy ball while singing at the top of his lungs, "Eggs, eggsy wegsy, eggs. I luvs eggs much more den pigs!" Graham Jr's mother and father joined him in the chorus, "'Cause pigs can't beat, a li'l baby chicken meat. I don't eat caviar from the sea, I eats eggs 'cause eggs is me!"

Three oblong bodies jiggled about room twenty seven in delight. A shudder of blue stucco attempted to quiet them, but nothing could suppress their inane mirth. With a resigned sigh, the blue menace withdrew, granting the Tunniwinkles general ablution due to insanity. Mr. and Mrs. Tunniwinkle exchanged happy glances, for Graham Jr. had suffered a scare that morning which had dampened his spirits. They watched him bouncing, a child of eight. They hoped he could forget about his poor snowman.

Kelley was fascinated by the remainder of Mr. Tunniwinkle's order.

"One dozen eggs scrambled, dry. One dozen poached with hollandaise and asparagus. One dozen sunnyside up. And, what the heck, one dozen soft boiled as well. Do you have enough egg cups?"

"Oh, sir, I'm afraid we do not serve eggs for breakfast. Could I get you some croissants and granola cereal?" Kelley shouted into the tube.

"Pickle?" Mr. Tunniwinkle screamed.

"No. I'm Kelley."

"Pickle served us eggs. Where's Pickle?"

Unbeknownst to Kelley, Pickle had served the Tunniwinkles large helpings of eggs during the previous two mornings. Mr. Tunniwinkle always paid cash. Pickle always kept a nicely voided bill in his pocket. After presenting Mr. Tunniwinkle with the rather large bill, Pickle pocketed the

19

cash. This added a nice fifty dollar bonus to Pickle's morning.

The dungeon like stoves and cast iron pots waited for Kelley. He remained adamant. There was no way in hell he would attempt to cook eggs.

"I'm sorry sir, Pickle is not here this morning and all the eggs are locked in the cooler. I'll bring you up a nice selection from the buffet."

Kelley hung up the brass earphone. He quickly gathered the coffee and croissants, placing them on a tray along with some fresh cantaloupe and cold slices of brown toast. Oblivious to the thunderheads gathering underneath the Manchurian slate, he climbed into the authentic medieval dumbwaiter and began pulling on the rope. Slowly, Kelley creaked up the shaft.

Running over three hundred and fifty feet, from the basement to the top floor, the dumbwaiter shaft stank like the gritty intestine of a burrowing tube worm. In complete darkness, crouched on the balls of his feet and hunched underneath the plank ceiling, Kelley was questioning his line of work.

Here I am, dressed like Little Lord Fauntleroy, working as a minion in somebody's perverted version of Xanadu. I haven't seen the light of day for over eighteen hours and seem to have forgotten why I'm here at all.

Right then and there Kelley vowed he would quit. At the door opening onto the top floor, he ground the dumbwaiter to a halt. He slid back the panel and stepped gingerly onto the crimson carpet. Before him stretched the hall leading towards the turret and room twenty seven. Drunk from the exertion required by the rope and pulley, Kelley swayed under the weight of the tray like Charlie Chaplin's hobo. Resembling the interior of a carnival funhouse, the hallway wound round corners before eventually leading up to the heavy wooden door of the room. Kelley rapped. Mr. Tunniwinkle emerged in an air of malodorous injustice.

He looked askance at the tray Kelley offered. He waved away the toast and cereal with a curt swipe. "Two hundred dollars a night, and no eggs!"

"I'm sorry sir. If you would like to complain I would be happy to notify my manager."

"Pickle served eggs."

Given the immensity of the order he had taken and the girth of the man he now stood in front of, Kelley came to the quick conclusion that he had better come up with some sort of explanation. This was an important matter, he decided, and time for a judicious lie.

"Please sir," Kelley wormed his way past Mr.Tunniwinkle. Mrs. Tunniwinkle and Graham Jr. greeted him with salivating eyes. Kelley slid the tray onto the wrought iron table (no tag on this one). He watched the tray for a hard second. He made sure no sudden quirk in the iron would dash it to the floor, before turning back to Mr. Tunniwinkle.

In the most ingratiating voice he possessed, Kelley addressed the Tunniwinkles. "I'm afraid this matter has a simple explanation, albeit, one I am loath to discuss where others may hear." Kelley pointed toward the door. "Yesterday afternoon my chef, Christian LeForrestier, fired Pickle for serving eggs at breakfast. In his efforts to please you, I am afraid Pickle managed to lose his job."

There was silence before Graham Tunniwinkle Jr., all two hundred and six pounds of him, launched his four foot eleven inch body in a lunge for Kelley's throat. Eight year old Graham Jr. had not been listening to Kelley. Rather, he had been focusing on the hideous, eggless tray. He was now out for Kelley's blood. He knocked a stunned Kelley Sapp to the floor and proceeded to pound his head with fat, white knuckles.

Dressed in his livery, Kelley resembled a Spanish explorer who had discovered that the indigenous tribes are, in fact, belligerent. With an open palm, he smacked the Tunniwinkle boy on the ear. Clutching his head, Graham Jr. tottered to the carpet. Graham Tunniwinkle Sr. was rolling up his sleeves.

Kelley ran.

Down, down the lapis staircase, he sprinted through brilliant sunshine past tall windows. Heavy footsteps pounded behind him. The storm clouds had broken, spilling sunlight into the high country of the Rockies. As he churned down the hallway even Kelley noticed how beautiful it was outside. He dove for the dumbwaiter's open door and scrambled to grab the pulley rope. A meaty hand clasped the plank roof before Kelley could get a grip. He was straining with all the leverage his cramped body could muster, the car did not budge an inch. Mr. Tunniwinkle's face rose in crimson eclipse. With the patience of the damned, Kelley waited.

A gaseous breath smacked Kelley in the face before Mr Tunniwinkle stammered, "I just wanted to ask you something, something I would like to know."

"Yes."

"Would your Chef wreck a little boy's snowman?"

"Oh my god."

"What do you mean?"

"I mean, oh my god, I mean, yes!"

"You saw him do it?"

"Yes."

"Thank you."

A hundred dollar bill floated into the chamber before Mr. Tunniwinkle released his grip. All the while Kelley had been straining against the rope. With a sudden jolt the car shot up the shaft like a missile before slamming into the ceiling and releasing the trap door on top of Kelley's head. Sunshine flooded the car. Kelley clambered through the trap like a newborn, and crawled out of the damp shaft blinking his eyes in the sunshine. A skylight hung over him, offering squared views of white cloud and cobalt sky. The clouds drifted in changing scenes. The only window in the dark gallery. Kelley watched as Monet blue and white floated overhead. Directly above him, fixed securely to a beam, hung the pulley apparatus. He stood on top of a solid ceiling within a little garret. The car hung beneath him. Its cubic interior lit up through the trap door. Spotting the hundred dollar bill, Kelley flattened himself on the floor and fished for it with his extended hand. Secured, he held it up in the light. A mixture of elation and sorrow filled him when he recognized Ben Franklin.

Long before he had ever heard of Vail, Kelley had cut the green lawn that surrounded his suburban childhood home. On School Street, at the top of Pelham Hill, in the air of upper middle class Massachusetts suburbia, was Kelley's two storey Colonial farmhouse. One and a half acres of grass surrounded the white house that had been standing since the year 1868. And Kelley's father, Emerson, a native Yankee who worked at Raytheon designing missiles, had decided that an important facet of his son's education would be the value of hard work, and the reward of money that came from it.

In the garage back home, stacked against walls and piled on shelving, was an array of power tools and agrarian implements arranged for immediate action. Four seasons cyclically circulated four varying sets of chores. And Emerson Sapp had made sure he possessed the tool for each one.

In the fall he would take down the screens and put up the storm windows. In the spring he would take down the storm windows and put up the screens. Emerson Sapp derived a great deal of satisfaction from these mundane tasks. It was his hope that his son, Kelley, would grow to love this work as much as he did. The overwhelming regularity Emerson sensed when he raked the brown oak leaves under the gray fall sky made him feel within the world. In his air conditioned office, under the fluorescent lights, his eyes straining at the computer screen, Emerson sometimes felt a distant pang of grief. Like a disquieting yelp heard through the window of one's comfy bedroom on a winter's night, Emerson heard the cry. It was then he would think of the leaves he must rake, the seed he would plant come spring, or the flagstone patio he could heal of frost heaves. He would sigh, and another warm blanket of calm would fall down and insulate Emerson for another day.

The result of these momentary insecurities was a white house trimmed with forest green shutters. Terraced levels of lawn, separated into steps with stone walls led up to the broad white porch that ran the entire width of the house. Evergreen holly hedges framed the length of the driveway. The flowering apple and peach trees stood as sentinels, one to each level of terrace. Dying elms screened the house from the road; and in back, under an arbor hung heavy with ripening bunches of Concord grapes, a young Kelley Sapp would sit in the chaise lounge sipping Kool-Aid and covertly eating the Twinkies he had purchased at the corner store.

At the age of twelve, he had already decided that it was time to avoid this thing called work. Kelley gazed about the recently cut lawn. Scattered on top of the lawn were heavy lumps of cut wet grass. Kelley nodded in satisfaction. He had been told repeatedly by his father that he must empty the catch bag on the mower or the bag would clog and the grass would clump. On all one and a half acres of grass Kelley had not paused to empty the bag once. When asked why he had done this, he would simply shrug his shoulders and say, "I don't know".

This, he had discovered, was the best thing to say, for it made Emerson very unhappy and left Kelley free for days before being given another task to screw up. Three days of freedom, Kelley figured. More than enough time to finish. He went back to reading his book, Tolkein's Fellowship of the Ring. This would be the fourth time he had read The Lord of the Rings trilogy in the past five years. Each time he found new reasons to be excited, new amazement from the same old characters.

Kelley put down his Kool-Aid and crept off the chaise lounge. His imaginary sword in hand, Kelley was un-afraid of the approaching armies of evil men and beasts. He leaped over a stone wall and tumbled to the grass beneath it. Thrusting his empty hand into the air, he impaled some fantastic creature. Kelley rolled on his back in the wet grass, the creature lay beside him in a thrashing heap. Emerson wanted Kelley to cut the lawn, trim the hedges, weed the flowerbeds, and clean his room. All this for a measly ten bucks a week. It was much easier to ask mom for money when he needed it. Priscilla Sapp worked as a librarian at the Acton Public Library.

"I'll never work for money," Kelley had told her. "I'll never do something I hate for a living. I don't care if I have money. I don't care if I have things. I'll do what I want to, and I'll figure that out later."

Priscilla Sapp had coddled her child. With the love of a devoted mother, she wondered what would become of her intelligent son. He had such an impulsive spirit. Her other son was so practical, but dense compared to Kelley. She hated to admit it, but Kelley was her favorite.

He was a dreamer, she knew. And all dreams must end someplace in someway. She wished that they would not become nightmares. So in the house on School Street, under the boughs filled with flowering apple blossoms, Kelley Sapp learned to entertain his imagination with books and more books. He never once questioned the lessons he learned during those summer days filled with day-dreams and girls whose figures could only be deciphered through black and white type. He lived on School Street, at the top of the hill. Though he traveled far and wide on page after page, he found it comfortable to remain where he was.

23

That static life had not lasted. He found himself on the rooftop of the Snowy Mountains Guest Lodge, a long way from New England. Like Arthur surveying his lands, he strode the roof of the Snowy Mountains Guest Lodge. Behind him, the glass door in the skylight lay open. He had crawled up the service ladder and out through the door. A six inch layer of snow covered the roof of the castle.

King of nothing, Lord of his own problems, Kelley Sapp gazed beyond the toothy parapets. Towers flanked him on both sides. Blue flags flew from the blue towers, in blue sky. In the cold and wind his skin turned cyanic. Everything was blue, even Kelley.

The one-hundred dollar bill was crumpled in his fist. The Gore Range was enveloped in cloud. White elephants danced around peaks, holding umbrellas with their trunks. Black thunderheads tickled the top of Mt. Powell. For a second, all was volcanic with smoke and fire. The air was silent. Kelley watched without enjoyment. Joyless and numb, he focused on the spreading wash of homes. Roads clogged the valley floor. Down there was Wal-Mart.

If he were King he would banish it all. He would wave a hand and it would go. All of it would go away. He turned back and crawled through the skylight, back down into the garret. He crawled into the dumbwaiter and assumed the position. Back in place now, Kelley reverted to the cog. Moving his hands mechanically, the dumbwaiter dropped Kelley back into place. He uttered a few practice 'yes m'ams' and 'thank you sirs', loosening up before returning to the fray. Dropping down, down, he reached the end of the shaft and found himself back where he had started at the bottom. He had gone to the top and looked around, and after a bit of thinking decided that nothing was changed. His life still turned his stomach. God, how he wanted to quit.

Except for Friday, *Au Naturel's* dining room was deserted. Used plates sat in heaps on tables in front of the empty buffet.

> Friday-"Where'd you go?"
> Kelley-"Room service"
> Friday-"For an hour?"
> Kelley-"God. I didn't think it was that long."
> Friday-"What did you do?"
> Kelley-"I don't know. I mean, I know what I did. But,it doesn't seem that long. It couldn't have been."
> Friday-"Don't worry, it happens to all of us."
> Kelley-"Really?"
> Friday-"Really."

Everything was out of whack at the Snowy Mountains Guest

Lodge. Employees disappeared for hours and returned with no clear recollection of where they had been or what they had done. It was a place of dream turned nightmare. Here, the sensitive and flawed served their life sentences without a complaint from their imploded heads. Spinning in static frenzy while the world laughed and danced about. "Where did the time go?" Kelley asked Friday.

"Don't worry. Please don't worry. I shouldn't have even asked you. I knew damn well what happened. Say, you're off tonight," he said to change the subject. "Why not come over to my place and we'll have dinner."

"Where do you live?"

"At the Silver Aspen condominiums."

"So do I. Seven o'clock, ok."

"Yeah. That's fine. Bring your ears. I've got some things to tell you about this place."

Kelley went back to work. He cleared the plates from the heaped tables and dumped them into the reeking wooden wash tub. Salvador, the dishwasher, dressed in his medieval dishwashing garb of sackcloth and rope belt, was hard at work with an authentically archaic wire scrub brush. Kelley slipped into a hazy pattern through lunch. He took orders. He cleared plates. He hardly spoke: but when he did, it was not to say anything of any real importance. At the end of the day, when he stumbled out of the employee entrance, it suddenly struck him that he had not once thought about skiing during the entire shift. He would quit. God, oh god, he would quit, damn it. He had to live. He had to quit.

Chapter 2:

In which the reader learns how Kelley Sapp moved to Vail.

When Kris Blaze called from Killington to ask Kellie Kay if she had ever heard of someone named Harvey Weintraub, Kellie Kay was flabbergasted.

"No!" she screamed into the phone with great enthusiasm.

"You're lying," Kris calmly assured her.

Last spring Kellie Kay had been introduced to Harvey Weintraub by Dieter Hump, a retired futures salesman from New York City. Dieter Hump was the kind of person who could take a name like Harvey Weintraub and dangle it in the air as if it were a diamond necklace.

"Harvey Weintraub," he had said, "would like to meet you next week. I've told him about you and he is very excited to go skiing."

Never mind the fact that the last time Kellie Kay had seen Dieter Hump was in the back seat of an Austin Healy with an eighteen year old Mexican heiress and a gram of coke: Kellie Kay liked Dieter Hump.

Dieter Hump always sent flowers *weeks* before he arrived. Dieter Hump was a considerate and well kept man. He never pawed, and he always booked her for a week of private lessons at the ski school. Each afternoon he would take Kellie to lunch at Rafters in Beaver Creek. They would sit down, Kellie in her blue uniform, Dieter in his Descente one piece, and begin their daily comedy.

"Have a glass of wine," Dieter would insist.

"No thank you," Kellie would decline.

They would eat lunch.

Round about desert Dieter would ask, "Why don't we stop skiing and go back to my hotel?"

"No thank you," Kellie would decline.

"You're so sweet," Dieter would say. "I don't know what I would do if you ever said yes."

Kellie would bat her eyes and wonder if this constituted sexual harassment. For the rest of the afternoon she and Dieter would ski trees. When three thirty rolled around Dieter would hand her a hundred dollar bill and Kellie would give him a peck on the cheek. "Some friends of mine are throwing a party," Dieter would say, or, "Please come out to dinner with me."

Kellie always accepted, and Dieter always drove her home before eleven. He had been a one week fixture in her life for the past three years, and had still never gotten further than a peck on the cheek.

Harvey Weintraub had been another matter. They had met at the base of Beaver Creek at nine A.M. and had immediately resumed their private lesson, fifteen minutes later, on the top floor of the Hyatt in Harvey's Presidential Suite. For four days Harvey Weintraub had schooled Kellie Kay in the art of skiing fresh powder of a different sort. Starting with the upper slope of Kellie's breasts, Harvey chased fluffy Peruvian flake all the way down the easy trail into her valley. Not that Harvey was any beginner. A Sean Connery look alike, he had left Kellie Kay five grams for a tip, and a promise he would return next year. Back to Dartmouth for finals, he had been on Spring Break.

Of course, this had all been before she and Kris were a steady thing. Kellie didn't consider herself wild. So, she rationalized: "What young man would have turned down a week long fling with Cindy Crawford?" Harvey Weintraub was very handsome.

Voices and music drifted over the static line. Kellie Kay held her breath before asking, "Where are you?"

"I'm in a bar," Kris shouted. "I just met him."

"Who?"

"Harvey Weintraub."

"Oh."

"He's very nice. He's bought me four beers and is insisting that I should look you up when I get back to Vail. He's here, he wants to talk to you now."

"Hello Kellie!" Harvey Weintraub's happily drunken voice came onto the phone. At the bar in Killington a line of flaming jello shots had been placed at the bar, free of charge for all ladies willing to lose their shirts. "Listen, just thought I'd hook you up with this guy Kris. He's a professional skier. Oh my God! ..."

"Harvey, don't say anything to him."

"What? I've got to go. Oh my God! I'll see you in the spring, Kellie!" Harvey Weintraub left the phone dangling.

"Kris, I met him before you and I had anything permanent going."

"I think Harvey was coming on to me." Kris covered the phone with his palm and paused the conversation for a moment while he relaxed and silently allowed himself to catch up. At his normally cold level of idealisim, he included Kellie in the general category he despised: - *homo sapiens*. That he himself was within the scope of his wide ranging disgust was something Kris realized in his own efficient manner. He knew she still managed to view him with romantic notions. Sometimes he even felt emotional tugs, hence the phone call. It usually happened on nights like tonight, with a few beers in his stomach, Kris found it easy to forget his goals, who he was, what he would accomplish.

"Are you naked?"

"Kris, you're really pissing me off."

"Get tested. He's a queer." Kris told Kellie before hanging up. A sense of elation filled him. He had stepped beyond the range of social acceptability. He felt justified.

Kellie slammed down the receiver. "Oh fuck!" she screamed. What a complete asshole. He had no right to do that. She supposed he was drunk.

Fifteen minutes later when Friday called for Kelley Sapp, Kellie Kay was more than flabbergasted; she was horrified.

"What are you calling me for?"

"Not you Kellie. I want Kelley, your roommate. He and I are having dinner, and then we're going out."

"Not you, ... and him?"

"Not yet."

Within a fifty mile radius of Vail, Friday Day was certainly the only gay black man not locked in a closet. Founding and sole member of A.A.G.M.I.V. (African American Gay Men In Vail, *'equal opportunity is our basic philosophy'*, Meeting hours are very flexible. 926-WORD), he had succeeded in opening a very small beachhead of multicultural awareness within the Vail Valley. Listed prominently in all public relations literature sent out by the tourism bureau, A.A.G.M.I.V. was token proof that the Vail Valley had a tolerant, even liberal community. Friday's quotes appeared in such wide-ranging publications as *U.S. News and World Report*, and *The Village Voice*. He was Vail's Black Gay Guy.

Not that Friday had been able to parlay his unique position into any sort of monetary gain. He knew Kellie Kay from when they had both slung hash at a best forgotten eatery. Kellie had at first been attracted before finding out that Friday was *Really* different. This itself had not deterred her from seeking his friendship. But a desperate scene at a party two years previous, a scene involving Kellie's supposed date, who later left with Friday, had left them bitter enemies for the past twenty four months.

"Say, have you been tested?" Kellie ignored the years between their last words and feigned some concern.

"Three times. I couldn't believe the first two."

"And?"

"I'm clean."

"Thank goodness you're safe," Kellie Kay exhaled a sigh of relief. Like a letter someone had never answered, a distant curiosity began stirring in Kellie Kay's head. *Wouldn't that be different*, she wondered? *Wouldn't that be exciting!* Wouldn't that put Kris Blaze in his place, that conceited prick. He thinks he owns me.

Even though she had lived in San Francisco, there were certain sexual curiosities Kellie Kay had failed to explore.

"Let me get Kelley for you," Kellie crooned sweetly.

Through peach light and apricot, Kellie Kay floated out of her bedroom. Gliding through the dark brown kitchen she refused to stumble even when her porcelain shin barked the cluttered coffee table. Nothing would stand in her way now.

"Wake up," she shook a dazed Kelley Sapp.

Wrapped like an orange glowworm in his sleeping bag, Kelley had been angelically asleep after his exhausting day at work. Resurrecting himself from the cocoon, he emerged in cherubic dishevelment. He stretched his arms wide in a butterfly embrace of the dark nest that was his room.

"Be there in an hour," he groggily told Friday.

It was after he had stepped from the shower and was dodging his way back into his bedroom that Kellie asked him with the rapid voice of someone who has been lying in wait, "You used to live in New York City, right?"

Like a Roman caught at the baths, Kelley stood dripping in his white towel. He answered, "Yes."

Kellie Kay was on the couch. Calves tucked under her knees, she knelt on the cushions as she faced Kelley. She had changed into a magenta tank top and her obligatory hiking shorts. Appearing wholesome and scrubbed, she asked, "What were you doing there?"

"I moved there with my girlfriend."

"Oh, really?" she struggled to keep the momentum up.

"Yes."

"Did you have lots of friends there?"

"I had some, I still do. Why?"

"I was just wondering. Were any of them gay?" she abandoned her delicate tactics and fired a brick of a question at Kelley, scoring a direct hit.

Home run! Straight over the fence. By the look on Kelley's face she had nailed him. Jaw on the carpet, eyes glazed and starry, Kelley *must* have been gay at some point. Nobody looks that guilty for nothing.

If only she had known the details of Kelley's strange odyssey. Kelley Sapp did have gay friends. Z. Kelley had played the little lord tangent to her circumference. And like any straight line, he had gotten burned by those with the ability to roll. The shock on Kelley's face was one of remembrance. He had been sucker punched by Kellie Kay, and in the several seconds it took for his equilibrium to return, Kellie Kay read all that she wanted to confirm from his enigmatic face.

"Yes," Kelley said quite amiably, "several of my best friends are bisexual."

"Really!" Kellie Kay was ecstatic. She would get candles and incense. "I've always wanted to have friends who are gay. But there are so few gay people up here. I think all the gay people I've met are *wonderful.*"

"They're just like anybody else."

"Oh, I'm sure you're right."

"They get hurt, hurt, and suffer the same as we do." *But why am I telling you this? Why am I spouting stupid cliches about a subject apparently irrelevant to my present situation?*

"Of course, of course. You must have had some very interesting experiences. In New York I mean. So many gay people." Kellie Kay continued on like a monomaniac who has found an unwary victim. The effect was somewhat understandable. Kelley stopped listening.

"That was part of the problem," Kelley slipped off into a dream. *New York seems like such a long time ago. I can remember the perpetual gray sky, the stone canyons, and constant barrage of noise. I can remember feeling absolutely alone in the center of a street near my apartment. The people streamed by like so many familiar relatives whose faces still echo in my memory.*

"Of course, it was. Too many, too many. Such hard decisions you must have had. Kelley, would you like to sleep with me."

Kelley Sapp woke up to watch her violin figure play a song with his heart strings. Vamping on the couch, she remained an open invitation. "I've already answered that question once."

"Would you like to sleep with me and a friend as well?"

So that's what she was getting at with all those questions, Kelley's confusion cleared. Him, Kellie, and one of her girlfriends... Kellie was a switch hitter. He regarded Kellie with the shock and amusement we all feel when life tosses us a curveball. He never would have guessed Kellie Kay had it in her. But there are quite a few things in life he would never guess unless he were told. The innocent, sweet beguiling woman he had moved in with was proving to be more of an enigma than he had imagined. That was fine. What he didn't realize during those moments between their even reciprocal gazes were the similarities between them. She was as curious and inexperienced as he was. They had both managed to stand at the edge of *avant garde* sexuality during previous years, but had never taken the plunge. Strictly hetero, sublimely curious, they mirrored each others' mundane curiosities and twisted what they heard into offers of what they wanted.

"What about Kris."

30

"As far as I'm concerned, he has no say in how I choose to live my personal life. Now I should ask you if it would be a problem with Friday?" Kellie felt it would be best to check.

"Why do you ask?"

"Well, he is gay."

"So?" Kelley failed to see the point. That Friday was gay seemed to have no relevance to him and Kellie. "I can't possibly see why he would mind."

"Good." Kellie's libido flip flopped as she envisioned herself, Friday, and Kelley under the sheets together. "I've been wanting to try this for a while now."

They both smiled at each other with knowing glances.

You little devil, Kellie sighed.

You little devil, Kelley sighed.

"How about tomorrow?"

"Sure. Three o'clock?"

"It's a date."

Now why would Kellie mention that Friday is gay? This question badgered Kelley Sapp while he made his way across the parking lot toward Friday's unit. Did she think that he and Friday were lovers? He supposed it might look strange, him getting a call from a gay man. Maybe she thought they were dating? Well, even if she did, he would make it very clear to Friday that they were not.

Pausing in the center of the parking lot, Kelley tuned his attention to the hissing snow guns on the slopes of Beaver Creek ski area. He would go skiing soon. How funny, he had been here for over three weeks and had not gone hiking, or climbing. The slopes had just opened, and he would go skiing soon. But, he hadn't felt any great urge to go out and be athletic. Isn't that why people lived here? Hadn't he moved to Vail for that?

Or maybe I just had no idea of where else I could go?

Focus shifted and Kelley's perspective skewed as if an animating lens had been screwed on top of his eyes. Finding himself alone, he forgot about Kellie Kay while the seeping insecurities of his life ambushed his solitary mind. Kelley's surroundings became immediate. The presence of the parked cars became tangible and malevolent.

"Jesus Christ," he mumbled. He was scared. An almost uncontrollable urge to leave swept him as he realized, for what seemed the very first time, that he was actually living in Vail. He would pack his van tonight and go. He would pack and drive away from his job, from his apartment, from this valley. Maybe he would go to Mexico. With these thoughts came

31

no relief from his sudden attack of anxiety. In fact, as he stood paralyzed in the parking lot, his troubles seemed to increase at an exponential rate.

And what would you do when you got there? You have to figure something out. What do you want? "Oh, fuck it. I want to go skiing. That's what I want."

Above him in the Colorado night sky a million stars lit the stage upon which Kelley had chosen to play out the soliloquy of his young life. High up on the mountains to the west the blue lights of the Snowy Mountains Guest Lodge shone in spectral majesty. A beacon for all the lost souls adrift upon the waves of uncertainty. Some would call them free spirits, others would simply say they are lost. They came to Vail out of necessity. It is home for people like them - the unknowing, the uncertain. That's why they are here.

We came to ski, but stayed forever. I'll leave someday. I know I will. At the end of this winter, I will leave. The Vail Valley: the skiing, the aspen trees, the healthy mountain lifestyle, the trailer parks, the thousands of low paying service jobs, the four golf courses, the gourmet restaurants. Kelley Sapp leaned forward eagerly into the night while he made his way toward Friday's apartment. As he watched the far blue lights of the Snowy Mountains Guest Lodge, his black eyes flashed into the night like wild, dying stars. God how he hated the little bubble of life in which he swam.

The entrance to unit 407-F was exactly the same as the entrance to every other unit at the Silver Aspen Condominiums. Like the wet dream of some Bauhaus architect, order prevailed in symmetrical utility. Up the gray steps, to the gray door, Kelley entered the gray embrace of the cheap clapboard and shingle construction.

When Kelley knocked he was on the verge of desperation.

Unit 407-F of the Silver Aspen Condominiums had the exact same dimensions, rooms, floor plans, and wallpaper as unit 201-B. Friday led Kelley into the living room.

"Oh, God," Kelley moaned. "I think I'm going crazy. I'm sorry, Friday, but can we go out some other night?"

It would be cruel to tell what this evening had cost Friday Day in anxiety and time. First he had worried that Kelley might not be gay. Then he had worried that Kelley was a homophobic bigot. And what if Kelley was gay? He could take rejection by a straight man, but by one of his own?

The possibility had terrified him. All these scenarios had been flitting through his mind while he waited for Kelley to arrive. When he heard the nerveless wail of Kelley Sapp's self-pity, all of Friday's indecisive quibbling ceased in mid-thought before plunging into forgetfulness. For even though Friday Day may not have achieved the economic status so often touted as the sign of a successful person, he was an extremely solid individual. Sixteen years of life as a minority among a minority had galvanized his self-esteem and made him impermeable to the various traumas life daily throws at all of us. In short, he drew daily strength from his self-validating lifestyle. He walked alone in the world, like John Wayne, James Dean, Georgia O'Keeffe, or Walt Whitman. To others he seemed to speak in riddles composed of nonsensical symbols. But his oblique thinking nearly always yielded positive results for those willing to listen to him. Friday Day may get the jitters about a first date. It would take an earthquake to shift the solid bedrock of his personality. He seemed almost too good for this world, a fantasy if you will.

"Do you want to talk about it?" Friday led a reluctant Kelley into the living room.

"Oh, shit," Kelley collapsed onto the couch and curled up in a foetal ball. "I don't even know how to express it. There's just this fucking fear inside of myself that's eating me alive. All I want is to stay in bed and never have to do anything. I can't stand people. People are shitty."

"You're depressive."

"I can't help it. The thing that brought this on. I was just thinking about why I moved here."

"Why did you?" Friday popped the question.

Of all the generalizations that can be made about Vail, perhaps the most truthful of these would be, *everyone here is from someplace else.* There will always be a Vail; somewhere. And there will always be people who will move to Vail; wherever it is. When these people meet they ask each other, *why did you move here?* Some will say work, others love, but it only takes a little while to figure out the real reason. Life and what to do with it? Nobody knows why they move to Vail. With the exception of self-validating persons like Friday who need no extraneous rationale, most have vacant reasons that explain their move. Like directions that lead nowhere: take two eggs, add milk, at the four-way stop flunk out of college, take your first left, scream at your mother, cook for two hours at three hundred and fifty degrees, garnish with fresh snow, and you will be in Vail. Why?

"Oh man, I can't even begin to tell you what brought me here. I feel like a stranger to myself."

"You could read Thucydides," Friday sat down on the carpet and leaned his back up against the couch. Looking out the window into his own reflection, he couldn't help feeling a little wonder slip behind his shell of emotional armor. It wasn't often that he was confronted with raw grief. He supposed he could tell Kelley to shut up. Tell him life was hard and part of the challenge was learning how to deal without becoming a drunk or a pothead. But he preferred to be a philosopher. Being a philosopher was much more constructive. He closed his eyes and continued talking. "Thucydides wrote the first modern history."

"Yes, I know, History of the Peloponnesian War. He outlines the fight between Athens and Sparta." Some measure of calm returned to

Kelley's face as he regained his footing on familiar ground. But it was still the same old, same old.

And if you want to we can go on Friday. We can talk about Walt Whitman, Sappho, and Henry Miller. I haven't spent more than twelve hours with you, which would in no way prevent us from having a nice little discussion of Quantum Theory. Let us stray from the big question for a little longer. But in the end what kind of relevance would any of this have for me, Kelley Sapp? Because when it comes right down to it those are the big questions. Who am I and what am I doing? Everything anyone has ever become stems from that self-reflexive quandary. Every great field, art, literature, engineering, started with those two related thoughts. There are those who never answer themselves, and, you see, that's what scares the living shit out of me. I have ambition. If I could ever get past that hurdle, then I might do something. Who am I, and what am I doing?

"I mentioned Thucydides," Friday continued, "because your problem is an individual dilemma. Thucydides is remarkable today because back in ancient Greece he managed to take the real-life horror of thousands of people and generalize about it in a logical manner. That had never been done before. What a fantastic invention. Glance over the suffering, reduce the fatalities to silent statistics, and glorify the cause of status quo leadership by focusing on it in a seemingly objective manner. It was the beginning of disinformation, and it started back in the golden age of democracy. Do you think that one book could possibly do justice to all the people who died miserably for either Athens or Sparta? People who did not care who won, who simply acted out their assigned role in the drama? Or the slaves whose lives didn't even show up as statistics. Their stories need a thousand books. A million books. 'My name is Agamemnon Seferiades. I was the lover of Sophocles Jones, who was a Spartan soldier before he was accused of cowardice and murdered by one of his commanding officers.'"

"Ok, so I'm an individual. I have a voice. What am I supposed to do now?"

"Stop being so pathetic for one thing. You remember the polar bear story I told you? Remember that I also said if we met again you would be one of us?"

"Yes. I thought you were very strange."

"Then you obviously did not understand what I meant when I said, us. You are one of us now. That means you are in the war for control of your own life. You can feel it. You can actually put your fingers on it at the Snowy Mountains Guest Lodge. The malevolence is there. That place sucks the life from you. The war for us is between our dreams and the reality that stands in the way of achieving them."

"Then everybody is one of us."

"That's true. But listen Kelley, there are some whose dreams are weak from the start. They don't have the courage to try for anything. They are happy, asleep almost. You're different. I can see you have the strength for the fight, but you lack focus. You're ripping yourself up inside just with living. If you go on like that you'll either kill yourself or turn into a zombie with a bottle."

"But what should I focus on? I'm fucking out of my mind, Friday. I wouldn't know which way is up unless you pointed me to it. And then I'd just be following directions. Focus on money? On sex?"

"If you want."

"C'mon, that's bullshit."

"Who says so?"

"Are you telling me money would make me happy?"

"Kelley I'm not going to say it would. But, have you ever had enough money to find out? What gave you the idea that being rich is bad? I'm not saying it's good, all I'm doing is playing devil's advocate to make you think about yourself in a critical manner. What stereotypes, even liberal left wing truisms, are unwittingly lodged in that skull of yours? Listen Kelley, think about Thucydides."

"Why?"

"Because ever since him there has been a long line of people waiting, pen in hand, to write broad sweeping generalizations concerning every period of world history. Some have done it better than others. I'm not judging them individually. You can be sure, Kelley, that the future historian who will put his indelible mark on your generation with his brilliant thesis has already been born. You're already a footnote to her, a number for him. I can even tell you what they will write. 'After the baby boomers came the lost generation. These guys didn't know what the hell they wanted. There was no real war to fight. All the good jobs were gone. Japan was kicking our ass. They were cynical fucks as young men and women, but became graciously generous as they grew into their old age.' Doesn't that sound nice Kelley? Can't you relax now? You're gonna have a hard time for a while, but things will probably work out fine in the end. Doesn't something sound like it's missing, Kelley? What did they miss? They missed the entire fucking war, that's what they missed! That's the whole story. What are people like you going to do so you can have a happy ending? You're gonna get the shit kicked out of you, that's what's gonna happen. School of hard knocks! It's coming and you better not close your eyes. So Kelley, start telling me about yourself. Tell me why you came to Vail. Tell me, because we have to figure out what you want."

"I already know what I want."

"What's that?"

"I want to be happy."

"Then let's start from the beginning and get our plan."

These were the elements of Kelley's childhood story: Mom, Dad, brother, school, and house. Case # 6,534,627 of the lost generation, Kelley Sapp. I.Q.: 121. Hair: black. Eyes: black. Future: uncertain. D.O.B. 12/10/68. Too late for Woodstock, too young for Punk, he had listened to Zeppelin, cried for Jimi, and had no doubt that he would have burned his draft card right underneath the man's face. But he never got the chance.

"I don't know where to begin," Kelley walked into the kitchen and grabbed a beer out of the fridge. "Ok if I have one?"

"Get me one too."

So they sat and sipped. Two silent bodies adrift on the seas of isolation. Drinking their beers, they sat together and apart.

Kelley Sapp, starry eyes, dreaming head, was lost in a vacuum of indecision. *Come out, come out from wherever you are and be somebody.* There was only one thing he could come up with.

"I love Z."

"What's that, a person?"

"An unknown quantity. You could say she's a person, but that's like defining the Atlantic Ocean as water. She dumped me."

"Ahh, unrequited love."

"Let me tell you about it."

In the town of Amherst, Massachusetts at a university run like a factory, a young lady by the name of Elizabeth Pettigrew once lived on a sweet nectar of student loans and feminist poetry. Occasionally, when Fellini movies were shown on the big screen at the student union center or when one of her poems was published in the feminist literary journal, Elizabeth felt a vague satisfaction with the period her life had reached. But most of the time she sat drinking coffee, smoking cigarettes, hating the season, the snow, the sun, her fellow students, the year, the day, the minute, the second, the...pause in time before the next moment.

For these reasons alone, Kelley Sapp fell in love with her. Blue haired, black vinyl covered snake of sexual confusion, Z and Kelley were an odd couple. They had met in the mosh pit at a Butthole Surfers concert. Z, fire eyed and nutmegging with her elbows, had been on her way to the front row. Onstage, a two-hundred twenty pound member of the Amherst Hammerskins launched himself like a stone onto the heads of the crowd. The Buttholes played on. In a cleared space Z lay flat on her back. Moving like a wave of water, the crowd closed in on top of her. Oh my God, Kelley watched her disappear. Fighting toward the spot, he reached a hand down and saved her. That night Z took him home.

Like iron to a magnet, Z moved to New York City after her graduation. Kelley followed in her wake. They found an apartment near seventh and B. Kelley worked as a waiter at Benny's Burritos East. Though they shared a studio apartment, Z embarked upon a series of compact, obvious

little affairs with bohemian ingenues of decidedly questionable innocence.
All of which Kelley could take since Z had yet to experience an orgasm.

She called these affairs, "The Quest". Her focus: sex. Her nemesis: the post-coital slide into bliss, the shared cigarette of satiated pleasure.
Z was forever churning in the perpetual motion of sexual frustration; Until,
that is, she met Bond.

"I came home one night and she was bent over on the futon with some man. He had tattoos all over his body in the style of a Japanese yakuza member. The tattoos covered his skin like a painting, stopping only at his wrists, neck, and ankles in abrupt lines. His name was Bond, and I don't know what he had that everyone else didn't, but I watched her come right then and there. I turned around and left the apartment, got drunk for a week, then packed up and left for home. Z moved in with Bond on the Upper East Side. I guess he's a lawyer and specializes in international tax laws. That summer I worked as a lifeguard at the town pool. When fall came, I packed my van up and came here. It had been two years since I graduated from college."

"Did you know anyone out here? Anyone who had lived here?" Friday finished his beer and set the empty green bottle on the coffee table.

"No. I don't know what took me out here. Some force of nature, I suppose."

"Go west young man!"

"That's about it."

Friday straightened his back and pushed himself up off the carpet. He fetched another two beers from the kitchen. Kelley was silent until Friday handed him the cold bottle. He held the green, anesthetizing bullet in his hand.

"I guess I'm looking for love," Kelley twisted off the cap and took a swig. "If I want anything, it's got to be love."

"A time honored tradition...yours is the oldest and most common quest of all."

Kelley relaxed as the alcohol made a fist at the pit of his empty stomach. Love, was what he wanted: love, happiness, a sense of security presently absent from his vagrant life. He could be happy, he could enjoy life, if only ... . The blue fog rolled in and clouded Kelley's eyes. Where would he be, and what would he be doing tomorrow at five o'clock in the afternoon? Behind two windows on a tower of the Snowy Mountains Guest Lodge the blue lights burned. The demon eyes gazed out at the world and waited with the patient knowledge that at five o'clock in the afternoon Kelley would walk straight into its mouth.

The uneasy bile rose in Kelley's stomach. "Oh fuck," he said, "It's coming back." What exciting pleasures awaited Kelley in the dumbwaiter? Had his friends the Tunniwinkles stayed for another night? Oh, the pleasant

37

servitude that awaited Kelley behind those blue walls. "Friday, I don't want to go back in there."

Farther off in space, Friday caught Kelley's plea on a neat tangent and carried the thought back to him as if he had been inside his head. "Ask yourself the lottery question."

"What's that."

"My name is Jeannette Peterson, and even though I won eighty million dollars playing Keno, I'm still going to keep my job as a clerical slave."

"People are stupid."

"Au contraire, they are simply past the point of no return. They can't envision any other life than the one they have. You will see them at work, the ones who have developed a symbiotic relationship with the actual place. You could say they are serious."

"I really think that place is evil. Everytime I come out of there I feel like I've been drugged."

"There are some things you should know about the Snowy Mountains Guest Lodge," Friday cleared his throat and prepared to give a short history lesson concerning the nature of the lodge. "I have never seen a hotel just throw money away like that place does. I've worked in quite a few hotels. I think there's a reason for it. Why would you pay a chef a six figure salary and not even have a decent computer system in the lodge? Why build a hotel that has twenty eight rooms and requires a staff of over fifty people on any given day? Can it make money? No."

What was really important at the Snowy Mountains Guest Lodge was understood. A giant blue lure dangled next to the shining peaks of the Rocky Mountains. The Snowy Mountains Guest Lodge was out for big fish. M. Posthelwaite, the managing owner, also happened to own the several thousand acres of forest surrounding the lodge. This land included the sizable backside of the mountain ridge supporting the lodge. Already, several houses on the scale of minor chateaus hovered like satellites in orbit about the towering blue walls of the castle. Other waiters had told Kelley that complementary dinners and weekend stays were not uncommon. Guests ooohed and aaahed about the views, then struck off on hikes to various knolls and rises. Blue signs, pinned like price tags to the trees, identified the lots as specific parcels of land. "What a darling view. Look, we can see the mountaintop from here!" Such is the stuff of which both dreams and second houses are made. With malignant speed, the cancer was spreading. The construction continued. Asphalt capillaries webbed through aspen groves and across meadows. It was only beginning.

"There's something screwy going on up there," Friday continued. "Posthelwaite's a smart businessman. He's already made a fortune. If they were on top of things they would find a way to make both the lodge and the real estate profitable. There's no reason for them to take a loss on that lodge.

"How."

"Why would you buy a lot at Snowy Mountains?"

"I wouldn't."

"That's what I mean. I think you, or I, if we had the money, would rather have a house on the side of Vail mountain, right?"

"If I had the money," Kelley agreed.

"What I'm saying is that right now Snowy Mountains does not offer any real incentive, other than a pretty view, to buy a lot. And they want half a million for a lot, just a lot! That's an awful amount of money to ask for a view. You can find land off the Snowy Mountains property with just as nice a view for, say, one quarter the cost and you get the same thing right now."

"Right now," Kelley was catching on.

"Exactly. It won't stay that way for long. The lodge is minor, in terms of money. But it got things rolling in an un-obtrusive manner. If they are interested in making a profit, they will expand. This means they need to have a draw. Posthelwaite has got to build a real draw. That means either skiing or golf. If you pay over a million dollars for a home in a resort development it should either be on the slopes or on the links. That's what people want, and Posthelwaite's group has the money and the land to do both. The lodge got it rolling. Now they'll do what they want. The whole backside of that ridge will be a ski area. The golf course will get built somewhere. With skiing and golf, Snowy Mountains would click into high gear and become a year round resort. It will happen."

"All that land will be developed," Kelley was amazed at the scale of Friday's vision.

"Of course," *Psssshht*, Friday opened another beer. "Right now, for Snowy Mountains, it's either expand or die. If they go on the way they are, they'll always lose money. It's catch-22. To remain static is to stagnate. They have to move forward, and moving forward means intense land development, felled forests, increased water use. It will affect the entire ecosystem of the valley. It's unavoidable if Snowy Mountains is going to survive. There's too much money behind it to let it die. No matter what they say about how environmentally conscious they'll be, how carefully they'll develop, that land will no longer be wilderness. The elk will move out. Roads will get paved over the ridge. Soil erosion will increase where they cut roads. Septic systems will be built. Wells will get dug. Less water will flow down valley. Fewer animals and plants will be able to survive with the decrease in water supply. This is how deserts are made. Only ten percent of the original forests of North America remain as wilderness. You might as well write Snowy Mountains off as another loss."

Kelley slowly shook his head.

Posthelwait's partner lives in Switzerland and also happens to be wanted in the United States for violation of the Securities and Exchange commission codes on insider trading. He made his money with Boesky and Milken. His name is Ricky Rico. He can't leave Switzerland, but he wants to get some of his money, maybe even a lot of it, circulating back in the States.

With the empty beer bottles Friday went into the kitchen, leaving a bewildered Kelley Sapp alone.

Inside Kelley's head the spine of the cathedral ceiling arched toward the sky, straining the buttresses, and the whole Snowy Mountains Guest Lodge lifted bodily into the air before landing with a shiver, the Manchurian slate roof clacking like loose reptilian scales. Bulging and bouncing the tower windows swam on either side of the heaving spine. With horror, Kelley realized the blue mirth behind their panes was aimed at him. He watched them laugh while he grew smaller, eventually disappearing under their glare.

"Dinner?" Friday dangled a raw steak over Kelley's bowed head. "Wake up, wake up, wake up! You can't fall asleep on me now."

Eleven fifteen p.m. . The drunken Bridge Street shuffle was going strong. Having deposited Friday's Celica in the multi-layered parking structure (Elk level, which was above the Trout level, but below Bear), the two handsome young men cut between the thin early-season crowd of apres-apres-skiers. Without a self-reflexive thought they passed under the covered bridge and arrived at the foot of Bridge Street, in the pedestrians only center of Vail Village.

Being at the foot, they decided to start at the head. Friday held them up for a moment. He had to find a head at the foot before continuing on to the head.

"There must be a head in here," he said, ducking into a basement bistro.

This is Vail.

Bar, hotel, restaurant: Vail.

Kelley Sapp stood in the cold night air. His breath shot plumed white ghosts into the black. If Vail is Mecca, then where Kelley stands is the Kaaba. More than any ski run, Bridge street defines Vail.

Imagine Venice and you envision canals. Paris is famous for her broad boulevards of light. And who could forget Rome, for all roads lead to her. It is always the roads which define the space around them. Though Bridge Street may seem a pitiful mockery of some of the grander thoroughfares in our cities, or a sad reminder of how pretty an un-paved country lane can be, it has a grandeur all its own.

Early mornings it is the heavy tread of ski boots that fills the air.

40

The bar windows are shuttered. Lifeless electric beer signs rest as the army of skiers come down from the hotels, from Pepi's, the Sitzmark, the Vail Village Inn, The Lodge, their skis slung over their shoulders like tools, and converge at Bridge Street where they march toward lift number sixteen in expectant silence. Locals file out of the parking garage, duct tape on the seat of their ski pants, they cross the covered bridge and join the tourists.

The hum of many voices and the unison clatter of boots, poles and skis clicking together as the skiers complete their early morning pilgrimage to the mountain is magic. All focus on the task at hand. *Do I have my goggles? And if I don't, will I need them today?* Other myriad complexities of preparation, some rote, some ritual, can be witnessed by the keen observer on these early mornings. Stiff fingers press against unfriendly metal buckles on ski boots. *Crank it down.* Snowboarders stand on the edge of the crowd in sacred vestments. A Carhart workmans jacket made of heavy brown canvas adorns one. It is so large his body has lost all proportion. He is the jacket. *We are rebels.* Amazonian blond women strike unconscious poses in their tight black spandex, husbands beside them in *G.Q.* splendor. They apply sunblock religiously while striding up Bridge Street. *We are success.*

Noon and the streets are graced with shoppers, mothers and fathers in furs. Mexican ladies with hands un-fettered flit from shop to shop like bright birds of paradise, their dark skinned maids laden with carefully wrapped pastel packages stride two respectful steps behind. The bars are awake now. Lunch is served.

Three o'clock and the skiers return to sit on the sun decks of various bars with a pint of Fat Tire. The sun is threatening to dip beneath the low eaves on its shortened winter arc. In the shadows is deathly chill. With cheeks aglow, skiers march back to their hotels. Bridge street is gray. The day is ending, and the light of the bars is beginning to take hold while a solitary, hardy cyclist weaves between skiers in crazy circles through the dying sunlight.

The bars. At The Club a solitary man with a guitar plays ribald folk before the fraternity boys up from Boulder. A woman with more moving parts than a clock stands beside him in a tiny bikini. The air smells of sweat, nicotine, and alcohol. Inside Serrano's middle aged pirates quaff margaritas and sing along with Jimmy Buffett. Down Bridge Street the crowd moves from bar to bar. Drunk on thin mountain air and cold beer, they sway in the wind. This is the Bridge street shuffle. A nightly samba of bright ski clothes from one ubiquitous bar to another. At Vendettas, where dollar beers keep a steady racket up all night, Kelley and Friday were bellied up to the font of eternal Budweiser.

Kelley Sapp was pondering his quest for love. "What about her?" He pointed to a small table occupied by three young lovelies, and nudged

41

Friday in the ribs.

"Which one," Friday narrowed his eyes and peered through the cloud of cigarette smoke.

"The one with the baseball cap."

"Jail bait Kelley, they're all jail bait. Mom and dad own a condo in West Vail. They blew off school in Cherry Creek today."

"How do you know?"

"Suit yourself."

Kelley finished his beer and walked over to the table.

"Hi," he said. The girls looked up at him with amusement. Kelley struggled with his inhibitions and lost. Embarrassed, he returned to the bar.

"Last of the red hot lovers," Friday drawled sarcastically. At that point Kelley was quite drunk.

"Cmon, let's get out of here."

They finished their beers and stepped out into the cold. Kelley and Friday stumbled arm in arm past the *faux*-European arichtecture of Bridge street, underneath the pastoral Tyrolean frescos of Pepi's Austrian guesthouse, into the cowboy bar, out and quickly into the disco, then quickly out again. Sneaking beers through in their jacket pockets, Kelley checked out the tourist women from L.A., New York, and Chicago. Bridge street whizzed past them in an intoxicated and schizophrenic blur of pre-formed concrete and displaced culture. Stumbling out of Vendettas for the second time, they found themselves back in the center of Bridge street. The snoguns hissed high up on the slopes, pumping out inches of artificial snow for the morning. Time slowed, and Kelley became indignant as he realized the night was drawing to a close. Disgusted with himself, he headed for the nearest snowbank to urinate. As ammoniacal warm fumes washed over his nostrils, Kelley leaned over and heaved the contents of his floating stomach into the white.

"Cmon," said Friday as he wrapped an arm around Kelley's shoulders, "let's get out of here." Like two old men they limped back to the parking structure. Windows down, Friday's Celica raced into Avon with Beethoven's Fifth pumping from the speakers. Kelley slumped gratefully onto his naked mattress, the orange sleeping bag twisted like a snake through his legs.

He slept. He dreamt into the white, dreams of Vail filled with family members and lost friends who ordered him to fetch beer and food. The dreams continued until he awoke, several hours later, with a terrible thirst, still drunk. He guzzled some water and urinated again before returning to bed. When he woke for good it was mid-afternoon - light was dimming and he would soon be leaving for work.

Chapter 3:
Birth of a ...

Kelley Sapp's correspondence comprised not only wistful letters and one sided oral dialogues with Z but descriptive journal passages which he fondly considered time capsules destined for commendation one future season by a repentant society.

The Silver Aspen Condominiums are neither silver nor located within sight of a single aspen tree. Three years old now, they are beginning to resemble abused children. Neglected by their landlords and molested by resident tenants, a shabby and depressing aura surrounds all six hundred identical units. Last night at my friend's unit, which happens to be located directly across the parking lot from my own, I endured a torturous sense of deja vu while ensconced within his living room. Surely no two places on earth can look exactly the same but you would be hard- pressed to find the difference between my friend's unit and my own. Like a sculpture by Warhol was all I could think. 'Kelley's Apartment Six Hundred Times' would surely be the title. If you happen to like Warhol; then perhaps, you would be interested in purchasing my section of the sculpture for a tidy sum. Personally, I have always found his work to be a gimmick containing more statement than substance. If I must be trapped inside an artistic vision of hell, please make it Bosch. He's much more exciting. And if I had my choice of any painting, it would have to be Matisse. I would join the circle of his dance and turn until, exhausted, I collapsed in blissful ignorance of the Silver Aspen Condominiums.

The morning of the *menage a trois*, Kelley put down his pen and wandered out into the kitchen for unspecific reasons. He found Kellie Kay ready and waiting. He had showered and drunk three cups of black coffee in an effort to chase away his hangover, and had consequently been peeing at an alarming rate. On his way to the sink for some water he passed the soli-

43

tary Kellie Kay. Enticingly wrapped in a black silk dress with a low slung decolletage and sequined peplum, she resembled a gawky prom date unsure of both her figure and her clothes.

"I thought you were never coming out of there. How do I look?" Kellie curtsied and swished her hips.

"Absolutely ravishing," Kelley pacified her. He got some water and sat down with her at the kitchen table.

They waited.

At a quarter past two Kelley got up to make tea. Kellie Kay anxiously peered out of the living room window.

"Any sign?" Kelley asked.

"No. Not yet."

They read the paper.

At two thirty, Kelley had finished his tea and was about to suggest that Kellie call her friend and find out where she was when Kellie declared, "I'm not even attracted to you, are you attracted to me?"

Hung-over and feeling objective now, Kelley had a peculiar feeling that if he were to follow up Kellie's jibe she would call the whole thing off altogether. He half-wished for this result when he asked, "Then are you sure you should be doing it?"

"I think a better question is, do you want me to do it?"

"You're a nice person Kellie, and I don't mean that in a condescending way."

"You didn't answer my question."

"I hope you don't mind my saying so, but I was more than a little surprised when you proposed this. I don't know what Kris did to piss you off. Perhaps our little get together isn't the best form of response."

Kellie Kay drummed her fingers on the kitchen table while Kelley realized he had made no sense at all. If Kellie Kay were bi-sexual then of course she had other lovers. Wasn't he about to meet one right now? She must think I'm an idiot, he softly scolded his stupidity.

"Kris has nothing to do with this," Kellie Kay matter of factly made her point. "He and I are one thing. You and I are entirely something else."

There was an uncomfortable silence.

Kellie Kay glanced at her watch. "Maybe you should call him?" she suggested.

"Who?"

"Friday."

"What's he got to do with this?" Kelley genuinely wondered out loud.Slowly, the truth began to dawn in a golden haze of missed communication that rose and crackled like static electricity between their eyes.

Kellie Kay was the first to laugh.

"You mean, you thought that me and Friday?" Kelley gesticulated with arms wide and open mouth.

There was no need for words. And in the breech formed by their carefully misunderstood maneuvering a vacuum of possibility began to form.

"Oh, God!" Kellie stammered. "I guess it's just me and you." She collapsed onto the linoleum. Her legs splayed out at awkward angles from her dress. She peered up at Kelley. He turned away from her.

"You still haven't answered my question," Kellie prodded him.

"Of course you know I'm attracted to you," Kelley announced. *You and every other woman with curves, breasts, hips, and a tight ass. It's no great accomplishment. Don't you know that?*

He went on within himself as he watched Kellie Kay slowly stand up while peeling first, one shoulder, then another. Her dress hung on her breasts. She shrugged and it fell to her feet.

"Are you sure?" Kelley asked her.

Kelley Kay turned toward the bedroom, her wispy blond head lingered just long enough to give Kelley a knowing wink.

She stepped out of her dress.

He followed.

Perhaps if Kelley and Kellie were to stop and think about what they were doing, if they paused for a moment of contemplation in order to consider the vast scope of the world, then a great blond specter would rear his fearsome head into the air and, like a pagan son of Odin, scatter Cupid's darts away from our lovers' nest with a fearsome bellow. For Kris Blaze was in New Hampshire that day and all of that week. He had been in Vermont the day before, and would be in New York during the coming week. He had not been home to Vail for over three weeks; and if truth be told, he had not made love to Kellie Kay in over two months.

The Eastern leg of the World Pro Mogul Tour consisted of three competitions held at Killington in Vermont, Waterville Valley in New Hampshire, and Hunter Mountain near New York City.

A nascent professional sport schismatically severed from the World Cup Freestyle circuit, pro mogul skiers like Kris Blaze raced head to head in single elimination races through steep mogul fields. Their lifestyles resembled those of not quite famous rock stars. The mogul skiers gypsied across the country five to a van, their gear stacked to the ceiling and piled on the roof.

Now, it is generally acknowledged that there are two kinds of moguls in the world. There were the kind that used to run kingdoms in the far east, and in contemporary times run companies like John Rockefeller's Standard Oil, i.e. oil moguls and such. The other kind of moguls are the bumps which form on ski slopes when they are left un-groomed. It is purely coincidental that Vail contains copious quantities of both moguls and moguls. However, those who ski moguls well are generally not moguls. Moguls, for most middle-aged white men from Texas, are deadly obstacles that should be avoided at all costs. Oil wells, for most World Pro Mogul Tour skiers, would be the blackheads and pimples on their nearly pubescent faces. Young knees, dad's insurance policy, and a willingness to risk a life of walking are all that a young person needs in order to sign up for the pro mogul tour. Moguls on the slopes are round and humplike and pimple the steep faces of certain expert trails that are legendary for their difficulty.

Moguls who run companies are generally white, round, and hump-like as well. On the slopes they can sometimes bear an uncanny resemblance to the other kind of mogul, especially if they have made the mistake of attempting one of the aforementioned legendary slopes. Other than the fact that he might be lost or drunk or both, there are perhaps only two reasons why an oil mogul from Texas would attempt to ski a mogul field. The first is that his second wife wanted to ski the legendary slope and, being a man from Texas, he feels obliged to keep up. The second reason is that his son from his first marriage wanted to ski the bumps and the oil mogul feels obliged to stick with him since their vacation is supposed to be filled with quality time. From hence cometh the mogul amongst the moguls, a rare and generally semi-annual event. Perhaps a third reason explaining the presence of an oil mogul in the mogul fields would be a combination of the two aforemen-tioned scenarios. But this wouldn't really be a new reason, it would merely explain why the oil mogul happened to be drunk.

Kris Blaze's father had been a mechanic in Happy, Texas back in the forties after he got out of the army. During the war he'd worked on jeeps all the way from North Africa to Berlin, greasing them, coaxing them, get-ting shot at in them. He'd come back to Happy with a dress uniform, Sergeants stripes, and enough army scrip to buy himself some tools to go into business for himself out of the back shed of his parents' house.

The land around Happy was flat and dry and full of cows. The sky sat like a blue plate over the flatness of the plain, sandwiching the few build-ings of Happy between pieces of brown earth and blue sky. The buildings of Happy were wooden and square. They stood out like cardboard cutouts, like square pegs pounded up from the earth by some unseen infant playing with blocks. And like infants who pound square pegs into round holes, Ike Blazekowski, his family, and his neighbors were used to making things that didn't want to work function well and run smoothly. When they needed water, they dug for it until they found it. When the house got blown over by a tornado, they crawled out of the shelter and rebuilt it. When their teeth fell out on account of how much snuff they had dipped, they made do with their gums. When a horse got mean, they gelded it. And when cars and tractors came around to Happy and eventually decided that they didn't want to work very well, Ike Blazekowski was just the kind of tough, son-of-a-bitch mechanic only Happy, Texas and the U.S. Army 'vs' Hitler could have pro-duced.

Ike mended axles, ground down valves, re-bored cylinders, drained the oil out of a thousand crank cases straight into the parched brown soil behind his parents' shed so that forever after and into eternity there would be a naked circle of brown earth surrounded by the brown grass of Happy to mark Ike Blazekowski's workshop. At nighttime, with the stars, would come a shower of sparks out the door of the shed along with Ike's furious voice, "C'mon y' sonavabitch, work!"

And the sparks would fly, and the oil drain, and in the spirit of Vulcan's workshop Ike Blazekowski forged on with his immortal will to triumph over the inanimate and insensate. He prospered. He moved out of the shed. He married. And in the first year of his marriage to one Jean Marie *nee* Purvis, he became a father to both a baby girl and a growing fortune sucked out of the ground of the West Texas plain by a drilling rig he'd salvaged from a scrap heap near Wichita Falls. He'd taken one look at the rusting heap and promptly handed over six hundred dollars to the owner of the scrap yard. The year was nineteen forty eight and the drill rig was pre-war vintage. Ike had been out of the shed for three years. He had his own garage and two mechanics working for him, but he took the rig himself and set to work on it out in the back of the garage. Welding and grinding, pulling and hammering, he beat the shit out of it. And lo! One day the gears meshed, the pistons sputtered, and Ike Blazekowski wiped the grease from his hands with pride as he watched the rig rumble to life.

He pulled Tommy Bird off his porch and handed him twenty dollars. "Get your sticks," Ike told him.

"What for, Ike?" Tommy asked, "You already got yourself a good well."

"It's oil I'm after," Ike told him. "There's oil hidden all over this state. And I got a drill rig and enough pipe to go down a couple thousand feet. You think your sticks will work with oil?"

"I ain't never tried to dowse for oil," Tommy admitted. "I really can't promise it'll work. Heck Ike, even if we do find oil do you really think we're gonna find what you're looking for?"

Ike ignored him and stood thinking his own thoughts for a while. He'd heard of scientists over at the university in Austin who studied the earth. Geologists. They mapped the folds of rock and dirt underground by measuring the echoes of sound waves as they bounced off the rock layers. But those scientists were funded by the big oil companies. They didn't care if Ike Blazekowski found oil or a dry hole in the ground. He couldn't fork up enough bucks for their expensive toys and that was that. What Ike needed was an angle. He had to have some way of finding oil that no one else had thought of yet. Now, ever since Tommy Bird had quit travelling the circuit from Happy up to Hidden Springs and back down, twenty three towns in all, he'd settled into semi-retirement on the porch of his house in Happy. He'd sit all day, facing south, and watch as the sun traced its arc across the sky. He'd sit and dip snuff, and pet his dog. And somedays a car would pull up, maybe a newish one, and out would step a skeptical looking young man

47

dressed in a new suit. And with this man would be an older woman who would point up at Tommy and say, "That man is the reason you could take a bath at home, son. Go on and ask him."

And the young man, a little bit bashful now, would approach Tommy, maybe stand with his hat in his hand, (remember this is still the fifties) and not really know how to begin. He would look up at Tommy's lean sticklike body, and grey head, his arms poking out of his shirtsleeves like the twigs of a leathery old tree and find himself at a loss for words.

"Need a well?" Tommy would ask after an appropriate amount of time had passed.

"Just built a new house sir," the man would say, "me and my wife got married two months ago. Mom says you can find us water. Says you're the only dowser in all of West Texas who was ever worth a damn."

"That's right," Tommy would say, then spit off the edge of the porch. He'd sit silently in his chair while the young man stood there waiting. Then finally Tommy would clear his throat once, maybe twice, and say, "Newlyweds, huh?"

The young man would look curiously at Tommy and mutter, "Yes sir."

"Well, let's get going. I reckon I'll do it for free too. No point in charging people when I don't need it, especially folks just starting out like you."

Then Tommy would nod at the young man's mother, or maybe even wink if he remembered her from when they were both young. And he would climb down off the porch and into that car. And Ike Blazekowski would watch as the car drove off into the distance until just a small plume of dust marked its progress toward the horizon. He would stare and watch Tommy Bird, the man with a mystical gift, drive off down the road. And when the plume of dust disappeared off the edge of the horizon Ike would turn back to his wrenches and hammers and start pounding on the tractor engine or whatever it was he was working on and yell, "C'mon y' sonavabitch, work!" And in his heart he was jealous of what Tommy Bird had, which was the ability to give unconditionally of himself. Tommy's labor was not real labor, it was a gift, a freak of one in a million. And in Ike Blazekowski's heart, he felt the gap between people like himself, ordinary people, and people like Tommy Bird who it seemed never had to try.

So when Ike Blazekowski had his oil drill working and his sections of pipe all stacked up behind his garage, he figured that the angle he needed lay in Tommy Bird's talent to find water. Water and oil: they were both liquid and Ike figured it was worth a shot.

Tommy Bird sat there on his rocking chair looking up at Ike.

"Are you sure you want me to do this, Ike?"

"C'mon, don't talk to me like a priest," Ike chided him, before gripping one of those thin arms and gently lifting the frail old man out of his

48

rocking chair. "Get your sticks and we'll give it a test first."

"I'll take nothing from you," Tommy Bird warned.

So Ike Blazekowski and old Tommy Bird walked off Tommy's porch in the noonday sun and made their way down main street until they got to Ike's parents' house. They walked around to the back of the house until they got to the old shed where Ike used to have his garage. There, in the middle of the brown grass behind the shed, was the brown circle of dirt where Ike used to drain the oil out of crankcases. It still sat there, bare and naked. Ike and Tommy walked up to the edge of the spot.

"There," Ike said, "try out your sticks and see if they work. There's gotta be at least a thousand quarts of oil under that spot."

Tommy Bird took out his whittled pine sticks and held them in a V with one hand, thumb on top where the sticks crossed, and waved them slowly over the spot. He moved his hand in a circular pattern as he edged his way around. "Strangest thing," he began to say.

"What?"

"Feels like it's pushing up," Tommy said.

Sure enough, Tommy Bird relaxed his thumb and the two sticks levitated straight up into the air like the antennae on a television set as they hovered over the spot. Tommy waved his hand back and forth, watching as the sticks drooped and rose again as they crossed over the naked splotch of oil soaked dirt.

"Oil," Tommy said, it had to be. For in the normal practice of dowsing it was the pull of the sticks down toward the ground that signified the presence of water. It's opposite signal could only mean one thing. Oil and water, they do not mix. One goes up, one goes down.

"It works," Ike said in amazement. "Tommy, I'll pay you by the day until we find a place to drill."

"No need to," Tommy Bird said.

"Why of course there is."

"No need. This is the place." Tommy pointed at the spot. "There's a lot more than a thousand quarts down there. Feels like an ocean to me."

They both stared at the hovering sticks. "I'll be damned," Ike cursed again softly, "Sonovabitch, this is gonna work."

And it was on the very same day that Tommy Bird discovered oil for Ike Blazekowski that Ike's wife, Jean Marie Blazekowski *nee* Purvis, gave birth to her and Ike's first of fifteen children. She had a baby girl, and Ike named her Mary. Ike came back from the old garage to find Jean Marie all curled up in bed, the midwife holding his child up in a pink blanket. He went to his beautiful young wife, for Jean Marie had not yet begun to show the strains of family life and multiple birthings, and gazed down at her radiant face that was all aglow with sweat and happiness and thought to himself that she must look as beautiful as the Virgin herself when she gave birth to the baby Jesus. Hence the name Mary was chosen for their first child, and

Ike's love for his wife remained strong and healthy through those first years of his success.

It was weeks later when Ike's drill bit punched through the last layers of dirt and spouted oil all over his parents' house. Tommy Bird was sitting on his porch and rocking in his chair when he heard the sound of oil rushing up through the pipes and exploding out into the parched blue sky that forever lay over Happy. And he just sat there and rocked and seemed not to give a damn that he'd just made Ike Blazekowski a rich man.

Long after the well had been capped and a pump was brought in to suck the oil out of the ground, Ike Blazekowski sat and waited for Tommy Bird to come and ask him for money. He sat and he waited and he played with his baby Mary on the floor of his newly built concrete ranch house, the first one in all of Happy to have central air conditioning. It got so bad that finally, one day, after about eight months had gone by, Ike Blazekowski drove his shiny new car to the front of Tommy Bird's porch and got out in his new suit and stood looking up at Tommy Bird, who was just as frail and sticklike as he'd always been.

Ike stood there thinking that Tommy Bird had waited him out. For deep in Ike Blazekowski's soul he firmly believed that Tommy Bird knew the value of his own talent, and that like some kind of strange savant Tommy Bird had been waiting on his porch for Ike Blazekowski, the man who worked with his hands, to come and pay him tribute. And Ike stood there not really knowing what to say, as he placed the keys to his new car at Tommy Bird's feet. He turned to go after giving what he thought was fair recompense, though his heart resented it. Ike truly believed that the brunt of the labor had been his and that Tommy Bird had only been the angle he, Ike Blazekowski, had used like a tool in order to get what he wanted. But Ike also knew that without Tommy Bird all of his labor wouldn't have been worth so much as spit in a hot skittle. Ike could have punched a thousand holes in the dry Texas dirt before he found one that yielded as much oil as sat in the car at that very moment.

So Ike stood there with his hat in his hand, looking up at Tommy Bird. Tommy Bird spit over the porch railing and looked down at Ike before he spoke. "I don't want your car. I told you I wasn't gonna take no payment from you anyway. If you wanna go look f'r another one of those oil wells then let's go," Tommy Bird said. "Don't stand there lookin' stupid like you don't know what to do. Let's get in that car o' yours and go. I been thinkin 'bout other places worth checkin out."

And in that moment when Ike Blazekowski was standing like a stupid rock in front of Tommy Bird, Ike realized for the first time just how cheap a million-to-one talent can really be. Ike and Tommy drove out of Happy leaving a cloud of dust to mark their trail all the way to the horizon. Where the Texas blue meets the Texas brown, they drove over the edge of that horizon and into a different world for Ike Blazekowski, who now knew that the truest talent in the world is the one which lets a person understand the value of things. And Ike's heart was glad, for he felt that he possessed this talent. He did not even stop to consider that it might be Tommy Bird who understood the true value of things, and that was why Tommy Bird gave freely of himself and of his talent.

With Tommy Bird as his angle, Ike Blazekowski went on a run of oil discoveries unlike any seen before in West Texas. Late at night Ike and Tommy Bird would creep across the flat Texas plain, Ike holding a torch and Tommy Bird his pine sticks. For nights at a time they would do this until Tommy Bird's sticks found the right spot. And Ike would carefully mark the spot with a pile of stones gathered off the dusty plain. Then Ike and Tommy would hike back to Ike's car and drive back to Happy, where Tommy would return to his porch and his chair and his snuff. And Ike would begin the long and nefarious process of extracting the land on which the recently discovered spot was located from the possession of its present owners. Not all the cattle that died nor all of the crops which were destroyed were the result of Ike Blazekowski's invisible hand. Sometimes hail did destroy a crop or two, or a natural disease took down a herd of cattle. But the series of calamities which regularly rained down upon the land marked by Ike and Tommy Bird with a small pile of stones was a coincidence too regular to be anything but the planned economic destruction of the current owners of the land.

For, from Ike Blazekowski's point of view, it was that little pile of stones collected on top of the brown Texas dirt which marked the true value of the land. For Ike, the pile of stones was an indication of the hidden wealth which lay waiting for him. And as for that same pile of stones, should it be stumbled upon by the rancher or farmer who currently owned the land, what would he think when he saw the heaped rocks? Would it take his mind off the most recent bank notice he'd happened to receive that day? Would he think that perhaps one of his children had buried a small animal under the stones? Would he not see the stones for what they actually were - a symbol of his own death? Death of a lifestyle, death of a family: all of these things were marked by the simple pile of stones.

For with these stones came famished cattle and dying crops as in Biblical tales of plagues recorded in the Old Testament. Eventually the bank would come in and foreclose, and the auction would be held, and one of Ike's employees would be there with orders to go as high as necessary, which was never too high. For only Ike and Tommy Bird knew what riches lay underneath the soil of one more dead Texas ranch or farm.

For fifteen years it went on, and with each additional year at least one oil well and one more child arrived for Ike Blazekowski and Jean Marie. Ike now had houses in Dallas and Martha's Vineyard, as well as Happy. He belonged to a country club in Dallas, a place where the brown Texas dirt was watered so profusely as to create an oasis of green pastures worthy of Ireland. And at this club he had the good company of fellows who called him

51

Captain, because he'd been in the army in the War. And this pleased Ike because in his heart he felt as though he should have been a captain, and not just a sergeant. But, he conceded, not everyone had the same gift for seeing true value like he did. So in his heart, he forgave the U.S. Army for its slight; and for the present, allowed himself to be called Captain as a concession to the way things should have been.

For fifteen years it went on as though it would never end. And when his fifteenth child was borne by Jean Marie, who nearly died while birthing him, Ike was called away from a business meeting in Dallas and flew home to Happy. Now the reason Ike flew home was not because his fifteenth child was being born. Another child was the least of Ike's concerns; for in truth his first fourteen had failed to elicit much fatherly love from Ike. With the exception of the moment when he viewed his first child, Mary, Ike had been routinely disappointed by his offspring. If the truth be told, they were far too much like Ike himself to interest him very much. With black hair and thick digits attached to their hands and feet, Ike and Jean Marie's children were as dense and brutish as Ike himself. So when Ike flew back to Happy on the tenth day of October in nineteen sixty three, he did so because the phone call he'd received in Dallas told him that Tommy Bird was on his deathbed in Happy and that he wanted to see Ike before he died.

With over fifteen wells producing oil, Ike was already a very rich man, and as he flew into Happy to visit Tommy Bird on his deathbed, Ike carried a dictaphone in his jacket pocket so he could record all of Tommy Bird's last words. Ike's thinking, of course, ran along the assumption that Tommy would be divulging the whereabouts of the last oil wells he had located. For the past fifteen years, Tommy Bird had located wells free of charge for Ike refusing the money, the cars, and the houses Ike offered to buy for him.

So it was without any preparation whatsoever for what was about to happen that Ike Blazekowski stepped into Tommy Bird's old house and leaned over the dying old man with his dictaphone on and began to listen as Tommy Bird spoke out of his swollen, cancerous mouth.

"There will be a male child born today in Happy, in your house," Tommy Bird began with his eyes closed and his stick figure all a trembling underneath the army blanket. "This child will be your last. And he will be both your greatest joy and your worst torment, for you will love him as you love no one else. You will love him because he is your son and he will become everything you wish your life had been. He will have the God-given talent that makes life seem effortless. He will be like me."

And with that, Tommy Bird's eyes opened and glared up into Ike's. And Ike knew that for all of the oil that Tommy Bird had found for him, and all of the times Ike had tried to pay Tommy off with a house or money or liquor and failed, he knew that the bill was being rung up now while Tommy Bird lay dying. And in his heart, he felt a sudden urge to rid himself of this son before he even became a problem.

"You will love him and you will hate him," Tommy Bird continued. "He will be your conscience like I never was. Ike, I know you've done a lot of terrible, terrible things. Don't think I've been ignorant this whole time. And I know you ain't likely to change. I have watched you wreck entire families. That's why I could never take a dime from you. I helped you 'cause all along I knew this day would come when I would talk to you like I am right now and tell you that your son and your family and your story will become the seed from which will blossom an even greater story. What that other story is I can't say now 'cause it's still working itself out. All I can say is that, your one chance at redemption for the wicked way you have led your life lies with your son. If you can earn his love, your memory will be forever cherished by the generations coming after our own. I can see it up there in the stars, like a picture, they're gettin brighter, oh my God!"

And with that Tommy Bird did the death rattle and gave up his ghost.

There was a moment of hesitation when Ike got back to Jean Marie's bedside and stared down at his black-haired infant son. This one didn't look remarkably different from the others, Ike thought. He stood there doubting Tommy Bird's prophecy. After all, the man had simply been a dowser and never a fortune teller before today. The little baby cooed and burped, then snuggled toward its mother. Ike was very careful not to wake Jean Marie while he pulled his newborn son away from her. Out into the desert he drove with his son until he reached a place where the lights of Happy no longer glowed on the horizon and the evening stars twinkled brightly in the red-tinged darkness of a Texas sunset.

And the baby started crying because it was hungry for its mother's breast.

"Shush," Ike told the baby, but the baby was hungry and kept on crying while the sun kept sinking lower and lower until Ike stood in complete darkness, his shadow cast by starlight, cuddling his son against his chest to keep him warm and safe from the night chill of the desert.

"Oh God, oh God, how can I kill my own son?" Ike asked out loud. He stared up into the stars, at their brightness, and wondered what picture it was that Tommy Bird had seen in them before dying those few hours ago. He pulled out the dictaphone and played the tape. He listened to Tommy Bird's prophecy while the fear crept back into him as Tommy Bird slowly spoke. It was not the child itself that Ike feared, nor was it even Tommy Bird's prophecy that Ike's son would be blessed with a million-to-one talent. For his own son, Ike could feel no jealousy for whatever talent with which he might be blessed. No, the fear Ike felt was inspired by one thing, that thing was the same thing that all men in positions of power fear most. Ike feared a power of judgment that he could not control. For Ike's redemption or damnation lay in the hands of a child, and like a politician who rails against the cartoonist who lampoons him, Ike wanted to stifle the voices that could rise up and turn against him and damn him forever in the clearer hindsight of history. He should end it now before it ever starts.

He went so far as to even pick up a rock, but at the last moment his stomach betrayed him at the thought of the blood. And then the idea came to Ike. It struck him between the eyes like the proverbial bolt from above. He had once read a book by Mark Twain while in high school that his church hadn't approved. Perhaps this disapproval inspired Ike to even crack the cover. He couldn't remember all of the particulars or even the title. All he remembered was that a slave woman had switched her son for the son of the master. The book had confused Ike on matters of black and white, which had always seemed rather black and white to him before. But like most ideas he couldn't bludgeon into submission, Ike forgot about it and left things black and white for simplicity's sake. But now, when the similarity between fiction and his own life became apparent, the story haunted him. He wouldn't make the same mistake of having both babies grow up in the same town. This, he remembered, led to the eventual discovery of the switch in the book. No, Ike would go to Dallas, to the hospital with the newly completed five million dollar Ike Blazekowski Memorial wing. For like most men in positions of power, Ike had recently taken up the hobby of philanthropy. He would go and get himself a new son and end this prophecy crap now and for good.

With an added burden Ike slumped toward his car. The stars twinkled brightly as Ike Blazekowski showed them and whatever picture it was Tommy Bird had seen in them his middle finger. The car door slammed with finality. He was ending it, he thought. The Texas dust flew as Ike's car shot south toward Dallas on that tenth day of October in nineteen sixty three, near the town of Happy, in the state of Texas, in the United States of America, in the northern hemisphere of the planet Earth, underneath that cloud of stars called the Milky Way. That's where it happened, and that's where it all began.

At unit 201-B of the Silver Aspen Condominiums Kelley Sapp said to Kellie Kay, "You're my girlfriend now." With her hand, Kellie Kay reached across and covered Kelley's mouth.

"Shush," she told him before rolling off the tramp and walking naked into the bathroom. She looked at her face in the mirror and came to grips. Kris would come back and she would wait for him. *God*, she wished, *don't let this man love me*, Kris Blaze hardly ever touched her. He was the man she still loved.

While Kris Blaze, adopted son of an oil mogul, raced among the moguls of the Appalachian mountains, Kellie Kay confirmed her love through infidelity. She closed her eyes and refused to acknowledge the traditional conflicts causing her angst. She was not cheap. If anything, she was dear. Kris Blaze would find that out, fast, if things did not change.

Chapter 4:

Back to Work

"I'm here," Bennett Beauregard tapped Sloth on the shoulder.

It was the night of the International Workers Union dinner and close to a week after Kelley's initial employment.

"I'm here," Bennett Beauregard repeated. This obvious fact was certainly regarded as no great cause for celebration by Sloth. After disdainfully noting the blue suited menace with an air of nonchalance, he turned without a word of reply and ordered a drink from the bar like a battle scarred soldier. "Cheers," he said, and took a sip before Bennett Beauregard's arched eyebrows.

That Bennett Beauregard was concierge of the Snowy Mountains Guest Lodge seemed a fated occurrence whose celestial appointment had been secured long before Eve ever thought about disobedience. If one believed in the immortality of souls and cared to venture a cynical guess as to how Bennett Beauregard had spent the previous millennia perhaps one would come up with something like this - He had fared poorly as an ant and failed to distinguish himself during a brief and tragic incarnation as a hydra. Carrying an immense load of karmic debt stored up through millennia of cannibalistic activities begun during the Jurassic period and lasting through the late Cretaceous, Bennett Beauregard's immortal soul now found itself at the very bottom of the evolutionary ladder. That he had gestated and developed within the normal boundaries of human experience belied the unquestionable destiny of his pre-ordained life. There could be no other place for him in this world. Though the changes wrought by time would manifest themselves in various forms, Bennett Beauregard's indomitable brownnosing had been a fixture since early childhood.

Like a feudal tenant, Bennett Beauregard belonged to the Snowy Mountains Guest Lodge. His navy suits embodied the concentrated malevolence contained within the periwinkle walls. His symbiosis was so sinister, so complete, that it was impossible to imagine Bennett Beauregard in a sunny field with a million black-eyed susans waving about his naked body. One couldn't plunk him down in Times Square or Bangladesh with any facility. Though many had tried, it was a futile struggle to imagine Bennett Beauregard as anything other than the concierge of the Snowy Mountains Guest Lodge. Misery spread like a virus in his wake. Bennett Beauregard lovingly greased the rods and gears of industrialized hell. He turned the crank with glee, pushing his weighted soul down another notch in the spiraling descent of his incarnations.

He strode past the Steinway and on past the polar bear with a serene look of placid determination upon his face. He cast a shadow upon Mrs. Grahmsham, who was picking stucco out of her coffee cup, but never once broke stride as he made his way into the dark grotto confines of *Au Naturel*. It had been two hours since Bennett Beauregard disappeared. He was back now; everything could continue.

At the wooden washtub Kelley Sapp was up to his arms in tannic suds. A small troupe of cooks and waiters were busily prepping *hors d'oeuvres* and salads, polishing glasses, wiping silverware, and stirring the black cook kettles. "Oh, here it is," Kelley produced a large knife from the depths. Clad in his medieval tunic and hose he resembled a young Ivanhoe holding a short sword. With a silent tread amid the clatter of the kitchen Bennett Beauregard crept up behind Kelley.

"I'm here," he said, touching him on the shoulder.

Startled, Kelley turned around with the knife. "What?"

"Don't hurt me," Bennett Beauregard pleaded. His cadaverously pale face shrank back from the cruel blade Kelley held aloft. The hundred watt bulbs, recessed and screwed into parallel sockets of his naked skull, lit up with alarm.

Kneel, Kelley thought, *and obey me.*

"Oh," Kelley put the knife down gently. A cloud of innocence floated in and pushed the dark storm away from his pate. Beaming a soporific, stupid ignorance that calmed Bennett Beauregard, Kelley swept his momentary lapse of sanity into the past and resumed his subservient role.

"Oh," he said again.

"I'm here, " Bennett Beauregard proclaimed. He waited for Kelley to nod in acknowledgement before sweeping away from the washtub. In his dark navy suit he cut a swath through the white coated kitchen staff. Bennett Beauregard was here.

As concierge of the Snowy Mountains Guest Lodge, it was Bennett Beauregard's duty to make sure that everything ran smoothly for the guests. His desk sat to the immediate left of the lodge entrance. Guests would sit and chat with Bennett, who was adept at reading *what the guests were really saying*. At the back of the kitchen in a dimly lit chamber that stank of mold and entrails Bennett Beauregard strode behind Chef Christian. He paused for a moment in order to watch the Chef work.

Whack, A sharp steel edge separated a live lobster from its tail. Bennett Beauregard flinched, then stopped to observe the shadowy bulk of Chef Christian at work.

Whack, whack.

Both claws were no longer part of the lobster. In fact the lobster wasn't really a lobster anymore. What used to be the lobster tried to crawl off the cutting board. It's antennae quivered with questions no philosopher has ever been able to answer fully.

"Eh! Where do you think you're going?" Chef Christian LeForrestier, the man responsible for the lobster's philosophical questioning, asked on a more mundane level.

Soon the lobster's antennae were gone. Each little claw was clipped with a surgeons skill until only one remained. *Sans* tail, major claws and antennae, the lobster spun on it's one remaining claw like a spider stripped of all legs save one. Chef Christian thumbed the edge of his cleaver. His face, in the dark, held a half smile of curious interest that lit his Gallic features. With a silver flash of the cleaver the belated *coup de grace* swept down.

In Marseilles, at the age of twelve, a young Christian LeForrestier had begun his formal restaurant training by shucking oysters. The short path of his formative youth had been spent ducking school and learning to smoke cigarettes down by the quays where his father kept a fish stall. He had dreamed of one day riding a Harley Davidson across France and into Germany, but instead found himself placed into an apprenticeship that resembled slavery and would have surely violated child labor laws had any existed.

For four years he washed the dishes and pots during service. No longer in school, his only day off was Monday, when the restaurant was closed. And even that was a busman's holiday for he spent the morning fetching anisette and pernod from the outdoor cafe while the older staff played boccie and dispensed wisdom on their young charge.

"Someday you will be a chef, Christian, and you may even be able to afford a nice Peugeot," he had been told by the restaurant owner. The other staff, all of whom had long ago committed themselves to life imprisonment in their secure stations, nodded their heads in grim confirmation. Their youth was gone and all their promise had dried up with the withering regularity of a steady paycheck and even steadier bills. Christian could see it all. Vacations at discount beaches in the Adriatic. Maybe a fling with one of the local prostitutes. Such promise his life held if he only stayed in place and did what he was told. And as he shucked the oysters and washed the pots a seed of cynicism lodged in the soft mantle of his brain to form a hard pearl of discontent.

At sixteen, he was presented with his first set of knives and began to receive a regular wage which he saved. For the next two years Christian learned how to slice vegetables into very thin slivers. Next came the terrines and pates. He made jellied eel terrine wrapped with leeks. Pate de fois gras and wild deer liver mousse were added to his repertoire. And always he saved. For what, he knew not. Like a Ragged Dick out of some Alger story he neither drank nor spent his free time on frivolous games. He joined the library and read Escoffier, thrilled by the story of the short man in oversized kitchen clogs who eventually won the respect of academics through his culinary scholarship. He read Proust and Rousseau, always feeding the nagging goad of discontent that dogged his current station in life.

Six years later he was Sous Chef, second-in-command of the kitchen, with an oyster shucker and vegetable cutter under his direct tutelage when the revolution occurred. Christian had been on his way to the market to buy the early morning catch from his father when he read the news that would forever change his life. As was his usual habit, he read the newspaper as he made his way down the familiar cobbled streets that led to the quays. There, on page two, was a picture of a Chef from Paris holding a plate that appeared to contain nothing more than rose petals arranged delicately about a tiny thimble of pureed meat or fish. Underneath the picture was the heading *La Nouvelle Cuisine*. The new food. The new style. Like the Beatles, Punk Rock, and Impressionist painting, Christian knew this would be big. He stood in his tracks underneath the azure sky of the spring morning and stared at the grainy micro-dot photo. No more terrines. No more pates. Never again would he knead goose liver with his bare hands. Everything would be light, like leaves on a plate. Taste would be everything. If you wanted sustenance, go home and roast yourself a chicken. This style, Christian could tell, would be as ephemeral and sweet as the spring breeze of the morning. He breathed deeply through his nose and exhaled through his mouth with joy. At last, he knew what to do with his money.

Two months later, when he opened his own restaurant three streets away from his old place of employment, Christian LeForrestier caught the high crest of a culinary wave that was sweeping Europe. Each chef was known for his or her particular style, and in the fashion magazines that were turning these new chefs into celebrities, Christian LeForrestier was best known for his wonderfully inventive use of almost raw fish. "I kiss it with a hint of steam, then I let it go out to the diner in an almost pristine state of natural beauty and flavor," Christian was quoted in one American Fashion magazine. Within six months, customers lined up around the block and waited for hours. Christian opened a second restaurant in Paris. He drove a Ferrari. He married a model he met at a fashion show in Milan. Together they collected art and went to parties where Christian would thrill everyone by poking a wine cork into the bottle with his naked pinkie finger. He had blossomed into a powerful, self-assured man.

Fifteen years later, and many times a millionaire, he found his star fading on the continent and made the leap to the Snowy Mountains Guest Lodge when the backers offered him a ridiculous amount of money to open restaurant *Au Naturel*. Once again his name and picture began appearing in fashion magazines. Only this time he was no longer the young lion he had been. Portrayed as one of the elder statesmen of *haute cuisine*, his arrival in America was heralded as a cultural *coup d'etat*.

So it happened that the French chef best known for his dishes of almost raw fish assumed control of a restaurant in the middle of Colorado. That the potential annual earnings of the restaurant could not hope to cover Christian's six figure salary, let alone the food cost, seemed to be of no importance.

"You think I'm watching you?" Chef Christian said to the dead lobster. "I saw you try to sneak away from me without saying nothing. But you cannot sneak away from me. I see everything." The lobster remained mute.

"I wasn't sneaking," Bennett Beauregard adamantly protested.

"Heh," Chef Christian turned around with his cleaver, somewhat embarrassed that someone had caught his one sided dialogue with the lobster. It was an old habit of his from childhood that most of the kitchen was used to: "He's in the back with the lobsters," went the usual refrain.

"No! Put that thing down, please," Bennett shrank back from the cold steel. "I'm back now, and I'm going to be watching you," he continued. "It's one thing to bully a lobster around, but little children are quite a different matter altogether."

"Heh?" Chef Christian peered across the dim room and recognized Bennett, whom he hated. Reverting to his Neanderthal tone of voice, one he employed with waiters as well as his performance with wine bottles, Christian raised his cleaver even higher. "I do whatever I want. So you shut up or I throw this at you," he enunciated perfectly.

Bennett Beauregard scuttled off toward the dry storage area in back of the kitchen.

Chef Christian couldn't help wondering what little children had to do with him, but he wasn't really in the mood to find out. All he knew was that his wife had purchased another one of those nine-inch Venetian bronzes. This one was supposedly thirteenth century. Upon microscopic examination Christian had discovered what he thought to be an obscured seamline in the cast. Regardless of whether it was genuine, he sincerely doubted it was worth the seventy five thousand dollar price tag. His wife was bored here. She didn't ski. She didn't like the cold. She continued to chain smoke as if she were still living on the runways of Milan. He felt her monthly shopping sprees in New York must be some kind of unconscious protest. With a sigh he remembered his new Warhol was due in today. This thought brightened Christian considerably. He plucked another lobster from the box in front of him and went back to work.

Bennett Beauregard found himself all alone in the dry storage area.

Surrounded by rack upon rack of paper doilies, jarred capers, and industrial sized slabs of Belgian chocolate, he very quickly became claustrophobic.

Rather than risk sneaking by the Chef again he ducked outside into the sub-freezing Colorado night by way of the loading dock.

A shadowy group of men smoking cigarettes was gathered a fair distance away from the dock. Dressed in fedoras and wool overcoats they resembled a stooped flock of cartoon vultures.

"Hmmph," Bennett snorted as he sneaked a glance at them across the ice bound lot. Cigarette smoking was not allowed in the Snowy Mountains Guest Lodge. Only Mr. Posthelwait, the owner, was allowed to light up his cigars on the premises. Bennett Beauregard looked down on all smokers, excepting Mr. Posthelwait of course. Smoking was a nasty, dirty habit and only rarely, as in Mr. Posthelwait's case of course, did it lend a dignified air to the smoker.

"Not like the docks out in Jersey," one of the group remarked. A chorus of cackles and laughs filled the cold.

Bennett Beauregard wondered if the comment had somehow been directed at him. On all fours, to keep from slipping, he scrambled down off the loading dock and slipped back inside through the servants' entrance, a door he normally avoided like the plague.

Once inside he perked up and made his way toward the employee lounge. Staff dinner had been served. Sloth, Kelley, and all of the restaurant staff were discussing the bill of fare.

"What is this?" Sloth rhetorically questioned. An impaled piece of nondescript flesh was raised for inspection on his fork. "I'm serious. Is it pork?"

Kelley Sapp, who had just taken a bite, would have answered had his jaw not been bouncing like a rubber ball. He thought it was beef. Or was it lamb? He couldn't tell, and carefully feigned coughing into his hands while palming the chewed bit of meat. He let it drop to the floor as his hands fell back to his lap.

"It's almost cooked meat, kissed with a hint of steam, then sent out to us in an almost pristine state of natural beauty and flavor," one of the other waiters commented dryly. Sloth was about to agree most vociferously when a windblown Bennett Beauregard strode in.

"Time I got back to work," Sloth quickly rose from the table along with everyone else except Kelley, who had been busy with a feigned attempt to tie his shoelace. By the time he had pushed the bit of chewed meat into a well concealed position under the center of the table everyone else had left him. He rose from the linoleum and found himself stranded, with Bennett Beauregard, under the fluorescent lights.

A complaining sigh escaped Bennett as he settled into a plastic chair across from Kelley and hypocritically lit a cigarette.

That the scene now resembled a police interrogation did not escape

Kelley. He was alone in a room with a man in a blue suit. The smoke from the cigarette drifted toward the humming tubes, and Kelley felt like a bit character. Dressed in his period costume he wondered if he might say something like, *you know me and Bugsy worked for the circus. That's all I can say about him. I'm just a clown, that's all. I'm a simple clown. I don't know what goes on.*

"I can be frank with you. He's drunk again." Bennett exhaled a cloud of blue smoke from his nostrils. "I've already talked to Mr. Posthelwait about him."

Of course he's drunk, he's always drunk. "Who, Sloth?"

Bennett nodded slowly. He was about to put Kelley in the picture. For in the topsy turvy world of restaurants, where up is down and down is up, the position of restaurant manager can be characterized as a promotion to the bottom. It is a position so little coveted by those underneath the manager that they will generally do anything to avoid it. Idealistic young graduates of hotel and restaurant schools willingly hurl themselves into these positions of great responsibility and little pay. But they are the idealistic zealots willing to sacrifice their persons in a kamikaze whirl of bookkeeping and sixteen hour days.

"Sloth will be lucky if he keeps his job into next week. What would you say to being Maitre D'?" Bennett dangled the glass jewel in front of Kelley. "I've studied your resume. You have a great deal of restaurant experience."

It was the first time in Kelley's life he had ever been offered a promotion of any sort. He had no desire for the position. Rather, it was a creeping guilt he felt. The guilt told him that if he were ever going to become something then he must be willing to accept responsibility. The clearer, saner part of Kelley told the guilt to go to hell. If anything, he wanted out of restaurants. Guilt won.

"I don't know if I really want to deal with the Chef," Kelley compromised when he should have flatly refused.

"I've also been talking to Mr. Posthelwait about Chef." Bennett Beauregard didn't miss a beat. "Mr. Posthelwait is very concerned about what some of the guests have been saying. One family said they were never ever going to stay here again because Chef came outside one morning, when they were helping their young son build a snowman, and kicked the snowman over right in front of them. Do you remember the Tunniwinkles?"

"Oh my God," Kelley Sapp said.

"They are from New York City. It was the little boy's first snowman. He had named it Frosty."

"Oh my God."

"You couldn't have imagined my shock. Do you want to know what Chef said to the little boy when he kicked over the snowman?" Bennett asked.

"No," Kelley said.

61

"Well, I'm going to tell you anyway. He said, *Frosty's dead little boy. He's dead, he's dead, he's dead. He's all alone now, and he's dead, and he went straight to hell because he was a rotten little snowman.*"

"That," Bennett Beauregard arched his eyebrows and drew all six feet two inches of his frame up while puffing out his double breasted suit so he looked exactly like a whooping crane, "is exactly what he said to the boy."

"Unbelievable," Kelley exclaimed with some detachment.

"I didn't want to believe it myself," Bennett continued in a somewhat less dramatic tone. "I found it very hard to realize that such a great artist like our Chef could be so insensitive. But once I got over the initial barrier of disbelief it was as if my eyes had been opened for the first time. The man is a monster."

"I've never had any doubt of that."

"Don't tell anyone," Bennett Beauregard whispered to Kelley. "Sloth will be the first to go, but Chef will surely follow soon thereafter. And remember," Bennett Beauregard reached his pale hand across the table and tapped Kelley on the shoulder, "I've recommended you to Mr. Posthelwait."

He turned with a flourish and disappeared down the dank tunnel toward the gastric noises of the rumbling kitchen, his shadow long upon the shaped and sweating stucco. Bennett Beauregard's stride was even and measured. As he receded into the dim light his shadow vacillated and fluxed as if at every moment his body were mutating into horrific and surprising shapes. Kelley could have sworn a curtain opened and swallowed Bennett whole. He gazed alone off toward the stage. The curtain was down. Kelley exited the set and headed off toward the first scene of Act II.

"I asked for peppers. What is this shit? Huh? What is it?"

The gangster hooked Kelley's arm and sank his fingernails into Kelley's flesh. Then, the old buzzard shook Kelley's arm.

"They're peppers sir," Kelley said. In the great dining hall of Restaurant *Au Naturel* the International Workers Union dinner was underway. "They're some kind of hot shit, that's what they are. They're burning like those goddamned things that I have to eat every time I go to my cousin's Mexican restaurant out in Newark. I hate that fuckin' place. Get this shit out of here and pour some more wine, my friends have empty glasses, you inadequate prick."

"Yes sir," Kelley snapped, while unhooking his arm. He lifted the offending plate of red and green serranos from the dinner table. *What idiot did this?*, was all he could think as he walked into the kitchen. The man wanted sweet peppers and olive oil, and he was liable to shoot everyone here if he didn't get them. Sloth must have grabbed the first peppers he'd found.

The International Workers Union fit every stereotype of the *Unione Corse* that Kelley Sapp had ever encountered in the movies or in books. The men were impeccably dressed in the worst possible taste. Their double breasted suits matched their double chins. Their wives or prostitutes all wore high heels, sequins, and flashed bountiful silicone bosoms. The reality of people who lived as grotesquely as these horrified Kelley. He was nothing but carrion to these vultures. He felt like a scared rabbit as he dodged around the dining room.

"Who are you guys?" Kelley had asked one man while passing *Hors d'oeuvres* out in the lobby before dinner.

"Us?" the surprised man had said. "Why kid, we're the International Workers Union! We represent the people who made America Great! The workers built the roads; they dammed the rivers; they filled the swamps; they built the tractors that pushed the dirt into the swamp and filled it up. We're the guys that make sure they get their fair share," he swept his arms in an expansive gesture.

Kelley solemnly had nodded his head; and was about to say something ingratiatingly clever like, *that must give you a lot of personal satisfaction*, when the man's face collapsed into his starched collar.

"What's this?" he pointed to the particularly exciting *hors d'oeuvre* crawling on Kelley's silver tray.

"Escargot, sir," Kelley had replied.

"Why is it still fucking crawling?"

"Because they aren't dead yet, sir. It's one of our Chef's specialties."

"Jesus F. Christ, I can see they ain't dead. Get it away from me."

Their first course had been a green salad with thin strips of salmon and raw lobster mixed into the greens. Immediately, every table asked for peppers, olive oil, bread, and more red wine too. Sloth reeled about the dining room like a broken top. His red nose pointed in the air as shouts of, *hey waiter bring us another bottle of this red stuff ... and more bread too! Hey, you moron! Listen to me!*, went up.

When the main course came out of the kitchen, Kelley knew there would be trouble.

"What the fuck is this? What the fuck is this?" the same man who had complained about the peppers screamed at Kelley. All around the dark dining hall outraged cries and curses swelled into a cacophony of cries for good meat, cooked meat.

"Jimmy?" the man's date burst into a recitative, "Jimmy—this stuff looks like it's raw," she sang.

Kelley stood stoically. Mesmerized by the sight of her swelling soprano breasts, he had hoped the shock of the main course would free them.

"It is raw skate -kissed with a hint of steam and sent out to you in an almost pristine state of natural beauty and flavor. It is our Chef's specialty," Kelley's baritone voice modulated without a hint of irony. He beat it quickly back to the kitchen before Jimmy could react.

Kelley brought out plates and dropped them as fast as he could. The chorus had grown into outright revolt as more and more union members realized they were supposed to eat raw skate.

"Hey, don't we get a little sterno or something to cook it over? You know what I mean. Like those pu pu platters we get at the Hong Kong in Rahway?", Kelley heard as he dodged the grasping arms and angry faces that reached for him as he ran back to the kitchen.

On his next foray out things had degenerated into open violence. Jimmy had managed to grab Sloth and pin him against a sweating blue wall. Flakes of stucco angelically floated about the crucified Sloth's head.

"What did I say I wanted," Jimmy asked calmly.

"Steak," Sloth choked.

"For who?"

"For all your friends."

"That's right, for all my friends. I want your chef to cook us steaks. I want everyone to get one. So what are you going to do."

"I'm going to go in back and get steaks for everyone."

"That's my boy." Jimmy patted him on the cheek. He turned around to his admiring peers. "Jesus F. Christ," he punched his chest. "I'm a fuckin' animal."

Backstage, in the kitchen, Chef Christian LeForrestier was not pleased. Among the wide range of culinary choices the world offers were some items toward which Chef Christian harbored a great deal of prejudice. Included in these items was a large category of food known as meat. Lamb, pork, chicken, veal, and, especially beef, he considered, for the discerning palate, inedible. As he had once explained to a reporter for an American fashion magazine, "What is the life of a cow in comparison to that of a fish? All a cow knows is one stupid field for his entire life. A fish? It knows the whole ocean. It is alive like no cow could ever be. That is why I serve only fish. Fucking farting cows disgust me." Chef Christian stood behind the kitchen line with his cleaver poised high in the air as he screamed at Sloth.

"I do not cook cow! Look at a cow! Look at it! All day it sit in a field and chew! Then it fart! The whole world is becoming warm because of the farts of cows! I do not cook cow! These people ... they are pigs! No, they are worse than pigs. They are cows!"

As so often happens, the real story was played out behind the stage. Kelley watched as Sloth slowly melted. His red hair began to wilt as his knees slid together. His clenched fists opened and the smile of a beaten man began to crawl across his lined face.

By the time Chef had finished it was as if ten years had been lifted from Sloth's withered visage. He had lost and he knew it. Slowly, he walked away from the kitchen line past the simmering cauldrons and away from ancient medieval brick.

Kelley followed him up the blue hallway and into the staff locker room. He watched without saying a word as Sloth slowly peeled off the white hose and embroidered tunic. Low rumbles of noise came from the kitchen as the waitstaff frantically searched for some indication that the mob in the dining room would eventually be appeased. Sloth stood in his street clothes, his ski jacket zipped and a happy smile on his face as he stared at Kelley.

"Good luck," he said and made for the door.

Kelley touched him on the shoulder. "Wait." There had to be more to it than this. "What will you do now?"

Sloth looked at the floor. A halo seemed to form above his head, beating back the blue light. He was outside of it now. "Kelley, I'm going to ski. I used to ski all the time before this job. In the summer I would ride my bike and fish. I'll get a job making six bucks an hour and relax."

He was on his way out the door when he stopped and looked back at Kelley. "Christ knows what I'll do when the kids have to go to college. Don't let the bastards get you down." Then he was gone and off into the land of no pressure and a low hourly wage.

When he returned to the kitchen sixty yellowfin tuna steaks were sizzling on spits over open gas flames while a quiet waitstaff waited impatiently for the sous chef to plate them.

From the back of the kitchen the low sobbing of the chef could be heard. "My fish! My beautiful tuna. Cooked!"

Kelley had had enough. He was sick of it. He was really sick of Chef Christian, the great artist, the sensitive know it all.

"Shut up you idiot!" he yelled. The kitchen became quiet and Kelley found all eyes on him. He was normally a subservient and polite person, but a blue rage suddenly filled him. "Shut your god-damned mouth! Shut it up and get out of here before I go back there and cram all that tuna up your asshole like you deserve! I'm gonna give you a tuna enema until you're dead, then I'm gonna go to your house and fuck your wife. I'm gonna fuck her and she's gonna like it. Then, I'm gonna drive your Ferrari and fuck your wife at the same time. And you won't do anything because you'll be dead. You're gonna be dead with a bunch of hot tuna stuck up your asshole. So you better get out of here unless you want me to do all that you fucking idiot! You fucking cow!"

The silence continued for about ten seconds before Chef Christian burst around the corner waving his cleaver in the air and screaming like a man gone mad.

"Ahhhh! I will kill you! I will kill you! I will kill you! Ahhhhhhh!"

Everyone ducked for cover behind cauldrons, into the dumbwaiter, behind the wooden washtub, and into the cupboards as Chef Christian charged toward Kelley.

"Come on you miserable fuck!" Kelley screamed. It was unnecessary for Kelley to encourage Chef Christian. Like two knights at the joust,

Kelley sprang forward to meet his charge. And as Kelley suddenly realized that this wasn't a movie and that the Chef really was charging at him with a real cleaver that could really cut him down, he quickly grabbed a dinner plate from the stack that stood in front of the kitchen line and hummed it frisbee style at Chef Christian. The plate solidly thumped into the Chef's stomach, stopping him cold and laying him out on the hard brick floor. He clutched the plate and slowly let it drop with a clatter before turning his head to the side so he could throw up the hot dog he had eaten for lunch.

Kelley stood victorious. "Come on people!" he rallied the troops. *The king is dead long live the king.* "We've got a bunch of steaks to serve."

The curtain fell on Act II. Kelley closed his eyes and listened to the applause of the blue walls.

The rest of dinner ran smoothly until coffee. Even though Kelley had been given no official indication that the Maitre D' position was his, he ran the dining room and no one questioned his orders. At some point Chef Christian managed to drag himself out of the kitchen and get home. Kelley should have realized he hadn't slain the dragon, but he was so pumped with adrenalin that nothing could put a damper on him.

It wasn't until the cognac and coffee had been served that Kelley saw Friday. With Bennett Beauregard he walked into the kitchen.

"Mr. Posthelwait wants to see you first thing tomorrow morning," Bennett Beauregard announced. A low smirk of congratulations danced around the corners of his blue lips. He turned and dashed out into the dining room.

Friday raised a quizzical eyebrow.

"I don't know," Kelley replied. "I just got fed up."

Together they walked back into the dining room just in time to watch one of the union members climb onto the table of Lumsden of Strathdrummond.

"He shouldn't do that," Friday commented.

In one hand he held a balloon snifter of brandy which he swirled majestically. He was about to address the dining room when Bennett Beauregard clambered up next to him in an apparent attempt to get him off the table.

"Now he *really* shouldn't do that," Kelley opined. With a startled crash, Bennett Beauregard found himself levitated into the air and hurled to the floor. The unscathed union member took a sip of brandy.

"Get down from there," a toppled Bennett Beauregard shrieked. It was a bad mistake.

"What?" the unaffected man asked. He was wobbling drunkenly, his double breasted suit somewhat askew. "Let go of my ankle."

Bennett Beauregard continued tugging.

The gun appeared suddenly from the folds of his suit. Fifty nine members of the International Workers Union and their significant others simultaneously hit the floor. Twenty nine reached for guns until they heard the guy on the desk shouting.

"You fucking pansy! I told you to let go of my ankle." He shot a round into the ceiling. Bennett Beauregard dove under the table while large clumps of blue stucco rained down from above.

"Wahooo!" the man on top of the desk spun his pistol and fired three more rounds into the ceiling. Laughing, the recovered union members regained their seats and waited patiently for their friend's impending speech. A snowfall of blue flakes wafted from the stucco ceiling, converting *Au Naturel* into a bubble of simulated winter.

"Wahhoo! Get up all of you! Get up. It's me, Vinny. I ain't gonna shoot nobody, you're all my friends. Except for you," Vinny added in a low voice for Bennett's benefit. His hair was now completely blue. In his mottled grey suit, twirling his pistol, and sporting a red nose, Vinny resembled a schizophrenic Santa Claus.

Underneath the black table of Lumsden of Strathdrummond, Bennett Beauregard cowered.

Occupied by gangsters, a prostrate sycophant, ski bums in medieval costume, and the token black male, *Au Naturel* had been transformed into a surrealist Christmas party for the final act. The blue stucco snowfall abated. All eyes went to Vinny for the culmination of Act III. Poised with brandy in hand, gun in the other, he delivered his line with aplomb and predictable anti-climax. This was Vinny's speech: "You guys are a bunch of fucking great guys! You're the best fucking guys in the world! Now let's get out of this fucking dump!"

The curtain fell as a chorus of affirming curses welled from the tympanous chests of the International Workers Union. Above the table of Lumsden of Strathdrummond the perforated ceiling collapsed under its own weight of soaked plaster. Sheltered by the grotto of black wood, Bennett Beauregard lay like some spectral nymph behind the glassy sheet of the waterfall now cascading from the ceiling.

Kelley and Friday waited by the exit. Kelley shook hands with the departing union members.

"Please come again," Kelley repeated with the genuine and heartfelt emotion that stems from rote repetition.

Fat sweaty palms smeared with liquefied blue paste pressed hundred dollar bills into the various folds and pockets of Kelley's costume. He robotically repeated his mantra while green bills sprouted from the most unlikely places behind his ears and out his collar.

Vinny was the last to leave. "You were excellent," he complimented Kelley while slipping a folded bill of unknown denomination into the top of his hose.

"Some of the food, I don't know about. But you were excellent." With a loving tap of his palm, Vinny touched Kelley's cheek. "Ciao, bambino. Take care of that guy under the table," he spun and left.

Underneath the carriageway of the Snowy Mountains Guest Lodge forty limousines snaked one at a time. Bearing away their precious cargo of blue haired men and young ladies, the caravan departed in the vigilant shadow of the spectral castle towers. Leaving the malevolent blue-eyed abode for the more mundane insanity peddled shamelessly within the muzak-permeated hallways of the Hyatt Regency, they drove away.

Now the coda. The curtain rises to an empty hall. Two characters remain onstage. No one claps. No one screams. It is played out quickly and motionless; as it should be. One glance tells all.

Blue fingerprints dot Kelley's face like warpaint. A spring foliage of grubby bills is his camouflage. Painted and revealed as a warrior, he poses next to the neat picture of urbanity that is Friday. In a navy suit coat, grey slacks, and red tie, he is civilized.

Who's the savage?

In the small office, by the front desk, a swaddled Bennett Beauregard chattered his teeth while attempting a conversation on the phone. The police had come and gone. At the desk Friday read the paper. Washed clean and garbed in street clothes now, a frisky Kelley Sapp paced behind the desk. With a well deserved glass of pinot noir in his hand and two thousand dollars in tips in his pocket, there were good reasons for Kelley's bubbly mood. He peeked into the office at the heaped pile of wet clothes by the filing cabinets. Bennett Beauregard's discarded suit, shoes, and belt reminded Kelley of that classic childrens' story set in Oz.

Turning to Friday, *I'm melting*, he mimed before collapsing to the floor. "Look at this shit," an un-impressed Friday tossed his copy of the *Vail Daily* onto Kelley.

"What?"

"Page two. The article on Killington."

Kelley read. "Crazy Eco-Terrorist Torches Houses at Killington. An unidentified person, or group of persons, set fire to an unoccupied vacation home at the Killington Ski Resort in Killington, Vermont. Police report that a source calling itself Lone Wolf took responsibility for the arson. 'I heard a great big howl, like a wolf, then noticed the flames,' sno-cat driver Jim Peterson reported. The fire was started at approximately midnight. A call to the police department by Lone Wolf stated, *it is criminal for houses to sit unoccupied while over half the world lives in a state of extreme poverty. I am Lone Wolf, soldier in the war against those who are our real enemies. The wealthy, the powerful, those who can afford to buy their way out of society's problems. I will cut them down. Watch my fires burn and know that this is my generation's enlightenment.* Movie star Rex Rexnor, owner of the house, was reached for comment in the Brazilian rain forest. From the set of his latest motion picture, in which he continues his role of Dr. Goody Tree, botanist by day, savior of the forest by night, Rexnor commented that, 'Insurance would cover everything, even the Picassos.'

Kelley stopped reading. "Cool!"

"What do you mean by, 'cool'?"

"I agree with him."

"With Lone Wolf?"

"Yeah. I agree wholeheartedly."

"Then why don't you set fire to houses?" Friday wondered.

"Because I'd get caught and thrown in jail."

"You'd be a martyr."

"I already am for myself." Kelley tossed the paper back at Friday. "That's enough for me."

Friday was about to delve further into Kelley's revolutionary zeal when the blanket-draped form of Bennett Beauregard emerged from the office. "Don't forget, Kelley," the ominous specter intoned with his distinctive whine, "Mr. Posthelwait wants to see you first thing tomorrow morning."

When Friday looked back at the floor Kelley was gone. *Typical*, he thought while the blue walls closed in and sleep shut his eyes. The clocks whirred in imprecise tocks. Time froze and the normal static state of the Snowy Mountains Guest Lodge returned to reign over all.

Kelley's Volkswagen teetered perilously close to the cliff before skidding back to the center of the icy road. Kelley gunned through the s-turns, one hand on the wheel, the other balancing his full glass of wine. Ghostly aspens, illuminated in the headlights, shot by in a blur of Corinthian columns, the straight trunks rising in bare glory to their capital branches. Kelley drove. When he got home to unit 201-B of the Silver Aspen Condominiums, he found Kellie Kay waiting for him.

"What is this?" she asked Kelley. On the floor of the living room sat Kelley's bag of wild hemp. Kellie stood up off the couch and walked over toward Kelley. Her face bore an enigmatic, Mona Lisa type smile. That Kellie Kay had searched his room struck Kelley as odd. It also pissed him off a little bit, but what could he do?

"That is marijuana."

"Do you know what could happen to me if this much marijuana were found in my apartment?"

"It was in my room."

"That doesn't matter. This is my apartment."

"But Kellie, it grows wild all through the midwest. I gathered it right near Iowa City off I-70 next to a Denny's for God's sake. Smoke some."

Kellie stared at Kelley Sapp. Her stare said, *You are stupid, and you should shut up.*

"We've got to get rid of it."

"Now?"

Two minutes later they were in the Volkswagen. Kellie Kay cradled the black hefty bag on her lap.

"We've got to throw it someplace where no one will find it."

"How about the dumpster?"

Kellie glared at him again. She wore a Patagonia fleece jacket, the one with a mayan glyph pattern, and spandex purple tights. Her scowling face told Kelley all he needed to know as he contemplated their current dilemma. "No," she finally said. "That would be stupid."

"Why?"

"Because it's right next to our apartment."

"And?"

"And if someone finds it—"

"—they'll miraculously trace it to us out of all six-hundred units. Of course that's supposing someone sorts through the dumpster and finds it. I know I do that all the time."

"Shut up."

"And even if someone does sort through and find it what are the odds they'll go to the police?"

"Let's just drive and get rid of it."

"No. I'm not driving anywhere. Here's what we do. You walk out of the van and over to the dumpster. Throw the pot into the dumpster like it's trash and then walk back to the apartment."

"You do it."

"Why me? I'm not the one who wants to throw it out."

"Please Kelley?"

"Oh, God."

Kelley stepped out into the cold night. With pretended non-chalance he walked toward the overflowing dumpster that sat in the middle of the parking lot. In his hand he held the goods. *This is so fucking stupid, why am I nervous?* A car pulled into the parking lot. Kelley walked faster.

It was a police car. The silent blue and red lights were mounted like a ski rack on top of the roof. The cops glided in a circle around the parking lot. With a searchlight they swept the parked cars. Head down and his eyes staring at the snowpacked driveway, Kelley walked straight toward the dumpster.

He reached the dumpster. The cops circled behind him. Kelley threw the bag into the dumpster. The cops drove out of the parking lot. With a racing heart, he steamrolled over to the Volkswagen and threw open the passenger side door.

"Can you just tell me what you were doing in my room anyway?"

Kelley panted.

"That was a cop!"

"I know it was a cop. What I don't know is why this happened. Do you know what they would have done to me if they had stopped me on a whim? I have two thousand dollars cash in my pockets. I would have gone to jail. Why did you search my room?"

Kellie stomped out of the van and past Kelley. Inside the apartment Kellie headed straight for her bedroom.

That bitch. Kelley leaned against Kellie's bedroom door and spoke through the keyhole, "You may have the lease, but that doesn't give you the right to search through my stuff. Only my mother can do that."

On the trampoline Kellie Kay bounced. The ski posters on the walls seemed to shift as she softly skipped across the nylon mesh. The truth was; Kellie Kay didn't know why she searched Kelley Sapp's room. Evidence. Of what? She was curious about this man she had slept with.

"Kelley," she yelled while bouncing. "I'm sorry. I really am."

Mumbling under his breath Kelley slowly crawled back to his bedroom. He had been under the orange sleeping bag for a scant five minutes when Kellie Kay crawled in next to him.

"You shit," she sighed, "you made me feel like a nosy bitch. If you want to know the truth I read your letters."

"The ones to Z."

"Yes. The ones you haven't sent."

"I can't. I don't even have her address."

"Do you love her?"

"I used to. Sometimes I think I still do."

"Where is she now?"

"She lives in New York city with a lawyer named Bond."

"Can't you find her address."

"I really don't think there's any point."

"Oh, Kelley. I know how it is to be in love. I'm in love right now." Kellie Kay tucked her legs under Kelley's and wrapped her arm around his chest. They lay next to each other like two foetal spoons. Kellie Kay grasped Kelley's hand tightly. He wondered what she had meant.

"Who do you love?"

"You should know."

Kelley Sapp felt his heart thickening. It slowed to a terrible stop as his body tensed. What did she mean?

"Well, I know it's not me. Right?"

"Of course."

His breathing resumed. Somehow, he felt almost a little disappointed. He squeezed Kellie's hand.

"Kris Blaze. I don't think he loves me. I think you and I have something in common Kelley. We both love people we can never have."

71

"How do you know that about Kris?"

"Nobody will ever have him. The only thing that will ever completely own Kris Blaze is death, and I wouldn't be surprised if he managed to cheat that."

"With Z I could never keep up. It didn't matter what. She did more drugs, she slept less than I did. She had more friends, she took risks. When I take a risk it's out of desperation. She did it for fun."

"Do you think we're regular people, Kelley?"

"Me? I'm convinced that I am."

"I don't think you are. I don't think I am either. I think other people may see us as regular, but that doesn't mean we should resign ourselves to it. Regular people stay in Boston or D.C.. We moved to Vail. We made the jump. We live what other people dream. Our everyday reality is a fantasy for some people. We live while they dream. We act while they think."

"Honestly, Kellie? I think we're pretty regular."

"Oh, fuck you! Why?"

"Because we worry about who we are. If we were special, it wouldn't even be a question. Something else would be driving us. What do we value? I love Z and you love Kris Blaze. We're like every other person; more interested in the small affairs of men and women. The greater themes don't concern us as they would great people. And I can't help it. Can you?"

Kellie Kay pushed him away. Across the dirty mattress she laughed ironically.

"Jesus Christ, Mr. Sapp. Do you always have to make me feel like shit?"

"Oh, come here."

When they had sex that night it was a fight against anonymity. Kelley put Kellie Kay against the door of his room and she threw him on the floor. They left the lights on and watched each other with intent eyes, as if they were each making sure that the other was proof of their own existence. This was how they would keep from becoming invisible. They would have a secret and it would keep them sane. For in life it is always the secrets that hold promise for the future. Time is the greatest of these secrets. But Kelley and Kellie had lost faith in time and what it might promise to them. Therefore they made their own pact with each other, and kept faith through action.

When they parted, it was with the knowledge that small affairs between men and women matter more in the long run than might seem proper. Before this night they had felt dead to the world. Co-conspirators, they had dared to trust each other with secrets. The secret filled them and now they lived.

The next morning Kelley woke early and drove to the Snowy Mountains Guest Lodge for his meeting with Mr. Posthelwait. As he walked up from the parking lot, he saw five snowmen positioned next to the carriageway in a circle. Facing each other and holding hands, their eyes were made with buttons and lumps of chocolate. Scarves wrapped their necks, and a blond wig cascaded down from the head of one particularly voluptuous snow-woman.

When he reached the circle Kelley ducked under a pair of arms and strode into the center. They were ghastly snow-people.

Two held frozen brochures for the Snowy Mountains Guest Lodge in what would be the side pockets of their blazers. The three snow-women sported faux diamond necklaces along with thick ropes of strawberry jam that formed their lips. A strange attempt to show breast definition on the females had resulted in their resemblance to primitive sculpture. Kelley felt an overwhelming urge to take all their heads off. But he knew only one mind capable of such an ostentatious lure as this.

He looked up into the carriageway window. There was Bennett Beauregard. All bundled up in a greatcoat with a hat, muffler, gloves, and camera. He was perched in the tiny garret window of the carriageway, a spot usually reserved for the nests of mating magpies and bats. Next to Bennett, Kelley noticed the distinctive stain of several year's accumulated guano.

"Achoo," Bennett Beauregard sneezed. He waved his hand in greeting at Kelley. "I'm here. Good morning. Achoo! I'm afraid I caught cold from that dousing last night."

"So it seems," Kelley shouted up to him. "What on earth are you doing up there?"

"I'm going to catch him," Bennett answered as though it were a sane and rational explanation. "I will photograph him destroying these snowmen. Achooo!"

"The Chef?"

"Yes. He will come up the driveway; and when he starts to destroy the snowmen, I will photograph him in the act. How could he resist? If I do say so myself, I have never seen snowmen the equal of these in all my lifetime. I think he's coming now," Bennett flapped his wrist at Kelley, shooing him into the foyer.

Kelley watched as Chef Christian made his way toward the snowmen. The ear flaps of Chef's Russian cap flopped in the gentle breeze. He walked straight past the carriageway without any indication of stopping for the snowmen until Bennett Beauregard sneezed.

"Achoo!"

"Heh! Hello, what are you doing up there with a camera?" Chef asked. He stood at a slight angle, bent over at the middle as though someone had punched him.

"Oh, this?" Bennett waved the camera, "I'm photographing birds."

"Birds?" Chef Christian liked birds. Birds were free, like fish.

"Oh yes, very rare birds ... Snow Swallows in fact," Bennett ad libbed.

"Have you seen any? I love birds. They are like fish, but do not taste so well when they are raw."

"Oh no, these are very rare birds."

"I've never heard of Snow Swallows."

"They are very rare and shy, Chef. In fact some people say they are extinct.

Chef Christian contemplated the snowmen. "I think I see what part of your problem might be. These snowmen, they are very ugly. Like scarecrows, you think? Should I get rid of them for you?"

"Oh yes," Bennett exclaimed, "that would be wonderful."

"Ok."

Chef Christian slowly began pushing the heads off the snowmen. With lazy aptitude he kicked their soft bodies apart. Plodding from snowman to snowoman, picking up buttons and necklaces as he continued under Bennett's whirring camera.

"Snow Swallows?" Chef asked.

"Maybe, I'm not sure. Keep knocking them down. I think it's helping." Kelley turned and went on inside.

Within the great dining hall of *Au Naturel*, workers were erecting scaffolding on a scale which hadn't been seen since the days when Michelangelo had to go to the bathroom from the top of the Sistine Chapel. A white tarp had been thrown over the table of Lumsden of Strathdrummond. Exposed water pipes and air ducts radiated from the eroded plaster like internal organs undergoing surgery. The pounding of hammers and clank of boards filled the air as the scaffolding quickly rose. Kelley spied Mr. Posthelwait.

Electrically garbed in a purple jogging suit and puffing an early morning cigar, Mr. Posthelwait tapped his monogrammed jogging sneakers next to a pile of plaster. As so often happens with middle-aged persons whose daily conditioning consists of three-martini lunches and anaerobic exercises with *hecho a mano* panatellas, Frank Posthelwait was not the most robust picture of health.

Back home in New York City, before the lawsuits, he had the reputation among his peers of being a brassy opportunist. The main reason for this reputation stemmed from his quasi-legal association with the Statue of Liberty and Ellis Island Foundation. Each year, for a set fee, Frank would rent the Statue of Liberty and throw a big party. At the party he would award people like the Secretary of Defense or the Sultan of Brunei with something he called a *Congressional Medal of Honor*. Seats at the banquet cost over ten thousand dollars a head; and were quickly snapped up by ingratiating lobbyists, rich socialites, and minor pols. Since over a thousand people went to the banquet every year, Frank Posthelwait got rich quickly.

One percent of his net revenue went to the real Statue of Liberty and Ellis Island foundation. For five years he fronted himself as a charity, accepting large donations from well meaning corporations and philanthropists. And it wasn't until *The Village Voice* put him on the cover with a single-word headline that read, "Fraud!", in two-inch high type across his forehead that Frank Posthelwait became anathema to all but the most corrupt politicians.

He had hidden some of his money in various losing enterprises, like junk bonds, which is how he met Ricky Rico. A criminal fraud case was filed against Frank by the New York D.A.'s office. Ricky followed it. Since Frank had never billed himself as a non-profit organization, and always made sure his corporate sponsors deducted their gifts as business expenses under entertainment and lobbying, the case got thrown out of court. Ricky Rico was impressed.

The "Junk Bond King of New York", many had heard tell of Ricky Rico. He had been head of the bond trading department at the brokerage firm of Pogo, Zippy, and Crouchback. Singlehandedly, he had charmed the entire savings and loan industry into selling their mortgage holdings through him in the form of bonds. His wealth ballooned while America's smalltown banking industry was deservedly flushed down the toilet in a frenzy of Las Vegas style speculation. Lawsuits were filed against him by the Securities and Exchange Commission. But, raised up like the blessed son of a blessed union, Ricky Rico beat it to Switzerland, where most of his five billion dollars were safely deposited. Warrants were served. Cut off from the States, Ricky needed an agent there who would be able to creatively re-invest some of his money. He needed a contact in America: someone he understood, someone like himself. He had his lawyer get in touch with Frank Posthelwait, and the seemingly ill-conceived Snowy Mountains Guest Lodge was born.

For there was, perhaps, a method to the madness Kelley Sapp experienced daily. Frank Posthelwait would deny it. Tapping his Gucci toes, he happily gazed upon the crumbling ceiling. We ought to have more gangsters up here, he thought. More gangsters, or someone who could really do the job. Blow the whole place into the clouds. Then he could re-build. Oh, the kickbacks from the contractors and the neat little loopholes he could find. Frank Posthelwait touched his Rolex.

It was nine thirty and he had an appointment with that woefully inadequate young man who would, no doubt, screw up the restaurant even more than it already was. He swung his excessive bulk in the direction of the lobby and made his way toward Kelley.

He looks just like a snowman, Kelley recoiled. Moving toward him was a living example of the frozen grotesqueries lately of the carriageway. Frank Posthelwait's legs chaffed silkenly against one another. His gnomon torso bulged like a water balloon. But it was Frank's head which took the prize. For within the corpulent confines of his waxed, capped, and dyed skull, underneath the irrepressible eyes, was Frank Posthelwait's mouth.

75

While gazing upon it one generally came to the uneasy understanding that every fleshy tissue surrounding the mouth once entered in another form and descended through that gaping portal to become part of Frank Posthelwait.

Kelley should have turned and run. He should have sprinted away from Frank Posthelwait's mouth. But he had made his choice and would no longer play Peter Pan.

They sat on a powder blue couch underneath a mounted emu. The polar bear loomed above them. Stucco floated through the air in mote clouds that tinted the rosy beams a delicate shade of purple. The dream descended and Kelley found himself stumbling forward through the straight and narrow like a pig in a trough.

"So, Kelley, you're here about the *Maitre D'* job. We've looked over your qualifications and decided that we would be pleased to have someone with your capabilities in the position." Frank Posthelwait rolled his eyes a bit before continuing. "But before you go I would like to give you a little of the history behind this lodge and The Dream which built it. Come with me please, Kelley."

Obediently, Kelley rose with Mr. Posthelwait and began to stroll beside him through the lobby.

"We brought Manchurian slate from China and Douglas firs from Oregon. Fuzzy Nicklaus and Chi-Chi Palmer are designing a golf course for us, and later this winter we will announce our plans and break ground for our very own ski area. Why, you may ask, are we doing this? Is it really to make money?"

Mr. Posthelwait and Kelley descended the main staircase. Midway they paused as Mr. Posthelwait spread his arms wide in front of the great bay windows that looked out on the Sawatch Range to the east. The sheer cliffs of Holy Cross and the backbone of North America rode like ships across the turbulent white clouds.

"No," Mr. Posthelwait exclaimed, "why, Kelley, I don't mind telling you that we are losing money here. The Snowy Mountains Guest Lodge is not about making money. We want to open up this country and protect it from developers less sensitive than we are. I love this land. I love this country. Did you know that I'm a Congressional Medal of Honor winner?"

"No, I had no idea. What war were you in?"

"No war. I won it for my duties stateside."

"During what conflict?"

"Vietnam. I ran a border patrol around Canada."

Kelley feigned understanding. But, it was all beyond him. Like so many, he mimicked understanding and pretended knowledge. That he did so consciously troubled him all the more.

They headed into the Snowy Mountains Guest Lodge boutique. Kelley watched with horror as Mr. Posthelwait trailed his fingers along the rack of fur coats. His cigar drew a hazy line of blue smoke in the alpine sunlight. "Kelley, think of us as your family here. We want the best for you, just like we want the best for this precious piece of God's country we caretake. I think I should tell you that there is another man, another owner, who lives in Switzerland. He loves this country as much as I do, even though he's been wrongfully branded as a criminal. Next month his lawyer is coming to the lodge and beginning work on the ski area. He's going to want bright young guys like you to help him with the project. You're part of a team here Kelley. You're part of Snowy Mountain's future. Never doubt that. Go now, and congratulations. We're very confident you'll do a great job."

When Kelley reached the open air outside the front doors he paused for only a second before breaking into a run.

It was noon when Kelley glided off the chairlift. The morning clouds had dispersed as if a great hand had swept them aside to reveal the deep aqua sky. Newborn sunbeams reflected in the naked snow.

Kelley's skis were new, as were his boots. The money he had been making at *Au Naturel* was not going into mutual funds. He kicked over to Spruce Saddle, keeping an eye out for Friday. At the picnic tables tourists dressed in the latest ski fashions were having their lunch. Stacked in rows like futuristic weapons, their skis waited for their return to the slopes.

A steady stream of skiers marched from the cafeteria.

Green bottles of wine, apples, cheeses, and bread were spread out on white tablecloths. Skiers un-zipped their jackets and panted in the hot sunshine. A radio played reggae music. Someone sang, "We are all Jah's children." A heavy set man pulled off his boots and massaged his stiff toes through thick wool socks. Little kids munched French fries from gigantic paper cups while their attentive parents devoured bowls of factory made chili.

Kelley drank it all in. He wondered what lurid stories lurked within these placid people? How many were slum lords? What shit lurked beneath their surfaces?

Tight family units abounded wherever his eye wandered. Mothers and daughters in matching uni-suit stretch pants sat next to their Andy Griffith husbands and sons.

Ahhh, America!

Land of the free, home of the trust fund snowboarder. Rad dude! *Like let's hit the half-pipe then duck into the woods for a bat hit before meeting mom and dad.*

"*Coors Beer,*" the radio announced, "*was brewed from fresh Rocky Mountain Spring water. Isn't now a good time for an ice cold Coors?*" it suggested to all.

The families arrived and departed in lines. Kelley imagined they were ants following a trail to some decaying carcass. They poled with their antennae and sniffed each other with curious eyes.

Lunch was hopping at Spruce Saddle, mid-station of Beaver Creek ski area and easiest meeting point for skiers from all over the mountain.

Kelley met Friday over by the stand of aspens that screened the picnic area.

"Looking hot!" Friday exclaimed as he watched Kelley approach. "How much did you pay for those bib pants?"

"Around two-hundred."

Friday leaned forward on his poles and stretched out his calves behind him. Grinning from ear to ear like the Cheshire Cat, he regarded Kelley with paternal curiosity.

"Oh Kelley, those pants will undoubtedly make you a better skier. They'll also make you happier, saner, and well adjusted."

"I can feel it already. Don't you see my smile. Can't you tell that I'm the new *Maitre D'* of restaurant *Au Naturel*."

"Really?"

"Yes!"

"Looking hot!"

They all looked happy. Sitting in the sun. There had been a sense of crisis inside Kelley until now. He would ski, and there he would find solace from the world as in some secular prayer.

Friday skated down toward the entrance to Rose Bowl. Electrical tape patched his faded ski pants. No neon chevrons graced his jacket. His knit wool cap was white, with a tiny pompom that bobbed behind him in the wind. Friday reached the first line of moguls and threw himself into their teeth, cutting a line so straight and pure that his head hardly seemed to move at all. The pompom rocked from side to side as the flat of his skis caught the side of each bump. Rocking back and forth between them he headed straight down the slope with the ease of an expert. From the chairlift above Kelley heard the shouts of approval sweeping down the hill after Friday, while he struggled to keep his shoulders from dragging and skis from crossing. He lost his memory, then himself, before his skis began to turn true.

An hour later, they ducked into the trees above Peregrine where a tiny break in the aspens opens up. Kelley followed close behind Friday, both of them ducking down on their skis as the narrow path funnelled them toward the unknown secret. They cruised under a nylon rope and were suddenly off *piste*, or 'out of bounds'. The powder flowed around Kelley's knees, checking his speed through the grove of quiet pines. They left the flat ridge and ducked down into the tight trees. Friday led the way, twisting a path through the tops of buried evergreens. They brushed branches out of their faces with gloved hands. All around them was silence. An occasional bird call echoed a warning of Kelley and Friday's approach.

The slope grew steeper and Kelley's turns more frantic. He doubted he could keep it up much longer before he caught a tip or lost his balance and hit a tree. But just as he was reaching his limit, ducking past one last tree top and grazing his jacket on another, he saw the break ahead and was soon in the clear skiing a wide open mountain glade. It was early afternoon on a day without end in a timeless place. The joy of motion let Kelley know where life was. Friday arced ahead of him in a graceful semi circle, his hips and body carving a long chain of the letter *S* downslope. Kelley followed behind carving his own trail in the virgin snow. He crossed Friday's trail, catching his rhythm and leaving figure eights in the snow behind him. At every turn a plume of snow shot up and rainbows hung in the air as the fine spray vaporized in the brilliant sun. The glade continued rolling down the slope. Kelley caught powder in his mouth, it shot onto his goggles and blinded him. Down the glade he floated, the snow bouncing off him, piling up in front of him like a white curtain at each turn that he cruised through and back into the light, a rainbow at his side.

They braked where the trees began. Stopping in the shadow of what they knew was to come, they listened. Through the woods Kelley could hear the hum of the high speed quad chair racing up the mountain at twenty-five miles an hour. He and Friday gazed up at the turns they had just made, so evident and fresh in the deep snow. They had written the story of their descent onto the blank page of the slope and sat back now with pleasure reading their own story.

"That was Goshawk Glade," Friday told Kelley.

"That was the greatest thing I've ever done," Kelley panted.

They ducked back into the trees and worked their way through the tight aspen trunks until they found themselves close to the base of Golden Eagle. Out on the regular trail the hard packed snow welled up in tiny bumps as hordes of skiers whistled by leaving their trail on an indifferent, more industrial snow. Somehow, Kelley knew, he would never again equate this kind of slope with skiing.

They ducked under the nylon cord and stepped back out onto the trail, emerging from the woods like two deer onto a road.

"Hey!" Kelley heard a voice call from behind him. "Hey you two, stop right there!"

"Oh shit," Friday tossed Kelley a worried glance as a tall blond ski patrolman cruised down next to them.

"We were just taking a piss, Billy," Friday said while the patrolman cruised to a stop.

"Oh yeah, Friday? Let me hear another one. You've always got a good story. Why don't you tell me about the time that you went and skied Goshawk Glade with your friend and had the bad luck to get caught by me, Billy, the big bad patrolman, the guy who's already let you off one too many times."

"We just took a piss that's all."

"How come there's only one set of tracks leading out of the woods? What are you looking at?"

Kelley quickly turned his eyes to the snow. It had been worth it even if they did lose their passes.

"Did you know there's a high avalanche risk on Goshawk Glade, or did you just follow this guy without thinking for yourself?"

"I just moved here a little while ago."

"Don't insult my intelligence, of course you did. Why else would you be wearing pants like those? How much did you pay for them?"

"Not that much."

"Two fifty if you can believe it," Friday cut in.

"Jesus F. —," Billy was in the process of swearing when he got cut off.

"Hey losers," Kellie Kay cruised to a stop. Her blond hair flew in the sunlight. She wore her blue ski school suit and seemed to relish Kelley and Friday's situation. She winked at Kelley.

"Un momento por favor. Esos son mis amigos," she explained to a fashionably attired gentleman who'd followed her to the edge of the trail.

"Do you like Kelley's pants?" Friday asked. Kellie Kay let her eyes wander up and down Kelley's body. A coy smile drifted across her mouth. "I like Kelley's pants."

"Ohhhh," Friday and Billy moaned in unison.

"Awful."

"Ugly."

"Do you know this guy," Billy stuck his thumb toward Kelley.

"Yeah, he's my roommate."

With a good-natured shrug Billy waved his hand. "Get going, Friday, if you weren't with this kid I'd haul your ass in."

With a longing ache in his groin, Kelley watched Kellie Kay ski off with her private lesson. With a similar longing, Friday followed Billy's descent down the trail.

"What an ass," they both commented.

Kelley drifted off into thoughts of Z. "I really miss her Friday. But every day I'm here makes her seem like a long, long time ago."

"I didn't say you had to find love with her. Just find love, Kelley."

"I don't know Friday. I've been thinking I need to find something else. I've been thinking I need to make a lot of money."

Friday wiped his forehead and gave Kelley a non-committal shrug.

"You could try, but that would take years and years. Tell you what. Next month Gerald Ford will be in Palm Springs playing golf with Bob Hope. His house will be empty. I'll take you in and you can have an inside look at the world of wealth."

"Smoke some pot there?"

"And we'll eat his frozen pizza."

"Excellent," they both agreed.

They skied off into the afternoon sun and headed for the chairlift. A ride up, one run down to the Coyote Cafe and some Mexican beer: the timeless cycle continued, from the slopes, to the bar, and next to bed. Wake, repeat. Wake, repeat ... .

Chapter 5:

Lone Star

"Red course ready, blue course ready," the starter counted time down to that sweet sucker dance. His hand on the switch, the gates seconds away from...

"Racers ready."

Beep.

They're off.

The echoes of the snowguns followed one another into the rounded distance of the ancient, Appalachian countryside. Hidden by the crusty New England snow, the droppings of last year's sugar maples rose up in white heaps. Kris Blaze charged down the blue course. Head to head through the moguls he took an early lead into the first jump.

This was the semi-finals of the Budweiser Pro Mogul Tour event at Killington. Strung up and down the course like mountain goats on the steep face of 'Outer Limits,' Killington's *numero uno* bump run, spectators leaned on their poles and dug their edges into the hardpack. Bundled in fluorescent Gore-tex parkas, space age bibs, and dyed wool hats, they hung like pennants strung up against a corrugated field of white.

Kris' opponent came from Breckenridge, thirty miles east of Vail and a world apart. Referred to as Breck by the hipsters with long hair and twenty pairs of skis, this Colorado mountain town drew a local population of a different sort from Vail. Not quite so famous, not quite so wealthy, the glitz at Breck flashed silver next to Vail's gold. It was a town where locals routinely skied with shovels in their backpacks and built ramps in the snow so they could launch themselves into the air in order to perfect their daffys, helicopters, splits, double daffys, backscratchers *etc.*. . But today was not to be for this Breckenridge local and member of the Spyder Pro Mogul team.

Leading up to the first jump the Spyder skier lagged a bit behind Kris. The ringing of a cowbell matched the staccato rhythm of both skiers' legs as they absorbed each bump with bent knees. Never once carving a turn they extended through the troughs and compressed over the crests of each steep mogul. Pole planting for balance, their arms and legs synchronized in a delicate ballet of electric reflexes and unconscious precision. The crowd hushed as Kris neared the ramp. He pointed his skis straight and popped off the lip. Fifteen feet above the snow he scissored into a single daffy that quickly reversed into a double. Gliding at his apex like some levitating saint of the slopes he spun three hundred and sixty degrees, completing a helicopter, before landing perfectly and catching his rhythm down on the snow.

His legs pumped like a single piston, his poles flicked, and the white trail he left behind hovered above the course like some thin mistral wraith conjured up from the nether world in order to honor Him and the majesty of his passage.

Kris Blaze now trailed the Team Spyder skier.

The cowbell clanked like an alarm, and the crowd's screams swelled. This is what they had come to see. They clapped their poles and stamped their skis in harmonic accordance as Kris Blaze passed the Team Spyder skier.

Nearing the second and final jump Kris held a slight lead. He launched again, this time spinning in two lazy circles. Arms spread like wings, poles telescoping from his hands, he mimicked the aircraft for which the aerial was named. Landing hard, he bounced backward with his tips in the air before recovering his rhythm to cross the finish line with his fist raised. He skidded to a stop in front of the hundreds gathered at the finish circle.

Pausing in front of the television cameras, the enigmatic Kris Blaze once again flaunted his disdain. That he lived in complete opposition to the materialistic marketing stratagems which supported his profession was reluctantly tolerated by the powers that be. Regarded as an eccentric example of American individuality, he was a lone iconoclast among a herd of unquestioning believers.

Why this was so had become a matter of local legend and constant speculation.

For on Kris Blaze's head sat a cap knit by his grandmother back in nineteen seventy two. His parka was a dark navy White Stag purchased with his own money several years ago. Chevrons of electrical tape graced the tattered sleeves where branches had torn the shell. He wore sunglasses handed out free at the Exxon in Denver with every fill-up. The skis he held up and shook at the crowd did not say Dynastar or Hart, nor Rossignol, or Olin. Their tops were painted over with flat black wall paint that covered the brand name. In large block letters over the black paint Kris Blaze had lovingly painted in high gloss white acrylic the words 'Generic,' on one, and 'No

Name' on the other. On the race bib he wore over his White Stag jacket Kris had crossed out the red Budweiser logo with a black indelible ink marker. Written underneath his number in the same marker was the alternative slogan, "Drink water."

In the world of professional skiing Kris Blaze had done the unthinkable. He had given the ski companies, the beer sponsors, and clothing manufacturers his big stiff middle finger.

The Team Spyder skier slid next to Kris and congratulated him while making sure his Rossignols managed to find the cameras. Garbed majestically in a Spyder hat, the finest Spyder stretch pants, and Spyder jacket, he resembled a walking billboard. His eyes scanned through Bolle goggles and his toes wiggled in Raichle boots. For this prime television coverage he would receive a tidy bonus of over six thousand dollars from his various sponsors. His prize money for making it to the semi-finals would be about two thousand dollars. He shook hands with Kris and strode away having earned more money than Kris would even if he went on to win the final.

There was a time in the not so distant past when Kris had worn the clothes and taken the skis. But a run of bad luck out at Lake Tahoe two years ago had given his sponsors the impression that Kris Blaze's days were numbered. Knocked out in the first round at Kirkwood, disqualified at Heavenly, and injured at Squaw, he had found himself abandoned in California with an empty gas tank while his former employers left him spinning into skiing oblivion. At twenty eight Kris Blaze had already resurrected himself once.

Never again would he champion the cause of those who had so callously dropped him.

He shouldered his skis and waved to the crowd one last time before heading to the competition tent for a cot and a fifteen minute meditation. After the finals there was work to do. The real work.

In the one square concrete house on the one main street in the one-horse town of Happy, Texas, there lived the last child of the union between Jean Marie Blazekowski and Ike Blazekowski. Christopher was his name due to the fact that he had been born with a fringe of black hair that miraculously transformed overnight into a virtual golden halo of yellow flaxen baby fuzz.

Perhaps it would have been better for Jean Marie to name her son after a less ambitious figure. But Christopher it was, as if she knew his fame would spread across the smooth surface of the world like ripples emanating from the unobtrusive cradle she rocked sweetly with her bare pink arms.

In all of Texas there are two natural resources which are valued far and above all others including cattle. The first of these is, of course, oil. Oil is King. It drives the Texas economy like a drunken barometer.

Oil built the fortunes of Dallas, Fort Worth, and countless other sagebrush towns that would have simply been nameless patches of gulch and dirt baking under the hot blue of the Texas sky if it weren't for oil. Without oil there would have been no roads built between Wichita Falls and Dallas because there would have been no good reason to ride your horse in a straight line between identical clumps of sagebrush. There would have been no roads, and without the roads there would have been no settlement. And without the settlement there would have been fewer people. And without the people there would have been no reason for new high schools. And without the new high schools there would have been no Texas High School Football.

Like pearls from oysters, the cream of the sons of Texas are annually plucked from among their peers during fall football practice. The process begins early on in the life of most Texas boys when a miniature football is dropped into their cradle by some adoring relative. Conversely, the daughters of Texas receive miniature pom-poms and bullhorns, learning at an early age their supportive role within the societal structure.

Similar to many species of tropical birds, whose bright feathers and aggressive fighting attract the most desirable females, the daughters of Texas find nothing quite as enticing as a star high school football player in his letterman's jacket.

Young Christopher Blazekowski played football extremely well. In fact he played so well that his mother, Jean Marie, would look up from her knitting in order to watch the offensive series of his team, something that Jean Marie had never done with her seven other male children. Christopher could dash the field triumphant. With both speed, balance, and a wiry frame that summoned more strength than seemed right for his age there was no mistaking his talent. He ran around the other fourteen-year-olds like so many sculptures frozen simply for his pleasure. Jean Marie would watch with pride and wonder from where the talent came.

The sun blistered bleachers and parched brown field of Happy High School (grades 6-12) seemed unquestionably minor league to her. Within Christopher, Jean Marie knew, lay the kind of latent talent that needed a larger venue for proper appreciation. When she called Ike in Dallas that December it was to deliver an ultimatum.

"Johnny Carson, did you read what the papers said about Johnny Carson?"

Ike felt all cold inside as he listened to Jean Marie. He had made his permanent home in Dallas for the past ten years in order to facilitate his business dealings. Business and extramarital affairs of varying degrees had drawn him away from the family in Happy. The separation had suited him and he had no wish to alter it.

Ike was a great man, with money, power, and land holdings developers coveted. At Christmastime he distributed presents to orphans at the city home. Through his friends he had managed to put his older children into the right fraternities and sororities at SMU. He had a beautiful mistress, a woman whose viola curves he stroked each night with his thick digits.

The floodgates had opened long ago. There had been other women. Wherever he went they were waiting for him. At parties arranged by business clients in Detroit and Los Angeles, they were lined up like tasty appetizers for his choosing. And it was true that he had even arranged similar setups for his own parties. All it took was one phone call and twenty women would be in his office primping and showing flesh through the tight gaps in their clothes.

That Jean Marie had tolerated and ignored Ike's life in town was testimony to the uneasy truce they had arranged. Each month Ike's large check came in the mail.

"Did you take a look at today's paper?" Jean Marie's hard edged voice pressed Ike.

"I read the Journal, but what—"

"Well I read the Wichita Falls Sun, excuse me, and there was a big front page article about Johnny Carson. Do you know what that article was about?"

"No."

"His wife divorced him. For infidelity. She got half the money." Jean Marie let this last bit of information sink in with a lengthy silence before asking, "Understand?" Her coffee had grown cold. She watched the yellow school bus pull away from the front of the house.

"What do you want?"

"All you have to do is take young Christopher in and keep sending those checks. I want him enrolled at University High and I want him on the football team. Now if that seems unsatisfactory to you then we can go to court and I can win and I can move to Dallas. I'll also take the house in Martha's Vineyard."

"I think we understand each other."

"For your sake I hope we do. Just remember that he is your son."

And then Tommy Bird's prophecy came ringing back to Ike, *you will love him because he is your son and he will become everything you wish your life had been. He will have the God-given talent that makes life seem effortless... .* "And he will have the power of judgment over me," Ike mumbled into the dead receiver.

That September fifteen-year-old Christopher Blazekowski left his mother's house and Happy, Texas forever. Ike chartered a single engine Cessna to fly his youngest son from Happy into Dallas. Christopher sat next to the pilot and stared wide-eyed as they circled over the Dallas Cowboys' stadium while waiting for clearance to land. Dallas and Fort Worth sprawled out beneath them. In the distance Christopher could spot the skyscrapers of downtown Dallas, the green lawns of the suburbs, and Texas State Flags flying in front of various municipal buildings. The glass and macadam stretched on and on like something great and glorious. Waves of heat swelled from the ground. The Cessna pushed her nose down and swept like a vulture for the tarmac.

Running from the plane to the air conditioned coolness of Ike's Cadillac limo, Kris sneezed. He found himself in familiar, yet alien surroundings. Here was the same sky he had known all his life, but the smell in the air was that of a thousand exhaust pipes and black tar.

Ike took Christopher's bags and handed them to the chauffeur.

"I'm real glad you're gonna be living with me," Ike lied to his nervous son.

Did it always smell like this here?

"I don't know what your mom might have said, but we're gonna have a lot of fun together."

Ike smiled a gap-toothed grin at Christopher across a slick desert of black leather.

The limo began to roll. It had been ten years since Christopher last lived with his father, and two since he had last set eyes on him. *This guy cannot*, Christopher recoiled, *he cannot be my real father.*

Now Ike had a plan about this whole football thing. He figured that just about anybody could make a mistake when it came to something as subjective as the athletic talent of a young man. And he figured that just because Jean Marie had watched her son run circles around the ten or twelve Chicano kids that Hidden Springs had tossed up against Happy in no way counted as proof positive that young Christopher Blazekowski was a ringer. At least that's what the rational side of Ike told himself.

So, before fall practice started at University High School Ike went on down to Elijah Starbuck's office in order to have a word with the coach about Christopher's prospects of making the team.

University High School was a big gothic structure made out of gray granite and meant to look something like Duke, which was supposed to look something like Princeton, which was supposed to look a bit like Cambridge or Oxford or some place back in Europe. Vigorously watered and weeded green lawns encircled the edifice. Two stone archways sat above the gray granite steps which, legend said, had been sandblasted into their worn and ancient appearance. Inscribed in the stone above the archways was the school motto that no one could read. Ike absently scratched his head as he stood on the steps and tried to mouth the Latin. He supposed it had something to do with God and knowledge, things he didn't care very much about.

Off to the left of the green lawn and looking like some strange alien spacecraft set down next to the Center of Learning was University High's football stadium. Banks of lights arced out like antennae from the tops of the poured concrete stadium seats. On Friday nights over fifteen thousand of the wealthier citizens of Dallas would arrive to witness the glorious shaping of young mens' Dignity and Character upon this field of sport. Not that these wealthier citizens of Dallas were entertained at all in the bargain. Nor did they mind the ten dollar admission price which the Center of Learning saw fit to charge them. After all, these were innocent high schoolers, amateurs competing for the pure joy of competition out on that field. Why some of these young men even came from underprivileged backgrounds in poorer parts of the city. In fact, the entire offensive line and defensive backfield was composed of these "Special Students" that the Center of Learning had so magnanimously scooped up from poverty.

Who could say that University High School was not sensitive to the plight of Underprivileged Minorities? Why, if one were to judge by their football team alone, one would think that nearly the entire student body of University High School was composed of Underprivileged Minorities. And who would not enjoy watching the Character and Dignity of so many Underprivileged Minorities being developed so much on that field when they Won?

Many of those wealthier citizens of Dallas would tell you that it was downright beautiful to watch those Underprivileged Minority students from University High win. In fact, they would tell you it was so beautiful and so touching to watch them win that they would also confess to you in the same breath that it was mighty unbearable to watch those same Underprivileged Minority students lose. In fact losing was worse than unbearable - it was unwatchable.

The administration of University High would readily admit that when you have so many Underprivileged Minorities on your team then you have a special Burden to Society to ensure that their Character and Dignity are developed in a proper manner. Now the wealthier citizens of Dallas would tell you that not very much Character and Dignity, at least not the right kind for Underprivileged Minorities, can be developed while losing. And when you're letting your Burden to Society down by not properly developing these young mens' Character and Dignity you might even begin to take some of the blame for their losses yourself. Consequently, you might stay away from the stadium on Friday nights and spend your ten dollars at the movies.

And when those impressionable Underprivileged Minority students would look up into the stands on Friday nights and see a stadium less than a quarter full, it could be said that their Character and Dignity were in grave danger of suffering near fatal wounds. And with the Burden of Society weighing so heavily upon his shoulders, the Chancellor of the Center of Learning would sit glumly in the stands and sadly take in the emptiness of the stadium and the disappointment of the precious Underprivileged Minority Students down on the field. He would sit glumly, brooding, a dark cloud above his head, an empty stadium in front of his eyes. And with the Burden of Society weighing so heavily upon him he might even do something as rash as to quietly take the coach into his office and tell him that he was fired.

Elijah Starbuck's team had been five and five last season. This may not sound so bad. For in life, if you manage to win half the time then you're probably doing a lot better than a lot of other people. But with so many Underprivileged Minorities on his team Elijah Starbuck knew that the great Burden of Society demanded his team go at least eight and three this fall and thereby generate some more interest in the Character and Dignity being developed at Alumni Field on Friday nights.

So with the season fast approaching Coach Starbuck and his staff had for weeks been preparing for the start of fall practice. They had been busily recruiting new U. M. Students who might happen to have a greater natural reservoir of C. & D. than the current crop of U. M. Students at University High. Arranged on the walls of Coach Starbuck's office were magnetic charts on which the coaches had listed every playing position, then sublisted, in descending order of ability, the player who might fill that position. On other charts they had arranged the names of certain fourteen year old U. M. Students, not yet attending University High, in descending order of C. & D..

Coach Starbuck and his assistants, Peace Silas and Dick Wishbone, would hold animated discussions for hours in that office. Re-arranging and shuffling the names on the charts, they would argue over whose name should go where and how high or low. They plucked the names off charts with special magnetic rods designed especially to work with the magnetic boards. About twice a day a situation would develop.

Magnetic rod in hand, Peace or Dick would pluck off a name near the top of one chart and radically shift it to the top of another chart on the other side of the room. Whereupon a great debate would commence which would sometimes last for hours and involve a great deal of shouting, swearing, and hurling of blunt objects. Together, the entire coaching staff referred to Coach Starbuck's office as 'The War Room.'

Dressed like a dignified businessman, Ike Blazekowski threaded the hallways on his way to the door of Elijah's office behind which a melee, such as the one described beforehand, was in progress.

Crouched behind the end table, arms protecting his head, cowered offensive coordinator Dick Wishbone. Standing on the couch with his arm cocked and ready to hurl a large three ring binder was defensive coordinator Peace Silas.

"You might as well eat this playbook you son-of-a-bitch if you think I can run my defense without Washington at free safety."

The three ring binder took flight toward the end table. Elijah Starbuck's mother-of-pearl ashtray exploded like glass. From behind the end table Dick Wishbone said, "You never could hit the side of a barn, Peace."

"Gentlemen," Elijah Starbuck's voice calmed the air with a neatly modulated twang. "I am prepared to sit here all day and all night while you two children fight like dogs under the furniture. However, that is not what I

88

would like to do."

Elijah Starbuck swung his black lizard-skin cowboy boots up onto the green felt of the snooker table he used as a desk. Laid across the felt were rods for the magnetic charts, pool cues, bridges, red and white balls, old newspaper, and file after misplaced file. Elijah Starbuck leaned back in his leather chair and brushed bits of stray snuff tobacco off his grey flannel suit. He picked up one of the snooker balls and balanced its heavy weight in his palm.

From across the wide neglected expanse of the felt he surveyed his two assistant coaches with a reptilian stare of authority before spitting triumphantly into the brass spittoon stationed by the still cowering figure of Dick Wishbone. Thirty-eight years old, a University of Texas football alum and five year backup quarterback for the St. Louis Cardinals, Elijah Starbuck was beginning to feel his own mortality. The daily travails of life as a coach; the old friends who were more successful; all these things were beginning to grate upon Elijah Starbuck like sandpaper against flesh. He stood up and took aim for the left corner pocket between two unsteady pillars of paperwork. The red ball skidded wide and rebounded into a collapsing pile of play charts. Elijah Starbuck sighed and lamented the daily ennui that dogged him with a foreboding sense of failure. Two weeks until Fall practice began and he still hadn't found a running back.

From underneath the end table Dick Wishbone asked the question Elijah knew was coming, "Didn't we agree earlier this week that our number one priority was finding a talented running back?"

"Yes we did," Elijah concurred. He gathered the loose papers and pushed them into an amalgamated stack.

"Elijah, how can you take Washington from my defense?" Peace Silas pleaded.

"I'm not saying we're gonna, Peace. All I am saying is that we should try Washington out at tailback. Peace, we need a running back. Lord God what I'd do for a running back.

A timely knock came at the door. The coaches' heads turned to see Ike Blazekowski's silhouette behind the frosted glass.

"Peace, get off that couch and see who's at the door for me please."

Now, when the important and respectable looking Ike Blazekowski strolled into Elijah Starbuck's office, Elijah's eyes involuntarily ran the circuit 'round their sockets. From underneath the end table Dick Wishbone peered out and started to laugh. Even Peace Silas's hangdog face broke into a smile.

"Good afternoon, sir. What can I do for you?" Elijah was out of his chair with his hand extended across the snooker table. Dick Wishbone crawled out from underneath the end table and made himself comfortable on the couch. Peace Silas leaned back against the snooker table with his arms folded against his chest. With the regularity of a smooth program, the assembled football coaches of University High School flipped their binary switches to the open position. For what? For Ike Blazekowski, wealthy businessman, obviously concerned father, and potential source of funding.

"Gentlemen," Ike was heading straight to the point. No sense in messing around. He was prepared to offer money. Just as long as Christopher Blazekowski did not make the team. "I'm here about my son who wants to play football this coming fall. He moved here specifically to play football, and I don't want to sound as if I'm putting any pressure on you gentlemen. But, I am prepared to–"

"Mr. Blazekowski," Elijah Starbuck cut Ike off with a wave of his hand. "I can assure you that you are not the first concerned father who has come into my office in order to enquire about his son's prospects of making this team."

"Now you wait a minute, you've got me all wrong here."

"Nonsense. No offense Mr. Blazekowski, I know that's not how you look at it. But try to see things from my perspective. I understand how you, as a father, are concerned about properly developing the Character and Dignity of your young son. Now you may say to yourself, *'What does it matter if they have one more kid on the team? It's just one more boy. They should be able to handle that.'* What you cannot understand, Mr. Blazekowski, are the logistical aspects of our problems here."

He thought about protesting. He held back. Ike Blazekowski lowered himself into the other man's shoes. What was he about to hear? *Of course, how stupid of me.*

"Logistical problems?" Ike said it real slow. He let his jaw drop. If he'd worn a hat, he would have doffed it.

Peace Silas' pitch came first.

"Why Elijah," he stepped forward from the snooker table and turned around to face his boss, "I doubt I could even squeeze Mr. Blazekowski's son in through the front door of our weight room 'less I greased him up like a pig and levered him in sideways with a crowbar. We got no more space. I doubt he could get in more than four bench-presses all year long, and that'd be the number if he managed to keep his place in line all season."

"Now Peace, I think we could manage." Dick Wishbone played his sympathetic hand. "Me and old Solomon went down to the basement yesterday with the dolly truck and searched around in those old crates until we found those leather helmets and pads from the championship season back in thirty-two. So your son would at least have a uniform, Mr. Blazekowski. I can guarantee you that, by gum. Course he won't have a face mask on his helmet, but neither did I when I started playing." Dick Wishbone wrinkled up a smile so Ike could count the various directions in which Dick's nose shifted on its crooked course down his face.

"Gentlemen, gentlemen, all your points have merit." Elijah

Starbuck interceded with a gentle thump of his gavel fist on the green felt. "There are many areas of significant need within this program; but as I was discussing with you all before Mr. Blazekowski so kindly dropped in on us, all of these points are moot unless we find some way to sod the stadium floor. As of now, gentlemen, we have no field upon which to play. Logistically speaking, I believe this is our number one priority."

There was a pause at this point which Ike understood was left purposely as a window for his gracious and benevolent charity.

"My son's name is Christopher Blazekowski, and you can all go to hell," Ike said. He then walked out of the War Room. Quietly pleased with himself, he shut the door behind him and strolled down the tiled hallway.

On the wall of the War Room sat a new name. At the very bottom of the least important chart, a chart listing the incoming non-recruited players, sat Christopher Blazekowski's tag.

"Four three?"

"What'd you say down there Peace?" Elijah Starbuck stood at the head of the sprint line holding a clipboard. The sun remained steady and calm in the still air. Sweat trickled from Elijah's neck all the way down his back and into his blue polyester coaching shorts. Elijah's hand involuntarily reached down in order to scratch the transition point between upper ass and deep crack.

"Four three!" Peace yelled back. From a distance of forty yards Peace could be seen jumping up and down, his lanky frame distorted by waves of heat rising up from the clipped grass.

"Fucking shit," Elijah cursed, "Fucking hot shit." He pulled his pen hand out of his shorts and marked the time down next to Christopher Blazekowski's name. He knew he'd pulled one out of his ass.

The players were lounging on the grass hill behind the south goalposts after practice. They waited for the coaches to come out and talk before sending them home to their various neighborhoods. Sitting in their streetclothes, showered, their athletic bags behind them, over sixty boys squinted into the low sun.

J.T. Green, special Minority Underprivileged student at University High, was pontificating to anyone who cared to listen.

"I don't care what Ms. Trumbull says, if she makes me write this essay, man, she's gonna get the whole story. I mean the whole story. She gonna hear how J.T. Green spent his summer vacation down in Louisiana, on the bayou, loving rich white girls in the backs of their daddy's Eldorados.

"J.T. shut up, man. What you gonna tell us now? You give 'em free crawfish and they jump on your lap?"

"They just want me," J.T. pirouettes, "ain't I the prettiest?"

A chorus of moans. A jock is thrown at J.T. . He just grins. A senior, J.T. is the biggest offensive lineman in the district. Last spring he won the role of Lear in the drama club production.

Two groups of players were on the hill. Those whose parents sent them to University High and those who were actively pursued by University High. Among the latter group were hispanics, blacks, and whites, including Christopher Blazekowski, who naturally made his decision to sit with this group. He grew up in a town where half his playmates were Mexican. The other boys in the group further down the hill seemed stiff to him. They laughed at things that weren't very funny and didn't talk to anyone but themselves.

J.T. Green would speak to anyone. "Look at that!" he whistled low. The cheerleaders from Methodist High School for Women had taken the field. A symbiotic relationship existed between the two schools. Without football there could be no cheerleading. And without cheerleading what would football be?

"Hey ladies come on up and let J.T. tell all of you how he spent his summer vacation. I'm the fastest, biggest, baddest man there is."

"Hey Muhammad Ali. Not to burst your bubble or anything, but you ain't the fastest by a long shot. Some Polish kid ran a four three," said Paul Rodriguez, captain of the defensive squad. "Blazekowski ran a four three. Coach Silas say he's gonna make a great free safety."

"Free safety!" J.T.'s eyes popped out of his head. "Who's Blazekowski? Who is he?"

"You?" J.T. stared disbelievingly at the thin boy with shocking white hair who had raised his hand as if he were in class. "What's your name?"

"Christopher Blazekowski."

"Look up when you talk to me man." He walked down the hill toward Chris. "You got the speed and I got the strength," J.T. said. "I'm gonna personally make sure you get a hundred yards a game even if I have to carry you."

The light burning in J.T.'s eyes was hope. Before he had been an offensive lineman without a running back, which is akin to a rider without a horse, or *vice versa*, whichever way you want to look at it. And in his senior year of high school, the recruiters from Southern Cal, Texas, and SMU were somewhat lukewarm on him.

"You wanna run behind me?"

Chris nodded his head in the affirmative.

"Climb on my shoulders, son. First thing we gotta change is that name of yours. Blazekowski," J.T. spat it out. "Now, I could be named Blazekowski," J.T. turned a three sixty to show his impressive girth. "Blazekowski's the kind of guy who goes up to the all you can eat buffet and bankrupts the place. You're no Blazekowski, you're just a Blaze, my four-three man. And that first name too. You can drop the second half of it. Chris. But make it harder like, K-O-O-L. Kris, K-R-I-S. Kris Blaze. Say it."

J.T., hands on hips, looking like John Henry; of course, Kris said it. "Kris Blaze."

J.T. moved forward and placed his palm on Kris' shoulder. In mock benediction he said, "I dub thee Kris Blaze. Knight of the World. Your name will be written down and remembered, translated, told from father to son for countless generations as long as there is a mankind to hear of you."

"Shut up J.T.," another chorus of moans. "Why don't you stick to acting, man?"

J.T. was struck with mock indignity. All were laughing except for Kris Blaze who watched one cheerleader with blond hair and freckles sink down into a split while her friends nodded approvingly. Dawn Signorello was a senior co-captain of the Methodist High School for Women cheerleading squad. This past summer her official reading list had been composed of books like, Pride and Prejudice, Animal Farm, and believe it or not, Planet of the Apes.

But Dawn's interests were not centered around nineteenth century England, nor communism. She had no fears that dolphins were smarter than humans, nor that apes possessed the evolutionary potential to beat out mankind in the long run.

And though she had been engaged to marry Dan Wagner since the junior prom last year, Dawn considered herself a contemporary woman and liked to sneak into her parents' bedroom and steal her mother's books. So, this past summer Dawn had read, The Feminine Mystique, and a collection of essays by Germaine Greer that were decidedly not on the Methodist High School for Women reading list. And though she had decided that unlike Greer, she was not bi-sexual, she was in accordance with the idea of liberating her sexuality in the very near future. Her interest in boys was direct and to the point now, a startling switch for shy Dawn from just a few months ago.

Kris Blaze leaned against the fence and unabashedly studied the cheerleading practice from close range. He had wandered down the hill away from J.T. and the others in an ambling, precise route that landed him exactly where he had planned to go.

"What are you looking at?", Dawn and her friends huddled like pioneers in a circle. Kris is the grinning savage. His skin is tanned and his hair stands up in the middle like a mohawk. He knows what he wants, but it won't be said. These are innocent times. Not innocent in a pure sense. Ignorance is more the word. The times were very much like a child of fourteen who gets his first job from his father and thinks he knows what work is. All we need is love, right. In short, it was a time when a woman could be both feminist and cheerleader. There was no contradiction.

The girls practiced their pyramid. Dawn, ever so lithe and popular, boosted herself up on the backs of her thicker friends and rose to the top, where she stood for a second before balance failed her. A tip of the scales. What weight could Kris' intent eyes have held? That recoil of Dawn's head, her tumble backwards, to avoid what?

She lay in the grass, her friends huddled about her.

"Dawn are you all right?"

"Dawn how many fingers am I holding up?"

"Three," she answered correctly before brushing her friend's hand away. Dawn stood and looked. All concerned eyes moved from her to the fence. Balanced on the fence railing in his bare feet Kris Blaze was posed like a gymnast. His soles cupped the warm aluminum tube that ran along the top of the fence. He bent his knees, and with a quickness born of certainty, was up and over; then down again, his feet centered on the rail as if a guide wire had been strung plum through him.

Like a girl in an audience who knows certain lines and how specific scenes were acted out with her in mind, Dawn watched Kris.

Two more back flips. The risk Kris took? Same as any actor's. He could seem foolish. He could forget his line and slip. Then the magic would be gone. Kris' feet plopped down true as if guided by magnets. Spin forward and dismount: say it now or don't ever say a thing.

"My name is Kris Blaze." There it was, the certainty again. He came forward like Krishna, or Christ, or maybe just the way we would have imagined they came forward. Hand extended. Calm, everything was calm. *My name is Kris Blaze*, the formality and politeness seemed so correct. Here's the subtext, here's what was understood. *My name is Kris Blaze and I am amazing.* He didn't have to say that. If the subtext needs to be said then don't bother.

Their hands touched.

Before Dawn could say anything he was gone. Kris ran back up the hill to sit next to J.T. and to listen to Coach Starbuck talk about Dignity and Character, and how much of it was on this year's team. Past the first group of boys he shot, and with him went the magic of the day. The steady humdrum returned and the mundane world rapidly smothered the drugged effects of youth upon youth. The memory was enough for Dawn. She would remember. Kris Blaze. Amazing. On up past Billy Wagner, Kris shot. Billy Wagner, who had watched the whole scene below. Tonight Billy would place a call to the Kappa Alpha house at the U. of T. in Austin and say hello to his brother Dan. He would ask how preparations for Old South week were going, and was Dan's Confederate General uniform looking good? And had he found a proper dress for Dawn so that she would look like the authentic antebellum lady of Southern society that all the girls would be impersonating? And by the way, not to get you nervous or anything Dan, but I saw something today... .

Unaware of the geometry at work, Kris watched Dawn. While

94

beneath him, in that awkward group of boys Kris had avoided at the start of the day, Billy Wagner squinted up into the sun and measured Kris Blaze with a cold, white stare. From Dawn to Kris to Billy, the triangle emerged.

"You what!"

Clearly, calmly, and for the third time in five minutes Kris Blaze told his father, "I made the team."

Out beyond the patio the grasshoppers chirruped in the irrigated lawn. The Texas blue sky arced overhead. Seated comfortably in wire chairs above the broad marble floor of the terrazzo, Kris Blaze and Ike were eating breakfast. Bacon, scrambled eggs, and ketchup were smeared like paint on the delicate palate of their *Limoge* plates. Coffee blended with chicory steamed from the eggshell thin cups.

Ike regarded this bit of information and for the third time came up with the same question. He asked it. "How? You're tall, but you're not big. You're too god-damned young."

"I'm the starting tailback because I'm fast and no one can get a clean hit on me. I also placed into Honors English, something I'm sure nobody else in the family has ever done."

"More coffee Master Blazekowski?" Jones the Butler approached the table with a silver thermos jug of coffee at the ready.

"No thank you Jones. Jones, from now on please call me Kris, with a K. That or Blaze. I've changed my name."

Ike choked on some egg.

"Very well Master Blaze," Jones smartly retreated to the kitchen.

"Who the hell do you think you are?" Ike's face had turned a pome-granate shade of crimson. "Ain't our name good enough for you anymore?" He pondered the enigma that was his son. Only Ike knew the truth about Kris. With the resigned fatality of a man caught in an avalanche, Ike surrendered his son's fate and ultimately his own to the fulfillment of Tommy Bird's prophecies.

He would love him and he would hate him. It was true. The pride Ike felt about his son making the team was matched only by the frustration it caused in Ike's heart. His son was not his son, yet he still loved him. Down on through layer after conflicting layer of Ike's soul lay the myriad answers to the simple question. Was Ike Kris' father? Yes and no. And so Ike spun through the revolving door of his own questioning.

Kris slurped from his grapefruit spoon. He sat calmly in his chair, arms neatly folded, eyes clear like the Buddha's. "Don't worry, Dad. It was my decision."

"Your decision. By what right?"

"Don't worry, I didn't expect you to understand. Dad, who's that woman who keeps coming over every night?" Kris neatly changed his tack.

Ike's face flushed to a deeper shade of crimson. "Her name is Ms. Tanner."

"I know that, but who is she?"

"She's my secretary."

"You're lying," Kris cut a piece of bacon with his fork when he said it. "She's why you live here instead of with mom, right? You see, I told you I understand you. I don't hate you though. You can't help it if you're weak."

There might have been a little remorse in Kris' heart as he spoke his mind. Who knows what each man's burden is? And who was he to damn the past and curse the present state of his father's life? There was a little bit of remorse in Kris' heart, but it sure as hell didn't stop him.

"You don't want me to play football, Dad. But Mom does. How come you can't order me not to play? I know you'd like to. What would happen?" Kris impaled the thin strip of bacon and brought it up to his mouth. "Would mom divorce you?" he asked with his mouth full.

There was a long period of silence before Ike screamed and tossed the breakfast table onto its side, shattering the gentle buzz of the grasshoppers with the sound of broken glass. The porous marble floor soaked up the spilt milk. Ike picked his way forward through the debris. Kris was folded in his chair, legs in the lotus position. A faint smile creased the corners of his lips. Ike knew it then. He knew that the prophecy had been horribly fulfilled. His son hated him. Kris was his son. The judgment had been passed. Ike's legacy was damned. And Ike still couldn't help but love this boy who was his son even though he was not his father.

"Yes," Ike said it inches from Kris' face. But there was no anger in his voice. He got right up close to Kris and let him look at who he was. "Yes, yes, yes." Ike turned away and left for the office.

Fifteen minutes later Kris padded into the kitchen.

"Jones, I'm afraid Mr. Blazekowski made a mess out there," Kris informed the butler as he made his way through the kitchen.

"Thank you Master Blaze," Jones watched as Kris moved toward the main staircase. There was still an hour before classes started. Breakfast with Father had been one of the more trying aspects of life in Dallas. It was a ritual Ike had hoped would cement the bond between father and son. As for Kris, all it had done was confirm inside of himself the growing suspicion that there was absolutely no way in hell Ike Blazekowski was his father.

When he reached the top of the stairs he turned right instead of left. Past the false Ionic columns that lined the open balcony at the top of the staircase, Kris headed into Ike's bedroom. His bare feet squished on the deep red pile. The clicking of jewels and springs from the lone Grandfather clock echoed through the vast emptiness of Ike's neo-Georgian palazzo.

The suspicion had been growing lately. It had gotten so strong that during those moments when Kris contemplated the idea that Ike might really be his father he began to get violently ill and wish himself dead.

Ms. Tanner's white, silk bathrobe lay on the floor in a discarded heap. There was the writing desk with locked drawers. Today he would continue his search for the keys to the desk. This would last for half an hour. Then, for fifteen minutes, he would start where he had left off on the bookcase, with The Counterfeiters by Gide.

Kris pushed the mattress off the boxspring and stopped for a moment to examine the pornographic magazines he found there. He emptied the unlocked drawers and pulled out spare keys of all sorts. None fit the locks as he tried them.

He had no idea what kind of proof he was looking for. He was only sure that there was something to be found.

He rifled through receipts, old letters, drafting implements, and maps with no luck. Half an hour up, he switched to the books.

The books were Ms. Tanner's touch. Within the cavernous space that was Ike's bedroom, Ms. Tanner had erected bookcases which covered an entire wall. More a library than a bedroom, the musty smell of old books mingled with the pre-fab conditioned air and nylon smell of the carpet, a combination which strangely evoked memories of both museums and the local Ramada Inn. Brass ladders ran on tracks along the walls and protruded from the shelves like archaic tubing or modern sculpture.

Kris proceeded alphabetically. He pulled down Gide and absently flipped through the pages of translated text in order to make sure that the book was not hollowed out. He replaced the book and proceeded on to the next one. His leg curled through the brass. He swung out from the ladder like a pirate on a ship's rigging while he flipped the pages.

Fifteen minutes gone, Kris padded out of the room. The maids were arriving to clean. He went into his own room and put on his socks and shoes and school tie before proceeding down the grand staircase. At the bottom Jones met him with his bookbag.

"The car is waiting, Master Blaze," Jones indicated the way toward the front door with his open palm. Paul, the driver, was waiting for him.
"Thank you Jones," Kris took the bookbag and made his way toward the door.

The spotlights glared in the night sky like torches strung in lines for the benefit of a million moths. Clouds of the fluttering insects swarmed beneath the false promise of their illumination.

Up, up, Dawn rose. At the apex of her flight her legs spread wide in a full split. She hung motionless, frozen in those spotlights for an eternal second, before plunging into the waiting arms of her spotters. The scattered applause of those who had seen and appreciated, mostly young girls and adolescent boys, peppered the air.

Out on the field the band was doing double time, marching to the beat laid out by the drum major's baton.

The girls from Methodist High School for Women began to lead a cheer.

Halftime sweat and strategy filled the pregnant air of University High's locker room.

"We have got to stop them defensively, Elijah." Dick Wishbone, Elijah Starbuck, and Peace Silas huddled together. This was the coaches' pow-wow. "Our secondary is getting eaten alive."

"Dick, I've tried everything. We've done zone, man to man, we've blitzed. He just keeps finding his receivers," Peace Silas was obviously at a loss. It was true. Even though University had seventeen points, Latin High had twenty one.

Elijah Starbuck scratched his head and decided to try something he had thought about implementing a long time before this first game of the season. He had contemplated it as far back as the second day of the Fall double sessions. He had secretly planned for it by giving Kris Blaze the defensive playbook and telling him to know it.

"Every play gentlemen."

"What?" Both Peace and Dick together.

"We're keeping our best player on the field for every play. Take Wagner out at free safety and put Kris in for him." Elijah instructed Peace. "Got that? Good. Now, come on. I've gotta go be inspirational in front of the team."

When the half was over the University High team lined up in the tunnel and anxiously scraped their cleats against the hard concrete floor before charging back out onto the field. Kris Blaze felt larger than he ever had in his life. In the first two quarters he had run for over eighty yards on ten carries, caught two passes, one for a touchdown. He had run almost exclusively to the right side of the line, behind J.T., and each time had encountered the prostrate bodies of defensive linemen who had attempted to stand in the way of J.T.. It wasn't until Kris was in the defensive secondary that he encountered standing defenders, and that's when J.T. would be screaming and charging up behind him for another block.

Kris would shift his hips. Gliding in second gear he waited for the crack to form between the safety and the linebacker. Fake inside. They bite. Boom! Kris' legs chewed the turf and he was past them for ten more yards before the cornerback caught his ankle. So it went. He shifted his hips and froze defenders. No one got a clean shot at him. With each tackle Kris fell to the soft turf, his ankle clutched by a desperate hand. He was up and ready for another run.

At the front of the team Kris and J.T. waited to charge out onto the field. Peace Silas tapped Kris on the shoulder. "Ready to go in at safety?"

"Thought you'd never ask! How 'bout J.T. at inside linebacker?"

"How 'bout it J.T.?" Peace put it to him.

98

J.T. punched Kris on the shoulder and nodded his grim assent. Then they charged out onto the field while the crowd went nuts, and the band played, and the girls jumped, and the bugs swarmed, and the hot air of the Texas fall lay over the stadium like a soft pillow.

How couldn't they win?

At safety Kris knew all the angles. He read every pump fake, then lagged until the ball was thrown, when he would break on it and beat the receiver to it. Two interceptions and he had stopped the Latin air attack as cold as J.T. had killed their ground game.

On offense they broke it open. J.T. in front steamrolled down the sideline until Kris broke out of his wake and swung wide out onto the chewed turf like a gazelle sprung from the draft of a truck. He raised the ball high, oh, how many times? It would be redundant to tell.

Suffice it to say: they won.

Outside the locker room J.T. grabbed Kris' arm. "C'mon, man, we're having a party at my place."

"Can we bring Dawn?"

"Only if she wants to come." A sly smile crossed J.T.'s euphoric lips. "Go grab her 'fore someone else does."

As it so often is with athletes who've not only won, but gone beyond and into the zone, Kris Blaze carried an air about himself. With an older athlete this aura may bless him with youth for yet another day. But when Dawn looked at Kris Blaze she saw a young man who was older, taller, and more worldly than his fifteen years on this planet should rightly grant him.

"I've thought about you," Dawn whispered. They talked by the cinder track, leaning over the fence toward one another. The crowd was slowly filtering out the gates.

"Let's go." Kris took Dawn's hand. Half an hour later, showered and clean, they met at the fence.

Into the night they drove, all piled into the back of J.T.'s van. Soon, the wealthy neighborhoods of Dallas disappeared and the rest of the world began to circulate around the van windows. They entered a neighborhood where the brick ranch houses were crammed in identical rows down each street. Each tiny back yard was fenced. Guard dogs barked and chased the van to the end of their leash. Dawn and Kris snuggled close to each other in the tightly packed van. Paul Rodriguez was there and so were some of those players Kris had chosen to sit with up on the hill that long month ago during Fall practice. Cans of Pearl Light were passed around along with a joint. J.T. punched the Sugar Hill Gang into the tape player and soon the whole van was rocking as the tightly packed bodies of University High football team swayed in time. Kris held Dawn's hand as they both laughed and pulled from their beers. He had never been happier. She had never been more confused.

When they reached the small brick ranch that belonged to J.T.'s cousin a case of beer was on ice in the tub. Dawn downed beer after beer in the backyard where J.T.'s cousin had the grill going and was cooking burgers and dogs. She heard J.T. say something about how he'd left his parents' place in order to get away from their neighborhood. He had said it so matter of factly that it made Dawn feel even more uneasy. She couldn't imagine what it would be like to live without her parents. Dawn had her own bedroom with white sheets and white walls and pink pillowcases. She sat down to dinner with her parents and had intelligent discussions with them about books and movies. Dawn respected her parents, and they had expectations for her. She couldn't imagine her family in another neighborhood. The thought disturbed her and she would have dropped it except for the fact that she was slightly stoned and drunk. How awful it must be, she realized for the first time, to live someplace that you hate. It must happen. Even to people like herself. How awful to suddenly wake up one day and find that you are no longer in your nice, big house with the wide, green lawn. How awful to wake up and find yourself living someplace, someplace like this place. She hated to think that because she liked J.T., but the thought of living in a one-story ranch house on a street where the neighbors could look in the front windows and the cars were parked up on the sidewalk scared the living hell out of Dawn.

But she would never have to face that. Dawn was going to marry Dan Wagner when she was a sophomore at the U. of T. . She would get into her mother's sorority since she was a legacy. It would all be so easy. All of Dan's family was perfectly respectable and had a great deal of money. She hated to think that word: money. But it came down to that, no doubt. It would be so simple for her to move in the same social circles she always had. But one needed money in order to live like she did. Coming here tonight was out of the ordinary. But then it was for Kris, and here she sighed. She did not think she was being cold-blooded. She was a progressive woman who happened to think Kris Blaze horribly attractive.

A sudden flash of hope made Dawn turn to Kris and ask, "What does your father do?"

Now Kris had no idea how important this seemingly normal question was. And in his slightly drunken mood he was in no way disposed to cast his father in a favorable light. "He can't help what he does," Kris cryptically answered. "He left my mother before I could even read. I think I'm adopted"

"Oh."

That sealed it for Kris. All Dawn could imagine was another sad family, split up and full of hate. What a pretty picture, her on a date with him and meeting his father. Maybe he drinks Schlitz and watches *Laugh In* from his Barco lounger. And he would still be in uniform. Yes, he wore a uniform. Some kind of non-descript institutional piece of clothing. A cap too. Something that identified him as one of those low arcing lives whose rise never saw the horizon and subsequent crash left him mired in a job with a monkey suit made out of khaki polyester and dotted with shiny, aluminum buttons. Dawn snuggled closer to Kris' arm. Did she really care what his father did? Did she even care what Kris Blaze might become? These were hard questions because her answer was: no!

Dawn tried to recall the lines of a dissident Polish poet. Something about the young men. The young peasants. How at the age of nineteen they would burst through the fields for one summer. Wheat on their back and the grin of youth in their faces. A year later, at twenty, they would be broken by labor. Somehow this made her feel sad. She told herself that she didn't know what she was doing. But she was lying of course. With a careless and relaxed abandon, Dawn let her inhibitions slide. Because even now, before the fact, it didn't matter.

When they drained their beers and headed inside it was Dawn who pulled him into the bathroom for his first kiss. That was all for the night. A wet, sloppy kiss and a promise of more.

For the remainder of that Fall, all through the shortened days and heat punched nights, Kris and Dawn had a thing, some kind of thing, going. Kris would wind his ten speed along the black ribbon of roads that twisted like capillaries into the residential heart of Highland Park.

He pedaled between the sculpted hummocks of golf course green lawns on symmetrical blacktop with names like *Alamo Boulevard* and *Lone Star Lane* that curled between the white frame houses and faux adobe concrete pueblos like an ancient streambed ox-bowing its way through the plain. On hills he switchbacked up, his balance swayed by the heavy duffel bag slung over his shoulder. All through the sprinkler-dotted landscape he made his way to Dawn's house. There, on the patio, in padded white cushion armchairs they would sip iced tea from tall glasses before departing for the white confines of Dawn's bedroom.

Under starched sheets and a prickly down comforter they nestled for warmth within the Arctic confines of the air-conditioned house and, like adolescents with a new toy, made ferocious, unaffected love.

A storybook romance in more ways than one. What twists and curves would Kris discover as he wound his way daily through the baking Dallas streets? Could such lush green lawns and properly homogenized homes lead only deeper into the labyrinth? How was he to recognize in them the dead end he had come to?

Even as Kris pedaled between those innocent flowerbeds, up past the parked New Yorkers and Lincoln Town Cars that sat like hallucinatory tanks in the short driveways, he could never have imagined that these things would push Dawn away from him forever. Another boy, perhaps, he could have handled. But the promise of things tangible, worldly goods and economic class, had shunted him into a role known well throughout history as *the other man*.

Both Dawn's and Kris' ignorance continued to run its blind course through their lives. For Kris, Dawn alone was enough. But not so for her. Had she only known whose son he was things would have been different. But she chose ignorance of what seemed surely distasteful. They met on the porch and sipped iced tea. The young football hero and cheerleader - of course it seemed to make sense. Of course nothing in life ever really does.

The season continued in fairytale fashion. J.T. crushed while Kris cruised. Decatur North went down in flames, as did Westside High. The Dallas Herald wrote a flattering article on, 'Coach Elijah Starbuck: Builder of Dignity, Shaper of Character.' A recruiter from Penn State visited J.T. at home, and Joe Paterno even flew down from Pennsylvania for the ceremony held at the University High Gymnasium. Where, in front of a packed audience, J.T. signed his national letter of intent that guaranteed him for Penn State. Coach Starbuck, of course, had his picture taken while he shook hands with the great coach. Then he framed the moment and had it nailed on the wall behind the snooker table. For everyone involved it was a great season that ended only after University High had disposed of legendary Odessa Permian High, in front of a packed house at the Astrodome in Houston, to capture the Texas schoolboy football championship for that year.

The first phone calls had begun months before the championship. The letters arrived by the hundreds, daily. Ike Blazekowski had to watch with a mixture of horror and amazement as his son basked in the glow of Tommy Bird's eerily fulfilled prophecy. His son, a sophomore in high school, was being recruited heavily. And though Ike loved him dearly, this was in spite of himself. At a sports award banquet held by the Dallas Herald, Kris met Tony Dorsett who shook his hand and winked at him. "I'm sure we'll be seeing you in few years," he said. Kris' head was spinning. It had all happened less than a year away from Happy, Texas, and he had no way of knowing that he would end it all so soon.

The Christmas holidays were approaching, and with them came Ike's bright new idea. He had been at a society cocktail party, martini in hand, with a frightful urge to get stinking drunk. The woman he had been talking to, a member of the illustrious Hogg family, had been conversing with Ike on a level elevated ever so slightly above that of the inanimate.

"Can you believe it is so hot!" the Hogg woman had said.

"No. Isn't it amazing?" Ike replied through a fog of alcohol.

While in truth, if there was ever an unusually hot day in Dallas, one could also remark with equal candor upon how extraordinarily wet it seems to be in Portland this year.

"Hot!" the Hogg woman wiped her dry brow.

"And dry," Ike finished his martini and ate the olive, his fifth.

"Oh would you look at poor _____!" the Hogg woman had exclaimed as she watched a female member of the illustrious Bass family, martini in hand, attempt to cross the room on crutches. The olives and half the gin splashed to the Oriental as she made her oblivious way toward the buffet. There, a plate of shrimp cocktail clutched at a perilous angle next to her leg, she downed the remainder of her martini and proceeded to leave a trail of jumbo sized pink shrimp and ruby red cocktail sauce behind her. Ike watched as she made her way back toward the bar with the sedated gait of one who mixes painkillers and gin.

"She had a simply dreadful fall last week!"

"Fall?"

"Yes. She was skiing someplace in Colorado. Someplace where all the Bass family goes. In the winter they ski, and in the summer they fish for trout. Flyfish I should say. I remember once remarking to one of the Bass boys that I could never put a worm on a hook and he looked at me as if I'd just insulted him. *You can just keep your bait to yourself!* he'd said."

"That's wonderful. Excuse me, but did you say she fell while skiing?" Ike turned to the Hogg woman with large eyes and newly aroused interest. "I mean that's a shame what happened to _____ Bass, but you did say she did it skiing?"

The Hogg woman's face did a bit of a jig. The corners of her fat cheeks rose like whiskers on a cat. She had always heard that Ike Blazekowski was a man of peculiar habits. His shady and somewhat malicious business practices were par for the course within the Texas business elite. No, there was nothing unusual about that, nor his country manners. Plenty of folks who'd made it big in Texas, and even some who'd gone to Harvard or Yale, played the country type. It came with the territory. Big Stetsons and silver belt buckles that grandpa won in a rodeo were treated like family heirlooms. But there was something about Ike Blazekowski that never fit this image. He was country trying to be city, and not vice versa. Ike's smoothest delivery could never eclipse the steady gruffness of his manner. He would always be something other than safe. Suddenly, and quite irresistibly, the Hogg woman found Ike rather attractive. "Didn't you just say, that's wonderful?" she asked.

"I meant it's wonderful that she wasn't hurt more, you know. I've heard skiing is horribly dangerous."

"Do you want to know how she broke her knee?"

"I thought she was skiing."

"Actually she was in the lift line. She bent over to pick up a kleenex and, *pop!* That was it."

"Oh."

"You seem disappointed, is something wrong?"

"I was just thinking of my son, that's all." What were the chances of Kris breaking his leg?

"Tell you what," the Hogg woman pinched Ike's ass.

"Hey!"

"I've got a Shelby Cobra in the parking lot that'll get up to a hundred and forty on the straights. I'll work the stick if you'll steer."

"Excuse me," Ike slipped away from the Hogg woman's wandering hands, "I've got to go speak to that Bass woman."

He hurried off toward the bar, where he found her, martini in hand.

"Please, let me carry that for you." Ever the gentleman, Ike graciously extended his hand and smiled.

"Nobody takes my drink," the Bass woman barked. She clutched her martini in defiance of Ike's offer.

"I'm not taking it from you, I'll simply hold it. You may have it back whenever you would like."

"Why are you bothering me?" The fog cleared from the Bass woman's face like a break in the clouds. She regarded Ike with a clearly questioning look, as if she had been awakened from a dream by a person unknown to her.

"Just tell me one thing. Where do you go skiing?"

"Vail. We go to Vail," the Bass woman relaxed her hold on the martini glass. Ike caught the stem before it could fall. It was then Ike noticed she seemed to be crying.

"It's so beautiful there. It's so beautiful. Sometimes I wish I lived there."

"What's wrong?" Ike did not want to become the center of any kind of scene. Tears ran down the small wrinkles that radiated from the dark circles underneath the Bass woman's eyes.

"Ohhh, Vail!" She turned toward Ike. "Sometimes, in the summer, we used to climb to the top of Mount Holy Cross. There, just above treeline, was a marmot, practically tame, that we would feed. The picas would scold us from the rocks, and we could see the backside of Vail Mountain. That is what's so amazing out there, you can see forever, Mr. Blazekowski. I know who you are. You think I'm a crazy old woman who's hysterical with crying for no reason. But I'm old now, and I can't ski anymore, and I can't climb worth a damn, and my husband's been dead for five years. I'm going to confide in you my greatest wish, Mr. Blazekowski. I wish I were young again and living in Vail. Now that would be a life."

And that was the first time Ike Blazekowski ever heard of Vail.

One day later Ike had the airline tickets and the keys to the Bass house. They would stay for two weeks, all of Kris' Christmas break.

One of the disadvantages of being a fifteen year old superstar is the illusion of freedom. Kris Blaze's name was known by every college football coach from Los Angeles to Orno, Maine. But that fame translated to a minimum amount of self-determination. He was still his father's son. Kris Blaze was not thrilled about going to Vail. He called Dawn.

"I'm coming over."

"Kris, it's dark out. You can't ride your bike."

"I'm driving."

"You don't have a license."

"I'll see you in fifteen minutes."

Who knows what urgent message impelled Kris to make that late night sojourn. What fifteen year old could resist seeing his beloved when they would be separated for a whole two weeks? Could he survive? What dire messages of everlasting love did he need to deliver? Surely the pledge of his eternal devotion would ensure the safety of their union through the void of these next two weeks. Paul, the driver, waited with the limousine.

Up *Alamo Boulevard*, down *Lone Star Lane*, the limo cruised like a black ship on a black river of asphalt. Past the silent air-conditioned islands that waited at the end of each short tributary driveway, Kris directed the limo through streets he knew well and regarded with fond affection.

They swung into the Signorello driveway. Diaphanous Dawn, in a white dress, descended the steps. At the limousine her blue eyes spoke of some passion, some fury. She opened the back door herself, not bothering to wait for Jones, and slipped onto the shiny leather seat next to Kris.

"Where the hell did you get a limousine?"

"That's not important, Dawn. I need to talk to you."

"Did you win it in a contest or something?"

"It's my dad's, if you really want to know. Dawn, I'm going away for two weeks and ..." Kris stopped. Dawn was stroking the black leather seat. She pushed a black button and watched as a wet bar of sparkling crystal decanters emerged from a side panel. With a pale hand she turned on the television before pouring herself a drink.

"My friend Kristen's father used to have one of these until he lost all his money. Have a drink? Oh, look a football game."

Kris shook his head.

"What does your father do? You never told me except to say that he was somehow irresponsible and weak."

"He's in oil."

"Kris!" Dawn cocked her head and scolded him like a nanny, "You should have told me that before now."

He could have said that it didn't seem important to him. He could have tried to explain that he wasn't really proud of his father. Kris could have tried to do all those things, but he didn't. He knew a futile situation when he saw one, and right then his heart was breaking. Because Dawn Signorello's hands were stroking the black leather seats and crystal glass. These were the things she loved more than Kris. He understood that now.

"Oh, Kris," Dawn snuggled up close to him. "Tell me what you wanted to say."

"Only this, Dawn. Only that we shouldn't see each other anymore. Goodbye."

Later that night, while Kris finished his packing, Dawn placed a call to the Kappa Alpha house at the U. of T. . She was crying when Dan Wagner, her betrothed, picked up the line. And she was crying even harder when she hung up ten minutes later. The triangle was broken. Lives that had been tied together were now running solitary lines through this world. Billy Wagner had called his brother and let him know what everyone at University High knew. Dawn Signorello was now a free woman and she hated it. Dan Wagner was now a man who no longer trusted. And Kris Blaze, what was he?

On the flight out of Dallas the next morning Kris watched the city open up beneath him. What had once seemed so grand and glorious that past fall now left him with an empty longing. The sparkling cars in parking lots, the Texas State Flags, the skyscrapers, and the grid of streets no longer thrilled him. He felt older as he watched the city disappear beneath the out-stretched arms of Ike's private Lear jet. Ahead were the mountains, the future, the unknown. He welcomed them.

Ms. Tanner was still reading. Kris leaned over her shoulder and began at the top of a paragraph mid-way down the page. "The overthrow of the king-father is a crime, but so is his restoration - and both are necessary for the progress of civilization."

"Kris, do you mind not reading over my shoulder please?" Ms Tanner didn't glance up from the page.

"Sorry," Kris mumbled. He remembered what she'd said to him at the airport when he had expressed some dismay over the weight of her suit-case.

"What's in here, weights?" he had asked.

"No, these are my books," Ms. Tanner had proudly declared. "Dear Christopher, the reason I live with your father is because he allows me the time I require to read."

"Oh," Kris had said.

Ms. Tanner twisted around to face Kris. The van was now winding down a steep section of highway. "If you aspire to read Marcuse, Christopher, I would recommend something else as a bit of a warm-up exer-cise." Ever since they had left Denver an hour before, the van had been climbing and descending mountains of such incredible scale that Kris had found it hard to stop looking at them in sheer amazement. Half the reason he had peeked at Ms. Tanner's book was out of curiosity. What, he had won-dered, could be so enthralling on those pages that Ms. Tanner never even so much as glanced up?

She was still looking at him. He had broken her concentration, so he supposed he should be polite.

"What would you recommend for a warm-up?"

"I'd start you with the Bible."

Ms. Tanner, Kris thought, probably had some very interesting things to say about the Bible. Of course he had known that the books in Ike's bedroom were all hers. For the past five months Kris had gingerly planned his steps around Ms. Tanner's comings and goings. That she was the other woman didn't bother him so much on a personal level. Kris knew his mother had actually lost interest in Ike. So the fact that Ms. Tanner existed didn't really get in the way of anything. He imagined there must have been a tragedy, a very deep one, at some point in Ms. Tanner's life. For her mood and movements always carried a hint of melancholy, formality, and pensive hesitation which Kris disliked.

To say she was beautiful would be true, though strictly in a classical sense. If something as distant from flesh as marble can be thought of in the warm vital terms of beauty, then Ms. Tanner was beautiful. She carried a parasol in the sun and wore long white silk dresses with hem lines at her ankles. Her shoulders she sometimes bared, but only to cast a frigid contrast to the balmy air of a warm Dallas night. She regarded Kris with the same indifference that she regarded everything. The fact that he made her uncomfortable she kept to herself.

That Ms. Tanner lived with Ike Blazekowski; this was the great tragedy in her life. And, unknown to Kris, this same situation was the reason for her frigid manner. It was her coldness alone that held Ms. Tanner aloof and saved her from the mundane poison of needing to eat, sleep, and find shelter. All these needs she fulfilled through Ike, while at the same time she attempted to wash her hands of it. Skiing was out of the question for Ms. Tanner; hence the books. In the front seat, next to the driver, Ike scratched away with his pen at some work. Except to look at roadsigns, his head had remained permanently bowed by the magnetic draw of the paper on his lap.

He had arranged for Kris to take private lessons with an Austrian ski instructor, whom the Basses had recommended, named Ulf.

"Shit," Ike mumbled. They had just passed another sign that read: Vail 47 miles.

"We're gonna spend half the day in this god-damn van."

Ms. Tanner sighed and flipped the page.

When they arrived in Vail, Kris was enthralled by the sight of people walking in the streets with skis on their shoulders. Women cloaked in furs mixed with the brightly colored ski clothes like woodland predators shopping within some strange neon forest. Perfect Stetsons, not like the floppy cowboy hats he had grown up wearing in Happy were perched at rakish angles on the heads of urban cowboys and cowgirls. Everything seemed perfect. The streets were for walking and shopping door to door. Cars kept to certain roads that skirted the actual heart of the village. They drove down past the bank and the church until they reached the entrance to Forest Road, where they turned right and proceeded up the side of the actual ski-mountain. Snowbanks had piled high on each side of the white snow-packed road. The chair lifts were still running. A long line of moving chairs, strung up the mountain, were filled with the dangling legs of disappearing skiers. Kris watched the chairs until they slipped behind the white ridgeline.

Forest Road was and is the most exclusive address on Vail Mountain. Winding in and out of the tight aspen groves at the base of the slopes, Forest Road skirts the lowest trails so that residents can ski into and out of their houses. Typical of other Forest Road residences, the Bass house was nestled among the aspen groves. Three stories high and built into the slope of the mountain so that the top floor peeked out of the crest of the aspens, the Bass house was screened for privacy.

Years later when Kris would think back on this visit to the Bass house, he would recall his first inklings of disgust. Perhaps it had been Dawn and her material values which had awakened this reaction in Kris. Or maybe it was the frigid beauty of a Rocky Mountain winter and Kris' innate sense of order which told him that this house was wrong. Whatever catalyst it was, the feeling was there. And like most reactions, this was a reaction against something that already existed.

His idealisms were his own. His actions would conform with his beliefs. What was he? Saint? Fanatic? Criminal? Role model? Christ figure? Revolutionary? Surely all these terms would apply in the future. But one thing is certain - in the heart and mind of a fifteen year old boy, who chose one of the countless bedrooms on the top floor of the Bass house during Christmas week in 1979, and who collapsed on the bed to stare out at the jagged peaks of the Gore range across the valley, lay the slumbering seed of a life that would be told and re-told through the ages.

They went to dinner that night at a French restaurant where the staff bustled about like life-sized puppets in red uniforms. With herky-jerky robotic starts and stops, they wheeled about the dining room with glowing red faces and sweating brows. Ms. Tanner read her book while Ike drank a three hundred dollar bottle of red burgundy. The irony of eating a scallop and salmon couloubiac in Colorado was not lost on Kris. He devoured every delicious morsel while mentally re-tracing the journey his seafood must have taken to reach his plate. They ate in silence. It was with relief that Kris finally went up to bed that night. In the morning he would be skiing.

One week later, Ulf, the Austrian ski instructor, sat with them at dinner in the French restaurant.

"Aaagghh," Ulf coughed into his napkin. "Excuse me," he folded the napkin into a neat white square and placed it onto the table before looking up. His blond hair was parted on the side. He looked to be in his mid-thirties, younger than his actual age of forty-two.

"In Austria," he continued where he had left off, "the government has programs for young men like Kris. They go to school in the afternoon. Mornings and weekends are for ski training and racing. I, myself, was in this national program until I was eighteen. Then I joined the world cup team. From these schools for athletes come all of our Austrian national team members and Olympic champions."

Kris blushed with pride.

For the past seven days Ulf had grown more and more amazed as he had watched Kris progress from a beginner to near virtuoso. Each morning Ulf had taken them to terrain with greater difficulty than they had skied the previous day. And each morning Kris managed to build upon what he had learned the day before. His aptitude gave Ulf the impression Kris was an animal. Like a bird that learns to fly through instinct, Kris Blaze skied with a natural grace that belied the learning process. Now Ulf felt it was necessary to state his case to Ike. Kris could be a great one, he felt, perhaps one of the greatest.

Ms. Tanner glanced up from the pages of her book for the first time that evening. With apprehensive eyes, Kris watched her attention lift from the pages to focus on Ulf. During their entire week in Vail Ms. Tanner had somewhat sanctimoniously voiced her belief that she had been martyred for the sake of Ike and his precious son. Trapped in athletic purgatory, she had taken to the books with more than her usual zeal. Her attitude could be compared to that of a cretin somehow stuck in a lecture hall at Harvard where red faced students and professors argued the existence of God. Ms. Tanner failed to see how anyone was having fun. How could they? It was so cold out. People broke their legs every day. She saw them in the restaurant with their casts elevated on chairs. Perfect weather for a cup of hot cocoa and a stack of Russian novels. She wished they would go back to Dallas very soon. And she especially wished she could shut up this Aryan ski instructor, sitting across from her, who seemed to embody all that she despised about Vail and this vacation. To Kris' horror, she opened her mouth and voiced her opinion.

"That sounds like a rather inane way to limit Kris' future." Ulf's and Ike's heads swung like owls. "It's all right to go to that sort of school if you want to be a ski instructor, I suppose." Here she paused and looked at Ulf. "But what if Kris has other potentials, other skills besides his athletic ones, that he would like to explore when he gets older? What will he do? It seems like a dead end to me."

Ohhhhh, Ike groaned silently. If there was one thing he wanted more than anything else, that thing was the removal of his son Kris from his own life in Dallas. A ski academy sounded just great to Ike.

"Dear, please don't interrupt Ulf. You've hardly let him tell us anything before you go jumping to conclusions. Please, Ulf, go on."

"Most of my schoolmates are now doctors and teachers," Ulf waved a friendly hand toward Ms. Tanner. "But, I'm sure you would agree, if one wishes to achieve greatness then the requisite risks must be taken. He would practice no more at skiing than he would at football. This I can promise you because I have in mind a school that my friend runs in Vermont. It is a very good school, academically speaking. But, it is also a ski academy. Kris would be ready for either college or international racing when he graduated from Alpine Academy. It is something all of you might want to think about."

When a young man or woman is talented and it seems to them as though the whole world is recruiting them to become the next great whatever, any flattery, even unwelcome, is received graciously. Kris nodded his head.

"Sounds like you might want to think about it," Ike hopefully advised.

"You would ski every day." Ulf's offer was tempting.

"He'd be lucky if he cracked a book," Ms. Tanner snorted.

Their table went back to eating. He was not sure how he felt. He loved football, but it was played on one-hundred yards. When Kris skied, he explored an entire mountain. The athletic differences between the two sports he loved were equally pro and con in the balance of Kris' judgement. But he could find no comparison between a mountain and a postage stamp field with chalk lines.

Two weeks later, Kris sat down at the modern desk in Ike's room with a blank sheet of paper in front of him. The family Bible sat open on the desk top next to the paper. The hollowed out pages of the centuries old Bible formed a neat cubby and had perhaps been used to stash a gun or liquor during frontier days. Or maybe Ike himself had hollowed it out for his own secret purposes. As for Kris' intentions, he had simply been following Ms. Tanner's advice. Start with the Bible. Not that he wanted to read Marcuse or anything like that, but he had simply been curious. He'd wanted to start at John, and read, *In the beginning was the word.* But the pages were empty, and in their place he had found a dictaphone complete with tape and a photocopied birth certificate bearing his own birthdate and the words 'Baby boy Sapp'. Kris wrote:

Dear Ike,

It was with great pleasure and relief that I
discovered the items concealed in your family Bible.
I say 'your family' for obvious reasons and can only
thank God for lifting the odious legacy of being
your son from my shoulders. You disgust me completely,
and it is with a happy heart that I leave you to
your miserable existence. From this point forward
you owe me nothing, neither monetary nor otherwise,
as a father would his child.

I will be leaving for Vermont today in order
to attend Alpine Academy, where I have happily
accepted a full scholarship for study. Once again,
I can only begin to express what a happy day this
is in my life. To be rid of your name completely

110

leaves me with a joy so fulfilling that I wish all
people could one day experience the way I feel right
now. As a rich man you are the envy of
many. But I would rather be a dog, or better yet
a wolf who murders with a clean conscience, than
you. I turn my back on society and step into
the world as an orphan. This is what I choose.

> Good Riddance,
> Kris Blaze

The night air at Killington was frozen as Kris Blaze glided through the trees on telemark skis. He moved with the skill and quiet of the wolf toward his destination. Up ahead the lights of a large empty vacation house brazenly shone in wasteful glory. Kris turned effortlessly on his telemarks. Heels free, he bent down into each turn and crunched the twigs hidden by the thin New England snow cover. The pack on his back balanced Kris as he cut neatly through the birch trees until he stood at the edge of the clearing where the house stood. Out on the trail, Snocats packed the icy droppings of the sno-guns. Kris watched as an animal might watch the machines of man. He watched with a cunning hatred before moving toward the house.

From his pack he took the can of gasoline and began with the large wooden deck. It had been shoveled recently and the gas soaked quickly into the dry wood. After breaking the plate glass doors with the gas can, he stepped into the house and began dousing the carpet, drapes, couch, and bookshelf. Stepping off the porch and back into his skis, Kris lit a match and tossed it before skating off into the woods.

As the flames began to rise he thought of the race he had won. He thought of the people cheering for him and his victory in the finals. The flames rose higher and higher as Kris Blaze felt the joy of certainty take hold of him. He sang it into the air in the wild howl of an animal who had not graced these woods for over a century. Here was the true victory of the day. Here was the real triumph.

Chapter 6:

Who loves New York?

It was a certain cartoon, one known to Kelley Sapp for years and years, that heralded Z's arrival at the Snowy Mountains Guest Lodge. He remembered it only after she had left for her room, and in retrospect found it an apt commentary on her sudden re-appearance in his life. The particular cartoon in question had at one time in Kelley's childhood hung on a wall in a poster frame at the home of a distant relative of Kelley's and can only be appreciated by a select few, though many would like to think they understand it, having visited Manhattan or knowing several people who currently live there. Its title: "A New Yorker's View of the World." But it is impossible to relate with New Yorkers and their city without having ever lived there oneself. Living in Manhattan cultivates an attitude of provincial focus, albeit one that is firmly affixed to the wide ranging multicultural horizon that is New York City. What's happening in Manhattan is easily mistaken for everything that's happening everywhere. And even when the New Yorker travels, it is hard for him or her to keep from viewing the local population with an attitude.

"A New Yorker's view of the world" is this: Madison Avenue, Park Avenue, Central Park as a large green field, the West Side as a strip of brown beyond the green, New Jersey on the horizon. Los Angeles is a dot, as are San Francisco and Paris. Now, if the cartoon were contemporary with the times, then perhaps there would no longer be such a blatant disregard for the heartland of America. At least one more dot would appear in the grey area beyond New Jersey and before the blip that is L.A. . Perhaps the cartoonist would even draw a tiny group of mountains with a woman in a fur schussing down the slopes.

It is both the good fortune and the misfortune of the people inhabiting the Rocky Mountains that the jaundiced eye of the New Yorker has managed to let his monocle slip and spy something of interest midway between the blip that is L.A. and Madison Avenue. And though it is still impossible to find a decent bagel in the higher elevations of the Rockies, the Mexican food is almost always better than what is being offered at Benny's Burritos East. Fashion boutiques with names like 'Ingrid's' or places where one can purchase red elephant skin cowboy boots for several thousand dollars simply reinforce the New Yorker's notion that all the world is really a poor mans' version of that golden stinking group of buildings teetering on the edge of the Atlantic.

And so it was that when a lovelorn Kelley Sapp spied from the *Maitre D'* stand a woman sporting boots much like the aforementioned absolutely no one but him blinked an eye. She was similar in every odd way possible to the others who had materialized out of thin air to walk the planned streets of Vail Village like so many peacocks escaped from their native habitat.

In addition to her boots, the woman wore black skin-tight leggings and sported a faux leopard skin fez. A black Yorkshire terrier stood by her side, which appeared quite immobile since the woman in red boots and black leggings kept stooping down to pull the dog along with her whenever she took a step. This caused some problems with her clunky black sunglasses, which kept falling down past the bridge of her nose when she leaned over. It also caused problems with her snake. A large boa constrictor wrapped about her neck and shoulders. Its tongue flickered out at the terrier in an inhospitable manner whenever the woman leaned down to encourage her dog along.

"Joey," the woman pushed the snake's head away from the dog, "leave Pudding alone."

Pudding let out a sharp yelp and jerked his neck with a robotic stiffness that made him appear more mechanical than animal. Up until that point Pudding had borne a remarkable resemblance to the various examples of taxidermy scattered about the walls of the lobby.

The little bell at the *Maitre D'* stand rang. Two hundred yards away Felicia Grahmsham tugged with her pinkie finger. Kelley picked up the voice tube.

"Yes, Mrs. Grahmsham. Of course. Yes," he shouted. "We will make sure that there is absolutely no raw fish on your plate tonight. Yes, we will try to keep the plaster out as well. What's that? ... Well, he has bought some eel which he says he can cook in good conscience."

Kelley covered the voice tube with his palm and let out an exasperated sigh. The cause of his melancholy was not the stream of obscenities pouring through six hundred feet of tubing. No, Kelley's sigh was centered about something far closer to heart than the daily brushes with absurdity that his job required.

In the lobby of the Snowy Mountains Guest Lodge the object of

113

Kelley's adoration continued to drag her dog and chastise her snake. That she had arrived in Vail was as inevitable as global warming and nuclear proliferation. This was her element, created for her and having more to do with her and the Upper East Side of Manhattan than it did with any of the dozen or so tiny, undiscovered mountain hamlets thirty miles distant. Vail and the Vail Valley are part of the great multinational web that encircles the continents with cutting distinction. St. Tropez, Val D'Isere, Monaco, Carmel, Vail, Distrito Federal, and West Palm Beach are all nexus points, connected by airline routes that grid the empty spaces where everyone else lives between these golden points. The Mexicans come to Vail during the Easter Holidays. They cross the Rio Grande like migrating birds and return south to Distrito Federal, with stunning regularity, two weeks to the day later.

New Yorkers are endemic. Like big, scavenging crows they set up ungainly house and work out of bedrooms with fax machines, leaving at will, returning whenever they want, with an attitude that all is theirs and meant for them. They inflate the price of cowboy hats, arid land, and fly fishing equipment. While in New York they stick to certain neighborhoods considered safe and lament the demise of Abercrombie and Fitch, but in Vail you are liable to encounter them almost anywhere at anytime.

A hill of luggage appeared behind Z as the bellmen slowly stacked suitcases and trunks on top of each other. Kelley studied her face, her hair, as Bennett Beauregard approached her. There was no doubt about it. He numbly drummed his fingers on the reservation book. Z had landed at the Snowy Mountains Guest Lodge. Z was back. The New Yorker had arrived.

"Madame, good afternoon. I'm afraid there are no dogs or pets allowed in the Snowy Mountains Guest Lodge," Bennett Beauregard applied his coldest, most cordial of greetings to Z.

"Bond," Z extended her hand, "the name is Mrs. Bond. I believe you have been expecting us."

Some shock registered in Bennett Beauregard's eyes. He did his best impersonation of a piece of wilted lettuce. His head drooped. His flesh collapsed upon his skeleton like jello on a rack. He kissed Z's extended hand, and even permitted Joey's forked tongue to lick his wrist.

When Pudding seized the hem of his pant leg Bennett mumbled, "Nice doggy," and reached down to pet him. With a sharp twist of his neck the terrier caught Bennett's palm with a ragged incisor.

"Ouch! He bit me!"

"What a wonderful thing. He only bites people he adores. You must take care of him while I'm shopping. Oh Pudding!" Z flipped Joey around her neck as if he were a scarf before bending over to rub Pudding's gelatinous belly. "Uncle Bennett will be taking care of you."

She straightened and glanced at the stack of Louis Vuitton cases assembled neatly behind her. "Bennett, please be so kind as to take me to my room. I believe the altitude is affecting my nicotine."

Z pressed the back of her palm to her forehead. "Do you have a cigarette?"

Without a word Bennett Beauregard reached into his double breasted jacket and produced a pack of filterless Lucky Strikes.

"Thank you," Z mumbled between clenched lips while Bennett lit the cigarette. "Mr. Bond will be arriving tomorrow afternoon. Please see that I am notified when he does. Which way to room twenty seven?"

"Follow me, Madame," Bennett clapped his hands and the Bellmen began loading the luggage onto carts. With worried glances they trundled off with their load to the hand pulled freight elevator.

"Room twenty seven is a tricky place to find." Bennett and Z sashayed around the corner toward the main staircase. Z carried Pudding beneath her arm like a piglet.

"Tricky to find? I don't think I've ever been in a hotel that's tricky at all."

"We are not your usual hotel. We have, how shall I say it, more quirks. If you ever feel disoriented or lost, please do not hesitate to call me. Sometimes I think I'm the only person who truly knows his way around this place."

"Actually there is one other thing you could do for me."

"It would be my pleasure."

"Rats."

"Rats?"

"Yes. Joey needs rats." Z stroked her boa's head with her index finger. "Hamsters and gerbils are fine and he's even managed with guinea pigs. There was the time he got the Trump girl's afghan. What a mess that was. He curled up on the sofa for a week and shat fur. But rats are his favorite. Joey has a delicate stomach for a boa."

"Of course, rats." Nothing would stand in the way of Bennett Beauregard's compliance. He laughed as if rats were logical. *Oh, yes there is one more thing. After you get the rats I want to take a broomstick and shove it up your asshole. Then I'll mount you out my window like a flag so my husband will know which room I'm in. Would that be a problem?* Nothing would ever be a problem.

At the foot of the staircase Z paused.

"Isn't there an elevator?"

"Funny you should ask, because actually there isn't."

"How's that funny?"

They proceeded up the stairs and rounded the corner out of earshot. Kelley caught one last fleeting glimpse of Z's ass, framed between the mounted heads of two startled emu, as she slowly climbed the stairs at an oxygen lovers pace. It had been a long time since Z's decidedly unique personality had been displayed before Kelley. Mrs. Bond now? Wife of Ricky Rico's hotshot lawyer, and still a rebel. She had graduated in life from her

115

former position as a low rent punk. Now it could be said she was genuinely eccentric.

To Kelley it seemed as if Z had re-incarnated out of thin air. What were the chances of randomly meeting one person on two different occasions in locations thousands of miles apart? Some people might say the world's a small place. But for certain kinds of New Yorkers, who move in certain circles, arrival in Vail is as certain as death and taxes. Z now moved in the upper stratosphere. That she had once been Kelley's seemed ironic to him for there was now a breach between their stations in life. Kelley was no longer in Z's peer group and this, for some strange reason, embarrassed him and made him feel like a failure. He was also, much to his tormented chagrin, still in love with her. Certain qualities, certain things about Z reminded Kelley of something else. Something paradoxical or ephemeral. Perhaps there was a French saying that would sum her up? But no. The only proper metaphor for Z was life itself. She mirrored the vast complexities of the world. He loved her. Did she make him happy? Not a chance.

It wasn't until later that evening, when Z appeared in a sequined gold jumpsuit, that Kelley actually conversed with her. Dinner service had been going for an hour and Kelley had been at the *Maitre D'* stand nervously awaiting her arrival.

When she descended the staircase with both Joey and Pudding in tow, Kelley ditched it into the bar and fumbled around while one of the waiters brought Mrs. Bond to her table. He doubted that Z had recognized him yet and was still trying to work up enough courage to go talk to her when one of the waitresses came up to him and said, "The lady at table eleven wants a steak, Kelley. She refuses to eat until she gets one, and says she won't leave until she eats. She also wants a bowl of water for her dog, and is it OK if she lets her snake climb the plastic fichus tree next to the table? She told me she wants to speak to the *Maitre D'*."

When he approached table eleven Z didn't even look up from her menu. "Hello, Kelley," she said with a flipness that made it seem as if two days had passed since they last saw each other. "What lovely views you have in your restaurant. Is there a law in Colorado against windows and elevators that I don't know about?"

Kelley sat down in the empty seat next to her. Z cocked her head and looked away from the sweating, frescoed walls of *Au Naturel*. She gave him a sly smile before they kissed each other on the cheek.

"I was wondering if you were going to ignore me all night. I spotted you at the Maitre D' stand the moment I arrived this afternoon."

He may have been foolish to avoid her earlier. But any embarrassment he felt disappeared in the wake of pleasure that now washed over him. For Kelley was flattered that Z had recognized him from across the lobby. All the times he had felt invisible at his job, like a walking piece of furniture, had been a constant source of depression for him. Z had recognized him, even garbed in his medieval livery. It didn't matter that Z, as always, had been one step ahead of him. Kelley laughed like he hadn't since God knew when. The warmth of genuine happiness began to take hold and shake him like a drug. It had been years. He had almost forgotten what it felt like to be happy. He signaled for Z's waitress and ordered a bottle of Tattinger.

The champagne arrived along with a tin bowl for Pudding. Kelley and Z toasted each other.

"You don't mind Joey? Do you?" Z pointed to the dangling boa, whose weight had managed to bend the plastic fichus into a drooping arc. Kelley glanced about the dining room. At various tables drowsy middle-aged vacationers toyed with their food. The damp air seemed to possess a fog, and Kelley laughed as he realized no one else had noticed the snake. It was as if they were in a bubble that insulated them from the general gloom pervading the Snowy Mountains Guest Lodge. Kelley shook his head.

"Sort of biblical isn't it. I think it adds quite a touch. Perhaps there's an appropriate term in French. Got an apple?"

Z's golden laugh cut through the thick blue air like lightning. Kelley could have sworn he watched it fly from her lips like a tangible line of music that ribboned through the air. Her laughter faded. They were now holding hands. "Kelley?" Z pursed her lips in a perfectly coy manner, then dissolved into giggles. "This place!" she finally whispered before rolling her eyes like a clown. "How can you, Kelley?"

"And you Mrs. Bond?"

"Oh, me," Z feigned boredom and waved her hand dismissively. "I get to fool around, play the vamp a bit. Dress in crazy outfits. For me it's all fun and games. But you work here. How dreadful, Kelley. I imagine it must be like hell. That Beauregard thing. Thank God I've found you, because I've been meaning to ask you a question. When are you and I going to leave for Rio? That's what I've been absolutely dying to ask you, even before I saw you in the lobby today. Even before I knew you were here I wanted to take you away to Rio. If you say the word, we'll leave tonight."

It was so typical of Z. She seemed so blase about the whole matter, as if it were a real possibility. And was it? Quite possibly. Kelley didn't know.

Though Kelley had yet to realize the problem, it was here that he and Z were at odds with each other. The same sense of duty that had pushed Kelley into accepting the job as *Maitre D'* was also telling him not to ditch it to Rio. He had an undeniably old-fashioned sense of a work ethic that could easily transform into a guilt complex. Leave for Rio, with Z? It was probably a joke. "Chile would be better," Kelley ran with it. "Santiago and then a trip into the Andes. We could ski at *Valle Nevado* and taste wine in the Maipo valley."

Z curled her lip before agreeing, "For you, yes. Lord knows how much I'd like to samba in the streets of Rio with postage stamps on my breasts and nothing but gold paint you know where, but for you I will go to

117

that other drab country. Who was their poet? The one who wrote about stones?"

"Neruda."

"Not exactly my idea of a good time, but if it's what you want, Kelley, I'm willing to go."

Kelley reconsidered. It wasn't as if Z had the most knockout body in the world. Her breasts were small by pornographic standards and unless they were tamed by tight lycra or underwires, had a tendency to splay out sideways. Her ass, though perfectly tight, was not ample, and when viewed critically could even be called bony. It was Z's face that held her most striking features. With an aquiline nose, short black hair, slight freckles on her high cheekbones and translucent white skin, she was a pale waif of a girl whose androgynous features somehow blended to produce what could only be described as an exotic appearance. The thought of her nearly naked and traipsing down the street like some mad elf caused a deep rumbling inside Kelley.

"OK, Rio."

"Thank God."

"But I can't leave tonight."

"Why not?"

"I need time to think. And besides, you're married now. You're Mrs. Bond."

"He's so boring."

"What about the sex and those tattoos?" Z's search for an orgasm had been an odd period in Kelley's life. He did not relish the memory of it.

She moved her hand down onto Kelley's thigh. "They washed off," she said. "A week later and all his tattoos were gone. I started pining for you then."

"They were fake tattoos?"

"There's a place in the East Village that paints you for a couple hundred bucks. He did it on a whim, met me, then they were gone. Absolutely took the wind out of my sails. After they washed off there was only a lawyer underneath. Three days of great sex, and then I'm taking a shower with him and the colors are washing down the drain. He starts talking about international tax laws and the next thing I know we settle into this routine. He goes to work and gives me his credit cards. I buy the stupidest things I can find, and he pays the bills. Joey cost me ten thousand dollars. I got him from a reptile man at the Bronx zoo."

"And Pudding?"

"Rare breed of Chinese Yorkshire Terrier. Given to female members of the royal household. Congenital arthritis keeps them from moving about much. Just the kind of dog to have if your feet have been bound since the age of two. Fifteen thousand dollars."

"Did he complain?"

"Never even blinked."

"I'm so sorry."

"You can't imagine what a bore life is for me. Can we leave tonight? I have some money. I've embezzled over a hundred thousand since we got hitched."

"That's not enough to live on."

"I know Kelley, but I'm desperate." Z pleaded.

"I'll only leave for Rio if we have enough money to live on."

That seemed to seal the matter, Kelley thought, until Z suggested, "We could kill him. I'm the sole beneficiary of his will."

"You can't be serious." He felt sick. Some large portion of his moral fiber was straining to comprehend what he had just heard.

"Why did you come here?" he managed to ask.

"Bond's client. Some man named Rico, owns this place. He's a criminal or something and sent Bond here to help put in a ski area. He arrives tomorrow with a suitcase full of cash and a lot of blank checks. We can leave before he arrives. Are there direct flights from Denver to Rio?"

"We are not leaving. At least I'm not," he said just as Z's waitress arrived. The waitress gave Kelley a funny look as she placed a slice of jellied eel terrine in front of Z. Adept with the ways of service at *Au Naturel*, she beat a quick retreat from the table without explaining the dish.

"Oh my," Z exclaimed, "a loaf of aspic. Pudding will love it."

She lowered the plate to the carpet.

"So, Kelley, do you have another girlfriend now?" Z lifted her champagne glass and tilted the bubbles down behind her adam's apple.

"Yes." Kelley tried to do the same with his champagne, but somehow the bubbles seemed to stick in his throat. He nearly exploded while holding the champagne down, and finally let a thin trickle escape out his nose to relieve the pressure.

"Charming," Z drolly noted as she wiped the champagne from Kelley's upper lip with her index finger. "Does she love you?" Z asked before plunging the wet finger into her mouth and sucking on it in an intimate and highly suggestive manner.

Kelley swallowed before gasping, "I think she can." Even then he knew it was a lie. It was all he could do to keep from choking even more.

"Too bad." Z commented as if she didn't really mean it. For a few moments she concentrated on twirling a lock of her short black hair around a finger. She released it and watched it bounce before turning to look at Kelley. "If things don't work out the way you want with her," Z looked at Kelley as if this were a certainty, "then promise not to be bashful. After all, I left you first. We're here for at least a month, probably more, so you'll have plenty of time to figure things out. My offer is of the standing sort."

She reached down toward Pudding as if she were going to pet the dog. But something was wrong, very wrong.

119

"Joey!" she screamed.

Sure enough, the boa had managed to slither down from the plastic fichus tree and wrap itself around Pudding without anyone noticing.

Starting with his mouth and finishing at his tail, Pudding was encircled with Joey's heavy coils. Z leapt to the floor and unwrapped the reluctant snake from the nearly suffocated dog.

"Honestly," Z was puffing as she strained, "I think Joey gets jealous when I feed Pudding. Oh God," Z's eyes went to her knees, "the aspic." Silence filled the dining room. Then an old woman screamed before fainting. The bubble had burst. People had noticed them. A thin blue laugh came from Kelley's mouth as he realized he didn't care. Nothing mattered. Guests would complain, but this concerned Bond and therefore Z was untouchable. For the first time ever the sweating walls of *Au Naturel* seemed friendly to him. The gaping ribs lodged in the ceiling became rustic in a homely, comfortable sense, and the black table of Lumsden of Strathdrummond no longer frightened him. Only the kitchen held horrors for Kelley. But in the dining room he was king. In his mind Kelley flipped off the blue walls. *You don't scare me anymore, you cocksucker. You don't frighten me.*

The rest of the night was relatively uneventful. Z retired to her room to wash the eel terrine out of her jump-suit. Kelley went back to work. Service ended, and Kelley had finished doing the check out before he ambled over to the front desk with a half full bottle of '82 Rausan Segla some Mexicans had kindly left for the staff.

Friday was typing manically at the computer station when Kelley popped in. He was about to tell Friday about Z's arrival when Bennett Beauregard popped his ever omnipresent head into the office.

"Just the man I wanted to see," Bennett smiled.

Inwardly, Kelley groaned.

"What can I do for you?"

"We're going to get him tomorrow," Bennett's eyes held a saintly, insane glow.

"Who?"

"Him."

"You mean Chef?"

"Of course. Tomorrow morning we're having a managers' meeting with Mr. Posthelwait and I am going to present my evidence."

"Will Mr. Bond be there?" Kelley asked.

"Yes. I saw you talking with his wife tonight. Charming lady."

"She and I are old friends."

"Mr. Bond will be there at eight o'clock sharp. Just see that you are as well. I don't think you'd want to miss this."

Bennett Beauregard swung starboard and left. He had much to do. He had arranged his photographs on the slide carousel and was in the midst of composing his written case against the Chef. There was that and the rats.

120

He had managed to get the rats Mrs. Bond required, only he needed to find a proper cage. They were presently gnawing their way out of the cardboard box beneath his desk.

Friday took a sip of his wine and eyed Kelley suspiciously."You look flushed," he said as if it were an accusation.

"With good reason," Kelley found a seat next to the computer.

He laid it all out to Friday, who listened to Kelley's animated account with an attentive ear. Appearing neither excited nor bored, Friday waited until Kelley finished before asking, "What are you going to do? I hear Rio's sweltering during the summer."

"I told her I have a girlfriend. Friday, I really don't want to go to Rio. Somehow I have this idea that I'd wind up begging for plane fare at the American Embassy while Z ditched it to the rain forest."

Friday contemplated this bit of information like a psychiatrist. His impartial demeanor gave no hint as to which way he felt Kelley should make his next move. While he waited for Kelley to continue he remained impassive. Kelley knew there was more he should tell. Friday knew about Kellie Kay, but this was Kelley's choice. Only he knew what the truth was in that affair.

"Of course there's no way Kellie Kay and I would ever be anything together. She's completely in love with Kris Blaze and I know that."

"Did you know that Kris is back in town?" Friday asked. "I saw him at the Coyote."

There was no reason this bit of information should have upset Kelley Sapp, but it did. Everything seemed to be rushing forward at an almost exponential rate. Kris was back now and Kellie Kay would be on her best behavior. Being cut off from her would only push him in Z's direction, he knew, and he would have to watch it. He teetered like a drunk underneath the sway of her intoxicating appeal. His aspirations seemed cloudy now. What he wanted, what he'd never figured out, could easily get lost in her grip.

He remembered what Friday had told him months ago. How Kelley needed to focus, and how the search for love was as good a place to start as any. He looked back on that night as he had many other times. But something was different tonight. Tonight he decided Friday was wrong. Love wasn't enough. Love needed other things working with it besides blind devotion. Love was luck, and Kelley had never been lucky. If he went with Z there would have to be some sign, some significant event, that occurred. Only then would he feel secure enough to trust himself with her. Things were still in limbo, as they'd always been with Kelley. He finished his wine and left before Friday began his regular nightly nap.

The clocks chimed in atonal, irregular intervals. The empty lobby of the Snowy Mountains Guest Lodge became an abandoned stage. Spectral dust drifted to the carpet where it sparkled like glitter dropped by a loose hand. In the ceiling above, stained glass glinted like the dull lead encasing it, no longer animated with sunshine that spun pink and blue circles through the lobby like searchlights. They were sterile and lifeless.

Kelley Sapp was leaving. The blue menace continued its reign, but Kelley Sapp no longer recognized the fear. He still didn't know what he wanted. But somehow he was calm with this knowledge. For his own insecurities no longer terrified him. Certainty came with time and only now did he realize just how young he was. He was that old. Old enough to know he was young. Things would come with time. Of that he was certain now. He might not find a pot of gold at the end of the rainbow, but at least he would enjoy the trip. He had learned patience.

Unlike most human beings who are sensitive about certain things concerning their significant others, Kris Blaze was remarkably tolerant with Kellie Kay. His trip back from the east coast swing of the Budweiser Pro Mogul Tour had been a less than satisfying experience, and even though what he found in the trash basket when he got back did not thrill him, it didn't really piss him off either. Perhaps this could be attributed to the fact that he wasn't a jealous or possessive person by nature. It would take a cynic to suggest that the real reason was his lack of love for Kellie Kay. Too bad that was the truth.

The trip back from Killington in the Team Spyder Van could have been the subject of a Homeric poem. Enough shit clogged their progress west that it would have been easy to believe a whole coterie of gods were bickering over the fate of the Team Spyder Van. Nothing against the Team Spyder guys, Kris liked them. There was a definite camaraderie between skiers on the tour and Kris was not immune to the notion that these men were his brothers. Sometimes luck is against you from the start, and that was the case on this swing back from the east coast.

Mid-way through Pennsylvania they hit a deer. It was two o'clock in the morning and they had just dropped down out of New York State on Route 219 on their way to join up with I-80. Past Ridgeway and on the way to Boot Jack, the doe stepped out into the hypnotic glare of the headlights and waited for the impact that soon followed.

Moments before the crash Kris had been reclining on the back bench seat. His head propped up on a boot bag, with equipment piled all around him like the sides of a nest in which he lazily reclined his long body, he had been comfortably asleep. The sweet smell of marijuana wafted through the van along with the Grateful Dead's Cornell '77 concert. The van, a nineteen eighty eight Kustom Koach Econoline cruised like a starship beneath the Central Pennsylvania night sky. White, with a large black spider web emblazoned on it's side next to a Spyder logo, the van had a streamlined plastic compartment attached to the roof. In this compartment all of the skis and poles were stored along with an unlicensed Remmington twelve gauge, rifled shotgun. Two boxes of twelve gauge deer slugs sat in a bag near Kris' head.

They hit the doe, skidded, and came to a frightened stop on the shoulder of the highway. One headlight pointed skyward now and small tufts of brown fur, lodged in the seams between the headlight and sheet metal, were surrounded by flecks of blood that had spattered with impact across the white paint.

They piled out of the van in one group and ran the twenty yards back down the road to where the deer thrashed.

"Oh Jesus!" one of them turned his back on the gory mess and started walking back to the van.

Five skiers, including Kris, watched from the front row of the silent winter amphitheater formed by the woods behind them. In a half-moon, they contemplated her shattered hip. Compound fractures had sent shards of bone through her skin along with muscle and tendons that shone with a vital wetness in the soft red glow of the van's taillights. She raised her head to look back at them, arcing her body, then collapsed flatly to the pavement every ten seconds or so.

"We've gotta kill her," one of them said.

He walked back to the van and rummaged around in the bags until he found a box of the slugs. Then, standing on the wide running board, he opened the plastic compartment on the roof and retrieved the shotgun.

Kris flinched when he heard the report. He spun around just in time to see the doe jerk violently for the last time, then stop. They were headed back toward the van when the blue lights of the patrol car eased onto the shoulder behind the deer.

Upon sighting, there are a few things that will cause a state patrolman some alarm. The silhouette of an athletic young man toting a long shotgun back to his car at two o'clock in the morning on a dark highway can be counted as one of those things.

Not that Kris and the other skiers didn't have a perfectly reasonable explanation for shooting the deer, there was no doubt about that. But when the owner of the shotgun failed to present a license for the shotgun, things got a bit sticky.

Two more patrol cars materialized out of the night. They searched the van.

Three ounces of marijuana and another box of slugs for the unlicensed shotgun were found in the bags. The cops pulled out the seats and opened the cushions with razor blades. After frisking and cuffing everybody they were loaded in the backs of the patrol cars and driven to the town of Du Bois. There, in one holding cell, they waited until morning.

Two Spyder skiers were arrested. One for the pot, one for the gun. Kris and the others walked down the flat road for a mile until they found a

Motel Six. Three days later they went to court and the judge set bond for the two skiers at a combined ten thousand dollars. Nobody had a credit card, and the bondsman refused to post bond for the two skiers since he had no guarantee they would be returning to Pennsylvania in the near future. Kris and two other team Spyder skiers were forced to sign over their prize money checks to the court.

Between the six of them they now had about four hundred dollars, barely enough for food and gas back to Colorado. They left at five o'clock in the afternoon, after being told by the state patrol that they shouldn't drive the damaged van after dark since the headlight would not pass safety regulations.

They drove for an hour, until it was dusk, then camped for the night in a rest area, drank beer and roasted hot dogs. It was thirty degrees out. They slept on the bench seats, layered like sardines head to foot, in their sleeping bags with wool hats and gloves on. An hour after sunrise they stiffly rose and scraped the frost from the inside of the windshield before running through the thin snowcover to urinate in the woods. When they crossed the border into Youngstown it had taken them more than four and a half days to get out of Pennsylvania.

The rest of the way back to Colorado Kris sat near the rear speakers, bombarded by bootleg Grateful Dead tapes. He listened to legendary concerts, Columbia '68 (taped on the roof of the student events center, where Jerry and the guys had played a free concert for the rioting students), Fillmore East '71. Once in a while a Jefferson Airplane tape was tossed in for variety.

He almost went crazy and was very happy when the team Spyder guys bade him goodbye on the westbound side of I-70 just before the Frisco exit, one mountain pass away from Vail. The van swung south toward Breck and home. Kris stood in the cold night air with his thumb out. His skis were stuck in the snowbank and his two bags were hidden in the ditch. Eighteen wheelers showered him with sharp pebbles and wind until, a half hour later, another V.W. microbus loaded with college kids from Boulder picked him up. Once inside the van they immediately asked if he had any pot. For another intolerable hour he listened to Grateful Dead tapes until the students dropped him off in Vail, where Kris went to the usual bars, The Red Lion, Vendettas, and finally The Coyote. He saw many people he knew, including Friday, while searching for a ride down valley to Avon.

When he finally reached the Silver Aspen Condominiums the door to Kellie Kay's unit was locked. He crawled in through the window and lay down, exhausted, on the trampoline.

He was broke again, without even enough money to buy dinner at the grocery store. He raided the cupboard and cooked himself plain spaghetti, with butter and garlic. Then he picked up his skis and began to work on them, filing the edges, checking the dings in the bases. He took out his portable iron and had already sprinkled the hard wax pellets on his skis when he looked down and saw the triangular burn in the white paint and remembered the last time he had waxed his skis on this table.

He didn't want to piss her off again, before she even saw him. There were no newspapers in Kellie's room, or in the kitchen trash. He went into Kelley's room and was rummaging through his trash can when he found the used rubbers underneath the newspapers.

He walked back into Kellie's room and opened up the top drawer of the bureau where he had kept his own rubbers. They were gone. He went back out to the living room and began waxing his skis as if nothing had happened. That she was sleeping with Kelley Sapp was understandable, he supposed, since he hardly ever slept with her himself. He finished waxing his skis and sat down on the couch with a back issue of <u>National</u> <u>Geographic</u>. But he couldn't concentrate on reading. He knew he should move out. That would be the right thing to do. But all his friends in the valley were just as indigent, living in cramped trailers and condos with too many roommates. He would make it last for a while longer, but it was dead. He didn't care.

When Kellie Kay returned home that night from another French dinner with her Mexican ski clients she was slightly buzzed off good Bordeaux and a couple of cognacs. She walked into her dark bedroom and nearly tripped over Kris. Asleep on the floor in his sleeping bag, he had cloistered himself off from her. She locked the door behind her and tip-toed to the trampoline. Then she lay down with a minimal amount of squeaking before she softly asked out loud, "Are you awake?"

Eyes open in the dark, lying motionless on the carpet, Kris Blaze didn't answer.

When Kelley Sapp returned home that night he was not surprised to find the door to Kellie Kay's room firmly locked. He felt a small flare of jealousy rise to his cheeks, but dismissed it almost as soon as it rose. *What a joke*, he thought before shutting the door to his own bedroom. He didn't need to get messed up in that situation any more than he already was. He returned his thoughts to Z, whom he knew with some degree of certainty loved him. A sign, some sort of sign was all he needed, and he would go with her.

When Kelley awoke at seven the next morning the door to Kellie Kay's room was still shut. He ate a bowl of oatmeal and walked outside to the parking lot before crawling into his Volkswagen van. He twisted the key and the van belched a cloud of black smoke into the clean Rocky Mountain air. Driving on the thin ribbon of Rt. 6 west, past the trailer park, he watched as three balloons slowly ascended from the valley floor until they floated high above both ridges of the valley. Like ornaments suspended by invisible wires they drifted neither right nor left and simply hung. Kelley's van climbed the road until it reached the Snowy Mountains Guest Lodge. By the time he pulled into the parking lot the balloons were on their way down and level with him. He could see the tiny figures in the wicker baskets, and watched as the flames shot up into the balloons, slowing their descent. It was a beautiful day, calm and sunny enough for balloon trips. After a minute or so he turned and started walking up the driveway.

Next to the carriageway, in the island of snow encircled by the gravel-strewn driveway, towered a snowoman on scale with an Easter Island sculpture. She had no eyes, no arms, and no mouth. Standing impassively, a glaring monolith of a snowwoman, her sex could only be determined by the absence of anatomically correct male organs, and the presence of two gigantically malformed breasts carved out of the snow above her protruding belly. At least three times Kelley's height, the snowoman did not tempt him in the least. He sighed and went inside.

The main conference room at the Snowy Mountains Guest Lodge had been named the America Room. Wood from over fifteen different species of trees indigenous to America embellished the walls, ceiling and furnishings. Silver wormy maple sconces that once stood tall in the Mississippi River Valley now glowed down onto a burled walnut conference table that sat in the middle of the room on hand-carved lion paw feet. Antique, tiger stripe maple paneling covered the walls on one side of the chamber. East facing windows looked out to the far slopes of Vail's gigantic back bowls. A cherrywood bureau was draped in white linen. Upon it rested the accouterments of every business meeting: coffee cups, creamers, water glasses and silver plated pitchers of water waited along with thermos jugs of coffee, both decaf and leaded.

On the walnut desk, pads and pens had been neatly arranged in symmetrically precise positions facing each applewood chair. Kelley Sapp stood in the doorway and took in the familiar surroundings of the America Room. He knew the scene well, for he had set everything up the night before.

A large projection screen had been erected at an exact distance from the end of the conference table. The slide carousel was waiting. Kelley was early. He made his way upstairs and through the lobby, on his way to the kitchen for a cup of fresh coffee. It was as he approached the black table of Lumsden of Strathdrummond that he saw Bennett Beauregard, down on his knees, clutching what looked like a butterfly net and burrowed underneath the table so that his ass poked out into the air like a target.

A high pitched squeal came from behind the table. Kelley watched with fascination as Bennett flailed about with the net. He wondered what Bennett was after until a large gray rat appeared on the top of the table and walked to the edge with an air of nonchalance. It eyed Bennett's bobbing ass for a moment before launching like a cat onto the pinstriped landing field. There was a momentary pause on both their parts. It must have been a foreboding sense of doom that made Bennett halt his exertions. As for the rat, it simply grinned at Kelley before opening his jaws and clamping down on the quivering flesh of Bennett Beauregard.

He screamed. A high pitched sighing wail halfway between orgasm and pain echoed from the depths of Lumsden's black table. Bennett Beauregard tried to stand up, hit his head on the nearly fossilized oak, and collapsed in a heap to the floor. The rat scurried off into the shadowy depths of the table. Like an unconscious man face down in a pool of water, Bennett Beauregard lay prostrate beneath the blackness. Kelley seized him by the ankles and hauled him out from underneath. He checked for Bennett's pulse and found it strong and steady before slapping his hands together and proceeding on into the kitchen as though nothing had happened.

One hour later Bennett Beauregard stood at the head of the conference table in the America room. His hair was messed and stuck out in two uneven clumps above his left ear as though he were a little kid and glue or jam had miraculously found its way to where it shouldn't. Kelley wondered if it was actually dried blood. The hair, coupled with the fact that his face was glowing red, forced Kelley to examine Bennett's fanatical eyes. An uneasy light came from the center of the pupils and radiated out like heat waves. It only took a second for Kelley to recognize the fact that Bennett Beauregard had snapped. His pants he hadn't bothered changing, despite the fact that a large tear in their seat was visible to everyone and displayed his bloodied white Hanes briefs to the assembled gathering of managers that had arrived minutes ago for Bennett's presentation.

The slide projector was on and the frozen image of Chef Christian's Ferrari pulling into the employee parking lot filled the screen. To Bennett's left sat Mr. Posthelwait, and to his right was the man Kelley had only seen once, when he had been naked in *flagrante delicto* with tattoos all over his body; Bond.

In a blue suit and British rep tie he no longer resembled the sinister freak Kelley had once thought he must be. His chin was square and cleft like Superman's, but didn't match his boyish mouth and baby soft skin. When Kelley had entered the conference room Bond had tipped his head in acknowledgement, as if he recognized him. Kelley had wondered how much he knew, and whether Z had told him anything.

An aluminum briefcase sat in front of Bond. His hands rested on the ribbed metal, folded as if in prayer. And his eyes followed Bennett Beauregard's harried gestures with no display of alarm or concern. If anything a slightly charmed display of innocence danced across his pink lips. Kelley regarded the assembled managers and Mr. Posthelwait as if he were separated from them. Like a spy in their midst, he masked his true feelings. The blue fog had once again descended over all. Benign smiles of ignorance and symbiotic concern cloaked each person. Was he the only one who recognized it? Bennett Beauregard was insane. What he was doing was insane.

The slide projector clicked and a new image of Chef Christian approaching the circle of snowmen appeared on screen.

"It is a pattern," Bennett continued, "of what I would term 'chronic snowman destruction'." He shook his head like a dog and tried to run his

127

fingers through the two clumps of hair, separating them even farther apart than before. It now seemed as if horns were growing from his skull.

"I have here a letter from a Mr. Graham Tunniwinkle, who was a guest at this lodge in late November of this past year. In this letter he details the blatant disregard for our guests that Chef Christian has exhibited on many occasions."

Bennett Beauregard cleared his throat and began to read from the letter like a senator before the house.

"Besides the exclusion of eggs from the breakfast menu, there is one other matter of importance which I feel must be touched upon. My son, a mere child of eight years old, was enjoying himself the afternoon before our last day at the Snowy Mountains Guest Lodge by building himself a snowman. Since we live in New York City, my son had never before had a chance to enjoy this traditional pastime. You cannot imagine how great my surprise was when after returning from my pedicure I learned from my son that while he was in the middle of constructing his snowman a man whom we later verified as the Chef, with the help of the ever so helpful Bennett Beauregard, had come up and actually pushed my son over into the snowbank headfirst. Whereupon, this animal proceeded to kick and stamp upon the body of the snowman, rendering it prostrate within a few seconds, all the while screaming at the top of his lungs, 'Frosty's dead! Frosty's dead! He's dead! He's dead! No eggs! Never!"

"This is the absolute truth, according to my son, and I have no reason to doubt his word as he has never once lied to me in the past."

With a red face and faux horns coming out of his skull, Bennett Beauregard folded the page into thirds and concluded his reading. He reached a hand toward the conference table and picked up the projector control. "Gentlemen, let me present my slides."

Upon the screen the life-sized figure of Chef Christian loomed among the circle of snowmen and snowwomen like one of his ancient Visigoth ancestors. He strode among the snowmen, tall and proud, a barbarian encircled by ... the strange icons of some dead druidic culture? Kelley didn't know. It had taken all his strength up to this point to keep from laughing out loud in desperation.

"Again gentlemen," Bennett Beauregard began his narration, "what we have here is clearly an example of, 'chronic snowman destruction'. Except in this case our subject displays what I would consider certain sociopathic tendencies which could be termed homicidal in a pluralistic sense of the word. Notice the relish with which he attacks the females, kicking them where it would hurt most. The males he simply decapitates with a clean swipe of his hand. In order to properly psychoanalyze this would require the assistance of an expert in the field of pathological crimes. But even without this expert, I think it would be safe to conclude that the man is dangerously suspicious. We don't know what he is. He is an unknown variable, in other words a cog in our gears that could go bad at any moment."

Bennett Beauregard karate chopped the conference table a bit harder than he should have for demonstration's sake. "Ouch!" He clutched his hand inside his suit like Napoleon, with his eyes closed, for five seconds. On screen Chef Christian stood frozen in mid-chop, his mouth hanging open, lazily allowing Kelley to inspect the saliva hanging like strings from the roof of his mouth. Positively carnivorous. Kelley had never seen such a frightful yawn in his entire life.

Bennett opened his eyes and withdrew his damaged palm in a way that reminded Kelley of certain documentary films about Nazi Germany.

"Hmmmmphhh!" Mr. Posthelwait's rumble echoed through the America Room. Bond had produced a cellular phone which now rested on top of the briefcase.

Bennett raised his palm. "Gentlemen and ladies," he glanced at his watch, "It is now nine-thirty, time for Chef to arrive. You will have, no doubt, noticed the snowoman standing outside next to the carriageway. This snowoman was constructed by me last night with one purpose in mind. Larger, more imposing and dominating than any before it, this snowoman should prove simply irresistible. I suggest that we adjourn to the upstairs hallway in order to watch as Chef Christian arrives for work."

Like a herd of buffalo, the managers' meeting dissolved and moved up the stairs in a pack toward the upstairs hallway windows. Mr. Posthelwait led the charge. In the wake left by his cigar Kelley and the other managers followed. On the way up the stairs Bond began dialing his cellular phone. At the windows they huddled about in half circles. Down below, the monstrous snowoman glared in the alpine sun. Godlike, her massively mis-shapen breasts pointed out and guarded against the approaching Chef Christian. Kelley sidled up next to Bond. The red Ferrari zoomed into the driveway. An unwitting and ignorant Chef Christian approached.

So far, it had not been a very good morning for Chef Christian. And without a doubt things were about to get much worse, though the repercussions of this day would not be felt by him for at least a few weeks.

He was upset again, as he trudged up the driveway, and with good reason. This very morning, at seven a.m., he had settled himself into the breakfast nook with his cup of coffee and found himself confronted with his wife's latest purchase. On the breakfast table, about as high as the salt shaker, stood a Piece of Art. It was a stone figurine, rough hewn, and grotesquely female. It seemed quite primitive or at least neo-primitive. He knew this was the fruit of his wife's latest visit to New York. Beneath the figurine was a sheet of folded notepaper. Chef Christian slid it out from underneath the figurine and read.

'Stone age fertility figure, dating from the last ice age. It was found in Poland.' Chef Christian skeptically eyed the figurine. Her legs were crudely represented by a single ball of rock that had been chiseled in half.

Her torso was another, larger ball of rock with conical protrusions that represented her breasts. A third ball of rock was her head. He supposed she was pregnant, which explained her role as a fertility figure. With a foreboding sense of doom he lifted the hand that had been covering the bottom half of the note and read on. 'Only fifty thousand dollars!' his wife had written. 'Just the thing for that tiny shelf in the bathroom.'

No, it had not been a good morning for Chef Christian LeForrestier. He slammed the door of his Ferrari and trudged up the driveway toward the waiting kitchen. He walked with his head down, mumbling to himself about the cruel fate awaiting the lobsters, when he caught the glare off the snow and looked up.

There it was; huge, white, mocking and pregnant. A gigantic fertility figure waited for him next to the carriageway. Chef Christian's hands quivered with ironic hatred. Why, he wondered? Why was this happening to him?

He charged forward and karate kicked the snowwoman right in the crotch. He kicked and pushed and punched her, hacking off her breasts with leaping chops, until she fell over onto the gravel. Then he ground her head with his boot. He felt powerful, vindicated even. It had been therapeutic. As he resumed his even tread toward the kitchen the bile that had been building in his stomach began to subside.

"Haaah!" Bennett Beauregard mechanically swung his hand in vicious chops. His rabid eyes were aglow with triumph. His spiky hair reminded Kelley of punk rockers he had seen in the clubs of New York. Bouncing up and down, swinging his hand, his Hanes briefs showing through the seat of his pants; Bennett Beauregard was a maniac. He spun in a circle, chopping and talking to himself. "Ha! Just like this. Did you see it?"

Kelley was listening to Bond, who had been doing a play by play into the cellular phone. "She's lying in the driveway now, defeated and crushed. A sad contrast to the gloating Bennett Beauregard, who continues to leap about. Don have you ever seen such a display of unsportsmanlike conduct before in your life? No, Howard, I can't say that I have," Bond did his best Don Meredith impersonation before switching back to a fairly accurate Howard Coselle. "This is an outrage, a positive outrage ..."

"The man is a lunatic!" Mr. Posthelwait broke away from the window with feigned shock. He knew that Chef Christian's contract was guaranteed for ten years at two hundred thousand a year. Losing him would keep them in the red for a long time. Of course he would fire him. Then they could hire another Chef at four hundred thousand a year ... "An absolute lunatic Beauregard! Good job. We'll see that he's removed. Now let's go downstairs, no lunatics allowed here."

Kelley touched Bond on the shoulder, "Who's that you're talking to?" he asked.

Bond broke away from the phone. "My wife. She likes it if I keep her abreast of every situation." Bond held up his hand and listened to the receiver for a bit before asking, "Are you Kelley? She wants to talk to you."

"Kelley?" Z's voice came over the static, "sorry to bother you. But I wanted to ask, since Chef will be fired does this mean you will lose your job too?"

"I don't think so."

"Rats. How's your girlfriend?"

"OK, I guess."

"If you don't ditch her soon we might miss Carnival."

"I've got to go."

"Give her up for Lent, Kelley. Do the right thing. Oh, no. Joey! Get off him! I've got to run!"

Ten minutes later they were all back down in the America Room. Mr. Posthelwait was expostulating.

"If we can get through the rest of the month, hire somebody else, then we can fire him. Kelley have we got any functions coming up where we'll certainly need the Chef?"

"None that I'm aware of-" Kelley was answering, but Bond cut him off.

"Gentlemen," Bond said, "I'm not sure if all of you know who I am." He introduced himself to the table, "I am Mr. Bond, and I represent a certain person who has a certain amount of interest in the Snowy Mountains property. The reason I am here today is to inform all of you that a major change is about to occur on the Snowy Mountains property. I have already spoken with Mr. Posthelwait about this matter. What we propose to do here in the next month is begin the construction of a large ski-area that is capable of becoming a destination-type resort. Now, one of the things that I want to have is a large party in about a month from now to celebrate the opening of the construction. It should be outside if possible, with food and tents. A ground breaking ceremony if you will, for the ski area. Perhaps we should keep the Chef until then?"

"Something to consider," Mr. Posthelwait agreed.

"I also wanted to ask all of you, " Bond continued, "if you have any good ideas about how to properly celebrate the opening of the ski area. I want it to be an Occasion. We will have potential homeowners here, and prominent people from about the valley. It should be quite spectacular."

Bennett Beauregard raised his hand. "I have an idea," he said.

With a wave of his arm Bond offered Bennett the floor.

"We should have a theme to the party. And with everyone so concerned about the environment these days, we should make the environment our theme."

"Good idea," Mr. Posthelwait agreed.

"Now, if we could manage to trap a herd of wild elk and pen them up near the party, even on the proposed site of the ski area, it would provide

131

a spectacular natural setting for the guests. The elk could graze tranquilly as we frolicked nearby. Then, we could get the members of the waitstaff to dress up. Some as condors, some as lynx and all that. It would set the proper tone, I think, and we should have skiing maybe?"

"Excellent, excellent," Mr. Posthelwait agreed.

Bennett Beauregard was glowing.

Bond opened his briefcase and pushed a wad of money toward him."Sign the receipt and get those trappers trapping," he said.

"And the skiing?" Mr. Posthelwait asked.

"Should we allow the guests to ski?" Bennett wondered aloud.

"No, no," Mr. Posthelwait killed that idea. "We want them looking at potential homesites, not crashing through the undergrowth. What if one got hurt? Kelley do you have any ideas about the skiing?"

He was on the spot. Kelley Sapp, who hated all that he was hearing, all that was being planned. Now he had to contribute.

"A celebrity," Kelley suggested tentatively. An expectant hush came over the conference table. All eyes were approvingly on him.

"Yes." Bond opened his briefcase.

"We should get a celebrity skier for the opening."

"Who?" Mr. Posthelwait was excited.

"My roommate, Kris Blaze. I think I could talk him into it."

"Kris Blaze, yes. The bump skier. We'll set up a course for him to ski, with a couple of jumps and all that. He can finish down by the elk. An inaugural run. I like that."

Bond pushed a stack of money at Kelley. "Sign the receipt and sign him up. Sign that Kris Blaze fellow on board."

Hours later Kelley was reclining on the sofa while watching last night's college hoops game on ESPN. He had the T.V. turned down and a Joni Mitchell disc in the CD player. A wad of hundred dollar bills, five thousand dollars thick, sat upon his chest. And when he breathed he could watch it rise out of the corner of his peripheral vision without having to shift his eyes from the newspaper he'd spread out on the coffee table.

He wasn't reading, he wasn't watching television, and he never concentrated on Joni Mitchell's lyrics because they always disturbed him with their nail on chalkboard shrillness or sent him into a nostalgic funk about nothing.

He was waiting for Kris Blaze to come home from skiing so he could offer him the money. He had contemplated offering only part of the amount and pocketing the rest, but had decided not to. Beside the fact that he was a generally honest person, Kelley felt a bit like the devil in this situation. He knew Kris never had a lot of money. He also knew that Kris never took sponsorship offers. Kris was like Jesus out in the desert for forty days and forty nights, starving for cash. Along comes Kelley Sapp, who waves five thousand dollars in his face.

He turned off the stereo and television before stepping into the bathroom for a hot shower. The water relaxed his shoulders and he slumped like an animal against the sweating tiles. A half an hour later he climbed out and was toweling off when he heard the door to the condo swing shut. Kelley walked out in his towel just in time to see Kris rummaging through the 'frige.

"Got half a pizza in there if you want any," Kelley offered, but got no reply. He shrugged his shoulders since he thought Kris hadn't heard him, and went into his room to change.

Kris Blaze winced. He had already eaten the pizza, cold, for breakfast. Having no money was a serious problem. Besides the fact that he hadn't had fresh vegetables for over a week and a half and was now surviving on the kind of junk Kelley and Kellie stocked the place with, he had gone skiing the hard way today and was now starving.

At the very base of Vail Mountain, just to the east of Bridge Street and the Vistabahn express, is an area of the mountain known as Gold Peak. Golden because of the aspens in fall, it is a gentle hill, almost Appalachian in slope. The kid siamese sister of rolling Vail Mountain, Gold Peak is the accumulated alluvial run-off of millions of summer thundersqualls, spring thaws, and fall hail, that have pounded the larger granite peaks of the Sawatch and Gore ranges since before there were memories to record them. It is the second son of a second son. The shifting, sliding, unstable amalgamated geologic slop that composes Vail Mountain has given birth to what we call Gold Peak. Twice removed from the high slopes of the Gore and Sawatch ranges, it provides the perfect setting for beginner skiers.

A one day lift ticket good for all lifts at both Vail and Beaver Creek cost forty-three dollars in nineteen ninety two. But there is a catch. One of the nice things about Vail and Beaver Creek is the fact that almost all of both ski areas have been built on public land managed by the U.S. Forest Service. Translation: if you want to hike up the hill no one can legally stop you, and it's free.

Earlier that past morning, at the base of Gold Peak, Kris had arrived before the lifts began running. Down by the Children's Center, a little ways off from the ski school building, he had begun his climb before the lights in the thousand dollar a night luxury suites and various administrative structures had switched on. The sno-cats were descending for a day's rest in the garage after a full night of grooming the wide, treeless runs on the front side. Trailing corduroy behind them, they powered down while Kris stiffly started up.

Stuffed inside the large rucksack he had strapped to his back were his heavy downhill boots. In side pockets, on the outside of the sack, Kris' black slalom skis jutted toward the sky in a triangle formed by the joining of the tips with a black plastic strap. Other straps along the outside of the sack held the skis in place. When viewed from behind, Kris appeared to be carrying the 'A' frame for a tee-pee. His telemark skis slid him into the gray light and on up the hill.

This was his warm-up. And even though it was not something he would do every day in the best of all possible circumstances, he really did not mind the exertion nor the emptiness of the slopes that were soon to be covered with thousands of skiers.

His plan was simple. Hike up the mountain without being spotted. Stash his telemark skis and switch to his downhills. Ski Chair 10 all day. They never checked for lift tickets at Chair 10.

With each step he sprang slightly up the slope toward the service road that led around the side of Gold Peak toward Chair 10. His telemarks were double camber, wooden with metal edges, and deeply bent in the middle like unstrung bows. The tails in the back curved up ever so slightly. These were skis designed to go up a mountain in deep snow. The camber sprang him forward. Glide wax on the tips slid smoothly along. Step wax in the middle of the bow, underneath his feet, stuck securely to the cold morning snow and propelled him up.

He found his rhythm and hit the road, bouncing as much as his heavy pack allowed, before swinging 'round a corner and into the abandoned base area of chair ten. By now sweat had drenched the turtleneck he wore next to his skin and drops of salty water had dripped from his brow to his nose and into the corners of his parched mouth. He stopped for a pull from his water bottle and examined the ancient double chair that silently reposed like a sleeping animal in the early morning gray.

It was time to get off the slopes and into the woods. Soon ski patrol would be starting their milk runs. Each day began with their early morning sweeps down the mountain, ostensibly trouble shooting runs that made sure warning flags were securely in place and trees hadn't fallen during the night to create an obstacle on a run. Milk runs were also fun time for the patrollers. On powder days they always got first tracks down the steepest pitches. Like tax collectors skimming cream from the top of the white bounty that had fallen the night before, these virgin runs they always took for themselves. The mountain, and the best the mountain had to offer, belonged to the ski patrol during those early morning hours when the lifts hummed up for them alone.

With skis on his back and boots in his rucksack, Kris knew it was not a good idea to let the ski patrol see him. One glance would broadcast his intentions at a ten decibel volume, and he'd be sunk. He swallowed another mouthful of water, paused while the liquid gurgled down his throat and into his stomach with a warmth like whiskey, and spread his legs apart until his groin muscles stretched like hot strands of warm camembert cheese, toned and pliant.

To his left, a stand of naked aspens rolled to a stop at the edge of the clearing. He moved up into them, stepping quickly through the light powder snow that reached his thighs in some places, and headed straight up the slope in a southerly direction. Through the aspen stand and on up into the higher elevations where the mast like trunks and evergreen symmetry of engelman spruce gripped the steep sides of the mountain like a furry velcro blanket. All was silent in shadow beneath the green and white canopy of their branches. Kris' steady breathing echoed as if in a chamber. Even the soft swish of his pants through the snow seemed to carry a resonance matching the sharp calls of the thick, gray birds, bouncing musically from branch to branch.

East of him, and finally coming out of shadow, was the cupped expanse of Mushroom Bowl. Above was the ridge line. Kris paused for some more water. Just about now the slow parade of skiers would be starting the early morning rush to the top of Bridge Street. He shook his head involuntarily at the passing image of that scene, and counted himself lucky. The crowd, the people, he had avoided it all this morning thanks to his indigence. What a beautiful thing to have no money. What modern angst and social convenience was he allowed to sidestep through his lack of dead presidents? No doubt he was missing a scintillating conversation with some Wall Street power broker/ Hollywood agent/ Mexican slum lord/ Banker-Doctor-Lawyer-Indian Chief on a cellular phone. He was nowhere. On the side of a hill, ducking the price of a lift ticket, and humping it a couple of miles up into the woods with a heavy pack, Kris Blaze wore a benign and radiant expression that the price of a million lift tickets could never purchase.

He reached the ridge line with an empty water bottle and stashed his pack and skis next to a tiny spruce. When he sat down in the snow and took off his telemark boots steam rose from his pungent socks. After clicking into his downhill boots and stepping into his bindings, he poled out of the woods on his slalom skis onto a cat track, which led down to the top of chair 10. Highline and the bumps were waiting. Warmed up and ready to go, he had made it up before nine-thirty.

During certain weeks in January, when the pro mogul tour is in town, lift number 10 becomes a popular spot for both skiers and spectators. The treeless face of Highline has the longest, steadiest and steepest pitch of any run on all of Vail mountain. Too steep even for the sno-cats to groom. Highline's bumps grow all year round and vary only with the snow conditions. On powder days the troughs fill with light snow and the bumps are soft and smaller than usual. After several weeks without a snow the bumps resemble miniature mountain ranges, some with flat spots on top where skiers perch like mountain goats in order to survey the terrain ahead.

On average, skiers carve their way through the bumps like blind senior citizens descending a staircase without railings, nor equal measurements between each monstrous step. Feeling with poles like antennae, and sliding backwards onto their butts during those rare moments when their skis point down the hill, they descend at a painfully slow rate of speed. This is the norm for the average skier. There are those who are better, who seem to navigate the bumps like a drunken sailor dancing across the planks of a rotted deck.

But during certain weeks in January, weeks when Kris Blaze and his fellow bump skiers are in town, the slow moving line of chairs chugging up the stubby poles toward the top of lift 10 becomes the best place in the world to watch Kris Blaze and his peers cut loose.

There is an etiquette to the way they ski. Like knights at a joust, they chivalrously bow to each others' wishes. Peers of the realm of skiing, they line up at the top of that half-mile face, arriving with a puff of white shot up from their edges, and pick their lines while leaning over on their poles. Eyes scrunched, they study the bumps ahead and plan their route of descent with professional scrutiny. From each trough to the top of each bump, they can see where the turns must be made. Hold the line. This is the key. Hold the line straight down. Never put your edges parallel to the slope. Deflect off the sides of some bumps, use your knees to absorb the next. Avoid the tourists switchbacking down the hill. Time to go.

Kris looks to his left, then right. He nods to another, one who hasn't made it past the quarterfinals yet. He's in his second year on the tour and sponsored by Power Bar. Kris nods again. The Power Bar skier goes, following the line Kris would have taken. He waits. Another slides up next to Kris. He doesn't even look. Five more seconds. The line is his now. Kris goes.

From the high chairs it seems as if they hardly touch the snow. That uneven staircase, so treacherous to others, is now a racecourse. They descend on skinny rails, dropping one after the other, like runaway locomotives, to bounce magically across the tops of each mogul with a weight so ponderous and precariously balanced it seems impossible they would manage to stay upright. But they do. Of course. To ski like Kris Blaze should allow for something more than the chance to be a walking billboard for Rossignol, or Budweiser, AT&T, or whatever.

When the long shadows of a winter afternoon stretched across the slope of Highline, Kris made his way back through the woods. After changing back into his telemark equipment he began the last descent of the day.

Zig zagging through the spruce groves, he free heeled it through the powder until he came out of the woods down at the base of chair ten. On the hardpack he skidded down like a newborn deer on skittish legs. His telemark skis rattled and bounced unpredictably across the snowpack. When he reached the base of Gold Peak, some six and a half hours after he had begun his climb, and smelled the canned chili and greasy French fries cooking in the lift lodge cafeteria, hunger hit him like a wall.

What he wouldn't have done right then for ten bucks would be criminal to reveal. Just how low he had sunk, Kris probably didn't even realize. He filled his stomach with icewater at the transportation center before catching the bus back down valley to Avon. When he arrived at the door to unit 201-B of the Silver Aspen Condominiums, he had one thing in mind.

Kelley had finished toweling off and changed into some jeans and a wool sweater. He went back out into the living room and was about to open the door to the refrigerator when he spied the empty pizza box leaning up against the plastic garbage container.

He cast a sideways glance toward the couch at the culprit, who was knuckle deep with a dill pickle spear into a jar of generic peanut butter. On the cluttered counter next to the stove two packages of Rah-Men noodles waited for the warming pot to boil.

Kris could have acknowledged Kelley when he sat down on the couch next to him, but he had other things on his mind now, things that had to do with Kelley Sapp.

On the back side of a long distance telephone bill that had been taped to the front of the refrigerator were the utility, rent, and cable television totals for the month, broken down individually. Kris had not been overjoyed with the news that he owed his girlfriend over two hundred dollars for his partial stay this coming month. But something else had caught his eye. At the top of the middle column, between Kellie and Kris, was the roommates full name: *Kelley Sapp* written out in Kellie Kay's looping pen.

Dramatic changes occur in the chemistry of certain solutions when a small amount of a specific chemical is added to it. Liquids can turn to solids. What was once chemically stable can suddenly become volatile. These changes occur at incredibly rapid speeds and are evidence of the wholesale molecular re-structuring that occurs on an atomic level. A new solution is created.

When Kris Blaze read Kelley Sapp's full name on the bill he did not actually turn to stone, nor even melt into a puddle of hissing acid. But the change was there and visible on his face. Dredging through the murky depths of memory, beyond doors long rusted shut, that had been waiting for the magic word to act like a key, the catalyst, that would throw open their mystery once again, he quickly found what needed to be remembered. That word was *Sapp*, and like abracadabra alacazaaam in the movies, things happened for Kris Blaze when he read it. *Baby boy Sapp*, had been printed on that birth certificate found by him long ago in Ike Blazekowski's Bible. He remembered now, before continuing his grab for the pickle jar. Kris Blaze's entire view of the world shifted focus as he wrapped his hands around the cold glass jar.

He had made the connection that he had always imagined. In his dreams, when he was younger and living at Alpine Academy in Vermont, he would sit awake in bed imagining himself as a Philip Marlowe/Sam Spade type character. Night after night he would re-enact the same basic story in a thousand different ways. Only after a twisted sprint through a labyrinthine web of deception that Ike had placed in his path, through dark men in alleys, femme fatales and other such adolescent notions culled from *noir* detective novels, he would burst through the black cloak of darkness that separated

137

him from his parents and their world that he never knew.

On that side, where the life that could be was waiting for him, a young Kris Blaze arrived at a house with parents who loved each other. They lived on a farm, maybe even in Vermont, somewhere near Brattleboro. Goats were penned in the front yard. In the summer Kris' mother would braid her hair in a long blond row that stretched to the small of her back. His father brewed beer and fruit wines. Their lives were complete except for their one son, who was fond of smashing apples and peaches against the stone fences separating the orchards. He blew up frogs with firecrackers, and guzzled his father's beer when left alone. With black hair and thick digits for fingers, he resembled neither his mother nor his father. Kris, together with friends from Alpine Academy, would arrive and drive the devil out. The epiphany of this imagined moment always dissolved into various mushy fantasies, all of which were idyllically similar. Kris becomes a professional football player. Kris wins an Olympic gold medal. Kris and his parents walk off into the sunset, happily re-united.

He had made several actual attempts to locate his natural parents. Phone calls had been placed to directory assistance operators for anyone named Sapp living in or around Dallas. Lacking much in the way of funds, these operations had yielded little except some amusing moments when he had actually been connected to a Sapp, someone, and stumbled for the correct line of questioning.

But in the present, contemporary life of Kris Blaze those fantasies had in hindsight passed into the realm of childhood whimsy. What had once seemed like a dark mystery waiting to unfold and reveal itself, had now been relegated to yet another one of the dead ends life tosses at everyone. He'd given up on ever finding a reason. Some stories never do get resolved. But Tommy Bird's prophecy was not the sort to be taken lightly. Twenty-eight years had passed since that day he died with a vision clear in the stars above him. Twenty-eight years it took for things to come to fruition. But the thread had been picked up, and was now back on line.

Kris was blase when he asked Kelley, "Where you from?" He didn't expect to hear what part of him feared he would. But the switch was thrown, and the electricity went through Kris, when a hungry and annoyed Kelley Sapp revealed that although he had grown up in Massachusetts he had actually been born in Dallas.

Questions led to questions. Banal, idiotic little niggling details of life were revealed by Kelley. It went on like a history exam. *What date? Are you sure? Do you remember which hospital? ...Oh, because my father's a doctor. It's possible he delivered you.* And finally, after all the discussion. *Do you have any brothers?*

"Yes," Kelley answered. He could have waited to give the details, but knew better by this point. Besides, this date and place he knew, as all good brothers should. He revealed them quickly and without any prodding on Kris' part. "He was born in Dallas on September 3, 1963 at twelve o'clock in the afternoon. That was five years before my father was transferred."

"What a coincidence," was all Kris could say for the moment. Kelley was quiet for the few seconds it took before Kris revealed in a matter of fact manner, as if it carried no relevance to their current situation whatsoever, "that's my birthday too."

So, he'd been born at twelve noon on September third. Kris Blaze stretched his memory backwards like a hand with a paintbrush and tried to re-construct his own birth.

"Kelley, do you like your brother?"

This young man sitting next to him on the couch, the same kid who was cuckolding him, must be his brother. The gap was too large a one to close in an offhand manner. He was at a loss.

Kelley scratched his head with his ragged fingernails. Kris' line of questioning failed to make any sense. He was worried that it all had something to do with Kellie Kay, and that all this was preliminary to Kris whaling the shit out of him. Nice fellow merely wished to know who his next of kin was. Perhaps he'd send a letter off to Emerson. *Dear Mr. Sapp: Before killing your son with my bare hands it was my great pleasure to get to know him for the delightful person he was. I counted Kelley among my greatest friends during those few minutes we talked prior to his untimely demise.* Good God, answer him. Why not?

"He's a complete loser. And he's an asshole. I think he works at Jiffy Lube and lives in my parents' basement. Everyone in the family thinks he's some kind of mutant redneck."

There was a frightening moment for Kelley Sapp when Kris Blaze beamed at him. What he couldn't know was that the radiance was borne of fraternal love. He was waiting for the first punch to shatter his jaw, and had closed his eyes, when Kris leaned over and hugged him.

They sprang away from each other, each as surprised as the other.

With no idea what emotions had caused Kris' eyes to tear up, Kelley saw his opening and took it. Now, he had decided, was as good a time as any to ask Kris a favor.

"Can you do me a favor, Kris?" He kept to the other end of the couch, tensed backwards, when he asked this.

"Of course." The moment softened like a wet sponge. All the uncertainty between Kris and Kelley now held a purpose. A favor had been requested.

Kelley slowly drew out a wad of hundred dollar bills, five thousand dollars thick.

"Actually, it's not so much of a favor. You'd be well paid for it," he said. "Do you think you could ski one run for five thousand dollars?"

Kris nodded.

That's how it went, brother to brother. One in the know, one out.

One destined for glory, one with no destiny but an anonymous life like so many others. One with a sense of purpose, the other as ignorant of himself as he was in general. Yet they were brothers, with much in common, as much at least as all men share.

Fifteen miles west of Vail, in a small side valley that could accurately be described as the tailbone of the Sawatch Mountain Range, is Vail's sister ski area; Beaver Creek. The small valley has a history of human habitation that stretches back to the days when Utes and Arapaho contested the land. In the recent past it was occupied by subsistence farmers who had homesteaded the high country and whose handiwork can still be seen in wilderness areas surrounding Beaver Creek. While hiking it is not uncommon to encounter forests of fifteen foot tall spruce stumps. These tell the story of men who couldn't chop enough wood during the short summer season to last them through winter. The fifteen feet of trunk sticking up like unfinished totems represent the snow level of some winter a hundred years previous.

Today, in order to gain access to Beaver Creek one must pass through a gatehouse which stands at the base of Beaver Creek Lane. When you pull your car up to the picturesque gatehouse a young man or woman will lean out the window and ask you in a very cordial manner what your business is in Beaver Creek that day. Things seem a far cry from the hard years of subsisting in the mountains. But if life has softened for some, the security person, a genial twenty-two or twenty-three year old, proves it has hardened along class lines. It is a strange transition point, this gatehouse at the foot of Beaver Creek Lane. Equal parts custom house and Disney World ticket office, only one aspect of it's *raison d'etre* is crystal clear; the gatehouse is a demarcation line. Like the old Berlin Wall or Central Park, it acts as a visible divider between economic classes.

North of the gate sits the sprawling town of Avon, Colorado. Home of the Silver Aspen Condominiums, Benchmark Trailer Park, the Avon Pet Centre, Comfort Inn, Pizza Hut, two liquor stores, a supermarket, and affordable rents. It is a town housing both middle and lower middle class Americans, illegal aliens, and your average garden variety domestic internecine crime. It is a company town, supported by and existing because of what sits south of the gate at the foot of Beaver Creek Lane.

With your pink cardboard pass neatly tucked between your windshield and dashboard you press the accelerator and leave the smiling twenty-two year old security person behind and begin the climb up.

There is an actual creek in Beaver Creek. The eroding power of the water it has carried over the millennia has helped shape the small valley into which you are now driving. The beavers are mostly dead now. They were killed in order to preserve the golf course, which passes on your left, from being flooded. Just as they have disappeared, so have the trees which used to line the banks of the creek. All that is left of the beavers is the name. In place of the trees are dwellings known in real estate parlance as, 'cluster single family homes'. They spring up like lines upon a painted graph. Black asphalt abuts green borders of square lawn.

In winter the flat white snow leads to the abrupt rectangular walls of white units that are larger, more spacious and gracefully composed than the Silver Aspen Condominiums. Still, they have that look of having been built with childrens' play blocks. Boxy, neat, homogeneous, and about as exciting to the eye as a monotone is to the ear, they are the second homes of well-to-do lawyers and dentists in Denver.

To your right passes a large snow covered embankment which is the beginning of the western slope of the valley. The road upon which you are driving winds along the base of this embankment and divides the valley into halves. Upon the right hand side of the road you spot the first of the castles which dot the landscape. Like miniature medieval kingdoms, immense homes that are direct architectural descendants of Tudor manors, Norman chateau, and Bavarian alpine fortresses, stand in close proximity as if they were similar sculptures arranged within the allocated space of a museum.

When it comes to beauty there can be little doubt that Beaver Creek is one of those special places blessed with a natural aesthetic appeal that lends itself, without effort, toward pleasing the human eye. But this is on a natural level. The color division between aspen and engelmen spruce divide the hillsides into patchwork quilts of color. Directly south, at the highest point visible from the valley, the bald tail of the Sawatch mountains tapers into the trees with an abrupt division that is as shocking and harmonious as a minor chord. That you can see without distortion through the thin mountain air lends a clarity and definition to the landscape that is unequaled anywhere at sea-level. Here you can see forever. When the moon rises over the ridge, and you are lucky enough to be there and fix it with your binoculars, the branches of spruce trees thirty miles distant stick out like jagged arms against the warm, pocked cheddar rising behind.

Splendid isolation. The houses grow in scale as you climb the road.

Certain ski towns, even rich overdeveloped ones, can warm the heart on cold winter nights. Old mining towns like Aspen or Crested Butte, places where sidewalks and tiny frame houses can capture the feeling of community between the streets, even if French restaurants and art galleries have taken over. There, and in places like them, people have actually lived and worked. You can feel that. But there can be nothing as sterile and lifeless, as the sort of pre-planned architectural community Beaver Creek is. Like the wet dream of some Bauhaus architect, all evidence that human beings live and work and sweat in various ways throughout our lives has been subsumed to a Master Plan of diabolical simplicity. If you are rich you may live in Beaver Creek. And being rich is obviously what counts.

At the underground parking structure you park your Volkswagen van. At the top of the stairs you turn right and exit at some double doors, follow a long brown hallway and find yourself in a courtyard. Welcome to the heart of Beaver Creek Village. Though it is cold outside, it is also sunny and a pleasant enough winter day. You would like to chat with one of the various persons streaming by you, but it is obvious by the way they keep their heads down and focus on walking *that they have something to do*. So you let them go and decide to take your tour without their company.

The fact that you are by yourself hadn't bothered you before. But now that you see all these people hurrying off to somewhere else you are struck by the idea that perhaps they are all hurrying to meet other people, people who love them, or lust for them, or happy families, or a party. You put your eyes to the pavement and quickly begin walking to the arcade of shops that you spot to the left of the public fountain. You are going to a store. Yes: that's what you're doing. Something drives you, you're not sure what it is, but at the same time you also realize that you have lost control of your feet and are now walking at an alarmingly rapid rate, one that would make it seem to others that you are in a hurry and must get someplace soon.

An overwhelming urge to greet someone suddenly obsesses you. You would like nothing more than to suddenly spot a familiar face among all those that pass you by. You search for familiar features, all the time imagining the happy embrace, the tossing of arms and cries of delight you would both utter upon sighting and stopping. With what eyes would others view you then? Happy people meeting happily in Beaver Creek. What joy to fold into someone you know. But you keep walking and looking, seeing nobody you know. Two people stop and talk with animated hands and loud voices about other people they know. A small twinge of jealousy attacks you. Your heart is beating faster than it might otherwise and you wish you had a cigarette even though you don't smoke.

The shops approach and you must choose and enter without seeming to hesitate. One is for womens' lingerie, another for womens' ski clothes, and a third for womens' formal wear. You toy with the idea of dropping into each and purchasing extravagant items for your non-existent significant other. The questions the clerk would ask and the answers you could invent. *She's six feet tall. Oh, god? You know I really couldn't tell you, but I do think that would pinch her in the bust. Do you have last month's copy of 'Elle'? She's on page twenty-six. What are you doing for dinner? So am I and that's never stopped me.*

Instead, you go into the art gallery and find yourself at the end of the store within two seconds. While staring at the lifesized, nude bronze of Bo Derek, complete with cornrows a salesperson approaches. Terrified of seeming like an indigent, you make out a check for the bronze and arrange to have it delivered. "Where do you live?" the salesperson asks.

Once again you are terrified. Where do you live? You don't know and can't remember. All you know about yourself is that you have just purchased a life-sized nude bronze of Bo Derek for fifteen thousand dollars. You laugh, *ha ha*, you laugh. What are you laughing about? You don't know. Things teeter on the edge of dissolving before you announce to the clerk that the bronze is for your new house, the one you haven't purchased yet, in Beaver Creek.

Come to lunch with me, the salesperson insists. At a table you fumble with a fork that feels like rubber and listen to a man the salesclerk has just introduced you to blabber like an insane idiot. You understand nothing of what he says and watch with fascination as his mouth opens like the aperture of a camera, spitting each word at you with focused incoherence. He jabbers on and you are unable to cut your steak, which seems like stone. The salesclerk disappears. You are alone with the man, who you now realize is a real-estate agent.

"Come with me. I want to show you this house," he says.

In his Lexus you drive past deer and elk, blackbears eating berries and on up you drive for what could be a long or short time until you reach a house that seems to have been waiting for you. At the door a small girl in pigtails giggles and runs upstairs to tell others you have arrived. But they are scared you won't want to play and will not come down.

"Those are Gerry's grandkids," the agent says, before grabbing a shotgun and walking out onto the porch. You follow him and he points across a field to another house that looks exactly like the one you are in except that it's different and says, "That's Gerry Ford's house. If you buy this house you'll be Gerry Ford's neighbor."

Who's Gerry Ford? You wonder to yourself before remembering that he was President of something at sometime. The real estate agent is pointing his shotgun at you.

"Buy," he says, before adding, "it's good for the economy."

Two people appear on Gerry Ford's porch. You wonder if they're watching. The real estate agent grabs you and drags you out to the Lexus then tosses you in the trunk. As you speed down the driveway the last thing you remember before waking up is that those two people on Gerry Ford's porch weren't friends with Gerry.

A crowd of concerned folk has formed a circle around you. It seems you slipped while getting out of your Volkswagen van and hit your head. *Are you okay? How many fingers am I holding up? Are you okay?* Somehow, you can't help but believe it was all too real.

"Looks like he was in a hurry," Friday blew a cloud of marijuana smoke into Kelley's face. They watched the Lexus speed down the driveway, it's tires spinning and spitting gravel off the snowpack.

They had been in Gerry Ford's house for half an hour now and had only managed to find their way through about two thirds of the rooms.

"Didn't one of those guys down there have a shotgun?" Kelley pointed to the recently vacated deck of the immense house abutting the Ford property. Above him and to his left hung the motionless chairs of the Strawberry Park chairlift. Skiing was finished for the day, and the last glints of daylight were filtering over the narrow ridge, bouncing down off clouds in the form of alpenglo, and casting a golden hue over the winter landscape of naked aspens and christmas tree evergreens. They had taken the last lift up that day, then skied down through the trees to the house. The door had been unlocked, as Friday had said it would be, and they had strolled inside as if they belonged there.

"Someone probably got kidnapped," Friday said as if it didn't matter. "Holy shit! How long have we had the pizza in?"

They had taken Gerald Ford's frozen Totino's pizza and placed it under the broiler some fifteen minutes ago. Kelley and Friday sprinted back to the kitchen and saved the pizza from incineration.

He cut the pizza into quarters and served it up on some of Gerry's personal china. Kelley lifted his slice in order to get a good look at the gold rimmed blue plates bearing the presidential seal in the center. They finished the pizza, silently wolfing down the slices of pasteurized cheese and dehydrated onion, while the presidential eagle stared up at them.

They finished the meal with some of Gerry's Chivas Regal on ice in baccarat crystal tumblers in the living room. Their legs crossed like middle-aged desk-weary-executives, they swirled the scotch and really tried for a few moments to put aside their cynicism and appreciate the leather couches, oriental rugs, and machine made furniture that cluttered the space around them. But they couldn't do it.

As far as palaces go, Gerald Ford's seemed a bit pedestrian. All the appliances in the kitchen were standard, top of the line General Electric, the stuff middle class American dreams are made of. The tall banks of windows looking out on Beaver Creek Village were triple glazed Andersen, and even though they stood fifteen feet high, Kelley couldn't help thinking that Gerry's place had all the warmth and coziness of your average hotel suite. The place was dramatic. Stunning views were everywhere. Bookcases and glass bureaus containing Gerry's football trophies and ceremonial golf clubs filled some of the empty space. But it was the same as all the other houses surrounding it. All the other palaces, including Gerry's, toed the architectural line of Beaver Creek. Nothing too flashy, no pink stucco or crisp, blue banners flapped in the air, as would befit a former head of state's household. Everything in the place, down to the paintings of Revolutionary War scenes, was something Kelley could have imagined without the aid of reality.

He knew it all. From the mock-Colonial period ottoman that sat in front of Gerry's armchair, to the Frederick Remmington bronzes, Kelley felt a recurring sense of both boredom and *deja vu* that had him wishing he had missed the entire industrial age.

He stared out at the mountains, a child of middle class America, whiskey in one hand, standing in un-buckled orange ski boots, wearing a green lambswool sweater and white nylon ski pants, and willed everything around him away. He melted walls, erased windows, killed lights and imagined himself up on the mountain. In snow up to his thighs, he struggled, a man like an animal. He lived in the mountains. He was an animal, instinctual and natural.

He let out a sigh at first. Just a small one, that grew to a snarl. He let it curl out of his lips in a long loose flapping growl before he howled into the ceiling. As the echoes of his voice died in the soft pile of the rugs, Kelley wished his voice could have carried out into the night air, where someone or something would have heard it. He stared into the trees outside the windows and imagined he saw something resembling a wolf glide across the trail and into the aspens. Shadows in the twilight, Kelley supposed. He turned and went back into the kitchen, where Friday was examining a framed photograph of Gerry and the former Shah of Iran.

"Let's smoke another bowl," Kelley suggested.

They put on their ski parkas and walked back out onto the deck. Friday loaded the bowl from his plastic baggy while Kelley concentrated on the emerging stars. Orion, the Seven Sisters, and other constellations Kelley knew but couldn't identify by name flickered dully in the early night sky.

They smoked, passing the pipe silently between them.

"So what's with Z," Friday finally asked.

"Still no decision on my part. All I know is I'm waiting for something."

"Like what?"

"A sign."

Friday laughed before coughing. "Go with her."

"I'm scared she'll run off with the first stewardess she meets at the airport."

"She's a lesbian?"

"She's bi-sexual."

"Funny how that stuff doesn't really matter. I'm gonna tell you something, Kelley, that I hope will convince you to take another chance with her. Since the first day I've met you all you've done is pine for Z. I think you owe it to yourself to take another shot at it. I had a chance once with a lover who wanted me to go away with him, and I think we would have been very happy together even though he was thirty years older than me. But I didn't do it, and the whole world had to suffer because of my mistake."

Friday knocked the pipe against the metal deck railing. Red embers spilled to the snow, trailing ghostly tails in Kelley's stoned retinas.

"How did this decision of yours have worldly repercussions?"

"Because the guy I could have lived with was Ronald Reagan."

"Get the fuck out of here."

"I'm serious."

"So am I."

"No, no. I'm telling the truth. We met at a de-tox center in Palm Springs one winter. He was trying to kick booze and pills, and so was I. We supported each other through the worst of it. I was really young back then, and it was so romantic, almost like a movie. Aging movie star finds true love with a young man sort of thing. But I knew it had to end. He was already talking about running for governor, and there was no way I would play second fiddle to Nancy."

"So, what happened?"

"He offered to move in with me and live in West Hollywood together. I said no."

"Why?"

"Because who wants to be married to an aging queen. I was young, and if we'd stuck together he would never have become President and I would have been bored of him in a couple of months."

"But you could have saved us from eight years of reactionary hell!"

"No I couldn't have. They'd have found somebody else. As it was they wound up hiring an actor. Except for his role in HUAC, Ronald was really a very nice person. Kelley," Friday turned away from the rail to look at him, "Z's a young, vibrant chiquita. You're obviously obsessed. Why not go?"

"You know," Kelley was just about to agree with him when they heard the glass break.

"Look, down on that porch." Friday pointed to the house they had seen the Lexus at earlier.

"I thought something weird was going on there," Kelley looked through the screen of aspens toward the neighboring house's porch.

They heard footsteps and watched as a single match flared, fell in an arc, then billowed into flames as it touched the gasoline fumes. Through the shattered glass doors they watched a man dressed all in black emerge, step into his telemark skis, and push off quickly into the night as the flames caught the drapes and grew higher.

"Lone Wolf," Kelley said.

"Who?"

"The same guy burned a house down in Killington, and one at Stowe."

"Doesn't he howl?"

It cut in above them, a cry so sharp and loud that it hung in the air and reverberated for what seemed like an eternity. He howled again, then once more. The flames climbed above the treetops and illuminated the Ford house in an eerie glow.

"Let's get out of here," Friday smartly suggested. They clicked into their skis and ditched it down the hill to the Coyote bar, where they drank four beers each before catching the bus back down past the gatehouse, where police cars and ambulances had gathered, into Avon.

In the morning when Kelley woke with a slight hangover from his post-bonfire partying with Friday, Kris Blaze sat on the couch in the living room with the morning paper. *"Eco-Terrorist, Lone Wolf, Strikes in Beaver Creek,"* read the headline.

"I saw it go up," Kelley casually remarked to Kris.

"Really?" Kris leaned forward with this news.

"Yeah. In fact I got a good look at the guy after he tossed the match. But since I was in Gerry Ford's house at the time, I don't think it would be a good idea to step forward as a witness."

"Probably not," Kris agreed. He glanced at his watch. Nine thirty. In twenty minutes he would leave to catch the ten o'clock bus to Vail. He patted the wad of money in his pocket. It was good to have cash again. He had paid Kellie the money she wanted for rent and bought himself some new skis. Today he would pay the premium on the medical insurance he had been lacking. All this for one run at the Snowy Mountains Guest Lodge. It still made his stomach turn, but last night's triumph eclipsed most of the ignominy he felt for accepting Kelley's proposal.

Kelley looked up from his oatmeal and gauged it's consistency by turning his spoon upside down and shaking it.

"Besides," he looked up from the steaming bowl. "I don't want him to get caught. I think I like the bastard."

"So do I," Kris agreed wholeheartedly, "so do I."

Chapter 7:

In which we get even more background on Kris Blaze.

In the weeks which preceded the ground breaking ceremony- days which could not, without irony, be said to have been spent in preparation for the great event- Kelley Sapp's life continued to remind him more and more, each day, of something far far removed from what he had previously thought of as reality. That the new ski area at the Snowy Mountains Guest Lodge was to be christened 'Snowflake'- and require Kelley and his waitstaff to dress in styrofoam costumes at the groundbreaking ceremony- costumes molded into the form of large, pink and blue snowflakes-sadly added confirmation to his theory that human beings are a generally base group, and best avoided by decent sorts.

He had just received news of the costumes during dinner service. It was a slow Tuesday night, with the restaurant half full of the usual sorts of people. Kelley had been standing next to one of the medieval cook kettles, humming a number from <u>Macbeth</u> and avoiding the customers, when an unwelcome Bennett Beauregard bounced up next to him with a package under his arm.

When Kelley had gone back to his small office he had unwrapped the package and stared unbelievingly at the floppy styrofoam. In his youth he would have scorned the costume even on Halloween, since he would most certainly have been labeled a faggot if he was spotted by another child while wearing it. Crystalline shaped pink and blue arms radiated from a central vest which encased even the head and transformed the face of the wearer into the center of the snowflake.

Kelley put it on. He walked back into the kitchen with his cheeks puffed and got several disbelieving laughs from his waitstaff before a small paring knife whizzed through the air and pinned one of the styrofoam arms to the moldy brick. Only then did Kelley remember that a certain person considered the kitchen his personal domain.

Knowing glances and small giggles came from the doughy faces behind the kitchen line. One eye winked at Kelley and went back to the steamer which was bathing each piece of raw fish in clouds of moist vapor before plating. Chef Christian had turned his back toward some unknown task and was diligently toying with the knobs of the great gas stoves. He fumbled with the dials, turning them left, then right, as if he were a child engrossed in some fantasy game with rules created and known only by him. Between Kelley and the Chef, waiters continued to pick up plates of food and disappear through the doors with trays piled high. They arrived and left in a highly irregular stream of comings and goings that did nothing to disrupt the tension strung across the kitchen. He knew what he had done. He also knew that Kelley knew, and absolutely nothing in the world could make him turn around and point his eyes in Kelley's general vicinity until he was ready.

Kelley reached above his head and tugged the knife from the wall, freeing himself. It is doubtful that in the recorded history of Western Civilization a similar sight to that of Kelley Sapp, the mad snowflake, moving across the kitchen with a paring knife in hand has been witnessed by anyone but those few lucky souls in the kitchen that night.

It was time, Kelley felt, to break some bad news to Chef Christian. For starters, Kelley grabbed a wooden cutting board from the salad line. He plunged the paring knife into the wood, twisted the handle, and snapped the knife blade like a twig. Then he sent the whole package, knife handle and broken blade, sailing over the line and onto Chef Christian's head, where they bounced as if they had struck rock and awoke the menacing giant.

A slow gleam of malice shone in Chef Christian's eyes as he turned around for what he envisioned would be the final showdown. His right hand held his trusty cleaver, and his left was balled up into a clublike fist. The stainless steel of the kitchen line separated the two opponents so that they looked at each other as if through a long, narrow window.

"You better leave," Chef Christian said.

It would be best, Kelley knew, if he could avoid a physical confrontation.

"I guess you've heard they're firing you?" Kelley asked in a tone that could almost be regarded as sympathetic.

The change his question wrought upon Chef Christian's face was immediate, as if the Chef had swallowed a bad oyster. The reverberations of Kelley's news filtered palpably through the other chefs as they all turned their eyes toward Chef Christian for confirmation.

"No way," Chef Christian said. "If they fire me then they still have to pay me. I have a guaranteed contract."

"That won't help if you're in jail," Kelley shook his head. "You should see this letter they got. Something about some snowman and a little

149

kid. I guess you went too far with that little kid."

"What do you mean? What kid?"

"You remember the snowman, but not the kid?"

"What are you talking about?"

"I hear his parents are suing for a lot of money. He'll need psychological counseling for the rest of his adolescence. Pain and suffering, all that. The total could be huge. You'll have to go back to France after the trial and whatever sentence you serve."

"You're making all this up."

"Hey, all I'm saying is what I hear." Kelley tossed his hands up in a dismissive display of innocence. "I'm sure you know what you've done. And if you say you're innocent, then I believe you. But I have also heard, from several different sources I might add, that you'll be gone as soon as we've finished the Snowflake party. Just thought you might want to know that."

"Who told you this?" Chef Christian gritted his teeth and took a step forward.

"Why weren't you at the manager's meeting two weeks ago? Or should I say, why weren't you invited? Think about it, Chef. Try to get a meeting with Mr. Posthelwait. I bet anything he'll stall you."

That night Chef Christian went to bed with an uneasy stomach. He tossed about like an ungainly bear, and was finally evicted to the couch by his frail wife, whom he obeyed with an unusual display of nasty indifference.

At four o'clock in the morning he fixed himself some chamomile tea with honey and sat down with a large, illustrated book containing prints and criticism of the work of Andy Warhol. Only then did slumber's sweet grip take hold and carry him 'til the morn.

When the sun had crested the snow-capped peaks of the Gore with a reflected glare so blinding it nearly knocked Chef Christian off his couch, the short peace he had known while sleeping was soon replaced with the questions he had mulled over all night. The best defense, he had so originally decided, was an attack. So when he called Mr. Poshthelwait's office that morning at nine a.m., it was in order to discuss the raise he felt he deserved and to demand the resignation of that incompetent *Maitre D'* whom he detested.

While dialing the number he had straightened his back and cleared his throat a number of times. His face he had washed twice and shaven meticulously. His hair was neatly brushed, and he felt in nearly every way possible the ideal employee.

So when Mr. Posthelwait's secretary answered the phone, Chef Christian LeForrestier's voice was the neatly modulated epitome of a well bred gentleman.

"Good morning. Yes. This is Chef Christian LeForrestier from the

Lodge. I was wondering if it would be possible to speak to Mr. Posthelwait for one moment. Of course."

He held patiently. Everything, he had decided, was going to work out just fine.

The secretary came back on the line.

"And this would regard?" she asked.

What business of it is her's? Chef Christian's smile cracked a tiny bit. He paused and cleared his throat before answering in an even suaver voice than before, "The restaurant. I wish to discuss the restaurant with him."

"One moment." He was on hold again. Impatiently, he drummed his fingers against the coffee table. His wife descended the stairs from the bedroom with ragged hair and a morning cigarette in tow. He hardly acknowledged her smile as she headed for the coffee maker.

Click. He was back on. He thought he heard faint voices discussing something and said, "Hello, hello?" into the receiver, before the secretary came back and said, "Wait one second."

Then the faint voices returned as the secretary covered her receiver with her palm, and Chef Christian realized with horror that things were not going to be OK.

"Two weeks," the secretary finally said, "after the Snowflake party is the first appointment he has open. Would nine in the morning be fine?"

"Yes," Chef Christian managed to say before numbly placing the phone back on the hook.

He glared out into the morning sunshine with a stony face. His wife came over and kissed his cheek with benign innocence. He clasped her hand to his and thought to himself that they would be sorry for this. They would be sorry, because he would not take it sitting down. He would do something. What it was he wasn't sure yet, but it would be dramatic. They would rue the day they cut Chef Christian LeForrestier loose, of that he was certain.

Today he would call in sick and let the Sous take over the kitchen. There was a bottle of '61 Mouton Rothschild in his cellar that he had been meaning to drink for a long while. He would go and purchase a big piece of beef tenderloin at the supermarket, or better yet send his wife down in the Ferrari for it. He would sear it first on the grill and roast it until the center was warm. With the beef he would prepare a *Marchand du Vin* sauce of red wine, butter, parsley and shallots. He would even roast some potatoes. Then he would sit on the deck in his warmest clothes, smoke a gram of hashish from his tiny brass pipe, and watch the alpenglow settle over the mountains. That would be his day. Yes.

Snowmen? What did any of this have to do with some stupid snowmen? Chef Christian suddenly stopped stroking his wife's hand. The vision of Bennett Beauregard's face that filled Chef Christian's mind was not a pretty one. There could be only one person behind all of this trouble. One per-

151

son only could account for the snowmen. Bennett Beauregard must die. Whatever Chef Christian planned as his revenge must include the demise of that fecund blight on humanity.

On the coffee table a two week old, yellowing copy of the *Vail Daily* caught Chef's eye. It was the headline, one he had read many times before, that jumped out at him. *"Lone Wolf Strikes in Beaver Creek!"* it read. *At seven thirty in the evening last night #2666 Prater Lane was engulfed in flames set by eco-arsonist Lone Wolf. Town of Avon Police Chief Dirk Gently released a statement earlier this morning that contained this message received over the telephone from Lone Wolf, 'One more down, a million or so to go. How can we have homes without people and people without homes? The balance must be restored. I will strike again, soon. Those who need fear me know who they are. I am Lone Wolf, and I strike for those with no voice.' Gently says the call was traced to a public phone in Avon, but also added that no suspects have been apprehended in the case. 'All we have so far are several reports from area residents that a loud wolf call was heard in the woods surrounding that area. This seems to be his trademark.'*

A predatory grin creased the corners of Chef Christian's mouth. He took up his wife's hand as the nascent threads of a simple plan began to form and take shape within him. She snuggled closer. Lone Wolf? What spurs a man to take on the whole world? Who was he?

Kris Blaze
May 6, 1981
Final Essay Revision
Ms. Foster

Once upon a time there was a kid who might have been a very different person. If a pretty girl wanted that kid she'd get all she wanted and more. That was normal. Since I'm graduating in less than a month this essay is supposed to be about How I've Grown Since I Came to Alpine Academy. It could stop right here because most of the changes took place before I arrived.

For three years I have lived in the worst room in the worst dorm for what seems like no apparent reason. I haven't changed. This room has no windows. It's cold in winter and hot in summer. If I weren't graduating and being told by everyone it's time to go to college or make the U.S. Ski Team, then I wouldn't move out. Ms. Foster, you said that this essay should be a summary of How I've Grown, and that I should illustrate How I've Grown with examples from my life here at Alpine Academy. Here are some examples you may not like. I'm sure that some of the stuff I'm going to tell you

152

isn't even legal, but since you're my teacher I'm going to hold you to an oath of silence like you're a priest in the Roman Catholic Church. Don't read any more if you can't keep your mouth shut. Please just flunk me instead.

None of this has anything to do with the way I win ski races. But it does have everything to do with people. I don't like people. That's why I live in this room. Two people can hardly fit in here, and when I shut the door I never answer it even if someone knocks. Which is why I like skiing more than, say, football. That's because it's an individual sport and I don't have to rely on any people who might be on my team and are not very dependable.

Here at Stratton Mountain most of the people who own big houses and read the *New York Times* on the chairlift come from New York or Connecticut. I don't like most of those people because I don't think they respect where they are when they come out here. They'd never think to ski off a trail and into the woods, even though that's what skiing really is, and they have the most expensive equipment for sitting around the bar. Some of them send their kids to school here at Alpine Academy, which is another reason I don't answer my door when someone knocks. It's so pathetic to watch people like Jenny Yarnell, whose parents live in the east nineties (that's a quote), fake an injury before the races and then go up to Daddy's house on the side of the mountain and put her foot up on the couch with a movie on the television. I don't care that she doesn't want to race, I just wish she didn't have to fake an injury not to do so.

If all this sounds like I don't like rich people even more than most people, then maybe you're right. I'm a scholarship student, which means I have to work in order to have any money. And this is where I might get into trouble. Because this past winter I worked as a ski tech at Precision Skis, which was a pretty fun job because we got to listen to the stereo and tune skis all night while we drank a few beers and smoked some pot. There was a rich guy from New York who started coming in last winter on the weekends. I'm not going to tell you his name, because if you know anything about this- which you should if you've more than looked at a newspaper lately- you'll know everything you need to know.

He was a real skinny person and not in very good shape. His calves were about as thick as his biceps, and his skin was a sickly yellow color that reminded me of fluorescent lights. He worked on the stock market trading something and was used to shouting whatever he wanted above the din of people who were always crowding the shop in the mornings and afternoons. We'd see him come in the door and sure enough, two seconds later, we'd hear his voice coming from the back of the pack as he elbowed his way through to the front.

If he caught your eye that was it, you were dead. He locked on like some dogs will with their jaws and shook you until you finally had to listen to him demand, "Kris, quick, my skis. It's important!" And then you'd drop what you were doing and go get his rental one eighties before going back to the people you were helping earlier who always looked at me with disappointment after those episodes.

Me and the other techs would go skiing some days on weekends when I wasn't racing and that's when I saw his house. It was under construction, with plastic tarps draped around it to protect the workers from the cold. It was right on the side of the mountain in a private nook carved out of the birch trees. He was just getting into skiing, which wasn't a bad thing, but he was a little too impatient. Mid-way through the winter he decided it was time to purchase his first skis, which was something he'd wanted to do from day number one. If we'd been like any other ski shop we would have taken his money. But, no. We convinced him to rent for the first months. Start on one sixties we told him. Two weeks later try one seventies. Then go to one eighties. Do it with rentals, you'll save money. He was a rank beginner and took our advice, which is something I really do think he appreciated. He bought all his ski clothes from us, Bogner suits for his girlfriend and quilted Roffee pants for himself. This guy looked like a million bucks out on the slopes until he tried to turn. Pat, the owner, even went out to dinner with the guy and we all started treating him like our star customer.

When he walked in the door we jumped. And it wasn't like we really minded because we all understood that's how the game is played. We fell all over ourselves for Mr. New York, and even competed with each other for his attention. We smiled brighter for him, stood straighter, and spoke better. For our services we received little cash tips folded into tight squares and pressed covertly into our palms like love notes received from a girl in seventh grade. What we thought about him was not in accordance with the way we acted around him. But that's just business, and something I learned about from my Dad's mistress, who probably had a much harder time of it than I did with Mr. New York.

He wanted skis on that Friday evening at seven o'clock when he pulled into the parking lot in his Range Rover, darted out of the cold and in past the magnetic gates Pat had installed at the front door to catch shoplifters. The afternoon rush off the slopes had died down about an hour before and all that was left to do were the ski tunes for tomorrow morning. Only myself, Eric Osborne, whom you know, and a couple of other techs were in the back of the shop running the edge grinder and waxing skis with the tunes turned up way loud on that night. I saw the headlights first and yelled, "Dibs!" before anyone else, put the iron I was waxing with down, took off my apron, and went out to greet Mr. New York.

Ms. Foster, if human nature can tell us anything it's that all of mankind are born fools. This is our natural state, and to try and deny it makes fools of us all the more. Wisdom, I believe, is a state achieved by a fool when he or she comes to grips with their own foolishness. I am not yet wise. I am too full of anger about what I see in this world. My daydreams are constant and usually center around the same fantasy, one where I am re-united with the family I never had and have never known. I am a foolish person, have known it, and when it comes down to it that's what this essay is all about: my foolish actions.

You see, I can't write an essay about How I've Grown Since I Came to Alpine Academy, because what I've done can't correctly be called growing. I've grown physically. I'm taller now, and heavier. But my mind has done something which I can only think of in terms of a big, black stew pot that's filled with broth and vegetables, and been on the fire for about three years. I believe the proper term is 'stewin'. There have been some wrongs in my life which cannot be corrected. My foolish actions? I try to remedy things which I feel are in need of a remedy. Is there a symbiotic relationship between the wrongs done to me in the past and my work as a renegade vigilante? I suppose there would be some truth to that supposition. But then again, I am a fool, and only a fool would believe a supposition as spurious as that.

Ms. Foster, here's what needed a remedy:

Up on the side of Stratton Mountain are gigantic houses owned by people residing hundreds and hundreds of miles away. Beneath the houses are leach fields for their septic tanks. At the power station coal is constantly being burned, or atoms split in order to heat the empty houses on the side of Stratton Mountain. In the Pacific Northwest we are cutting timber for more houses. Houses that are, in my estimation, superfluous, and an unnecessary burden on our already strained ecosystem. Am I crazy or is this wrong? It turns in my head, a simple chain reaction of push and pull, spinning like a bad machine. Cut the trees to make room for boxes made of dead trees. Burn the trees for heat. Will we have a planet resembling New York City, a place where everything beautiful has been labeled and purposely left, protected from economic predation? Will we survive with only isolated pockets of natural beauty that are surrounded by roads, houses, convenience marts, and gas stations? Will the vast interior of the United States finally be filled?

How's that cliche go? *Lord, all I ask is for the knowledge of what I can change, and the wisdom to leave alone what I cannot.* Well, I know what I can't change is the economic momentum of this country. But, call me a fool, I can't help trying in my own little way.

He wanted skis of his own, and he already had them picked out. Atomic GS skis. The ARC Bionic system, which if you don't know, has the best graphic design, brightest colors, and biggest advertising campaign behind them. Almost all of the Austrian National Ski Team uses them. They're excellent stiff skis, and the most expensive, of course. He wanted a 190 cm length, which was too big for him at that point. He'd been learning on recreational K2 skis at a 180 cm length. Skis of that type flex easily; they bend around bumps and troughs, which is what a beginner skier needs.

Switching to the Atomics would be akin to strapping greased railroad ties to your feet after skiing on the K2's. The Atomics would not flex without some serious leg strength. Mr. New York was going to find himself riding a wild horse before he knew what was happening. Point those Atomics downhill and you're going fast before you know it. Try to turn? If you aren't used to them it will take a long, wide jarring traverse of the slope, with your edges scratching the ice, and your feet cramping with the effort. No, I had some reservations about sending him out on those skis, but there wasn't much I could do to stop him.

So, of course he needed bindings. And the bindings he wanted were Markers, MRR bindings. In the vernacular, "Mr. R's" are a race binding with a pivot heel that will not release in a light fall. Racers like them for this reason. When we race we jar the skis much harder than even the most aggressive recreational skiers. We need a binding that only comes off in the most extreme cases, otherwise we'd constantly lose our skis while we were still on our feet. We know the risk we're taking with bindings like these. It's a necessary risk, one that must be taken in order to race. But for Mr. New York? I could not, in good conscience, send this man out on the slopes with those bindings. I knew he wanted them for the same reason he wanted Atomic skis, Roffee pants, and Descente jackets. There are no limits to the power of vanity. All the 'real' skiers use Atomics and Markers. Mr. New York was as human as any of us.

Finally, I excused myself for a second and went to the back of the shop where I called Pat. He owns the place and it would have to be his call whether or not Mr. New York got to buy MRR's. I explained it all to him and there was a bit of silence before he said, "Go ahead, but make sure you set them way low."

That night I took the twenty dollars Mr. New York tipped me and bought the shop a case of Budweiser and a fifth of Jack. We were there until eleven o'clock finishing the ski tunes. As I mounted up Mr. New York's Atomics with the Markers I had a feeling that things were not going to turn out well.

The next morning he was in early and I went through the release tests with him. We got him up on a bench, in the skis with his boots on. I set the bindings on low resistance. Then I had him try to twist out of the bindings using just his leg strength. He still had a lot of trouble, so I lowered it as far as it would go, which was better, but still pretty stiff for him.

Hey, I had washed my hands of it at that point. When he walked out that door with those skis over his shoulder I really hoped he'd still be on his feet the next time I saw him.

It was that Sunday, one day after I had set him up, that the inevitable happened. What possessed him to try the bumps in his Atomic GS boards I'll never know. But, miracle of miracles, he managed to spear a nearly impenetrable mogul with both skis and rocket forward so that his head bounced against the ice and the skis popped up behind him in a sort of delayed somersault. What this did to his knees was flex them in the wrong direction and blow out both of his Posterior Cruciate ligaments. Translation: major reconstructive surgery and serious problems walking in his old age. Those bindings hadn't released like I knew they wouldn't, and boy oh boy was Pat sweating it for a good reason. The letter came in the mail about a week later, which is why Precision Skis is no longer a living business. I'm sure you've driven by and seen the 'for rent' signs in the window. It was Mr. New York's attack dog lawyer that did in Pat. They settled out of court after his negligence had been well established by the star witness: myself.

But they didn't stop there. They were going after everyone. Pat and the entire Stratton Mountain Corporation were getting sued. Mr. New York wore a neck brace and stared balefully at the jury from his wheel chair during all the court sessions. I didn't hold back. I testified truthfully that Mr. New York had been a dumb ass too. Pat kind of deserved what he got, but in a way he really didn't. Somebody else would have sold him those same skis with those same bindings if we hadn't. I know that.

In the case against Stratton Mountain the jury was only out for about one hour before they came back with a decision that granted Mr. New York exactly one dollar for his pain and suffering. This didn't go over very well with him, and he and his lawyer started an appeals process. It's still going on today and could last longer than a decade if they keep it up.

That's the reason Mr. New York stopped the construction on his house. It was a small way for him to stick his middle finger up in the air at the entire Stratton community. If it was going to take a decade for this court battle to get settled, Stratton Mountain was going to have to deal with the eyesore of a half completed house on its slopes. He finagled a court injunction barring any interference with his house and property pending the final outcome of his court case against Stratton Mountain.

He left it as is. Piles of black shingles sat next to ice covered lumber. It resembled an ugly, bleached skeleton the way the frame weathered. The plastic tarps, tattered and flapping, were like so much decaying skin.

That, I think, is what really got me. At least completed houses grant your eyes the illusion of a healthy environment. But this house, the incomplete, decaying child of a sick capitalist, represented everything that was wrong with the world. This house was not an affront to the community of Stratton Mountain. This house was much worse. It denied the nobility and grace of nature. Would you let a festering canker or a pus ridden boil go untreated on your body? Of course not. So why let one sit in your community? Why let a court sanction its existence?

I realize that not everyone shares my views. Many of us can't look past our own needs. I think I owe my world view to my father, who taught

157

me everything that is of no value. I want to eat, and I want a place to sleep. If I don't need a car that's even better. But I can't help looking at what everyone else covets in this world. When I watch television I almost get physically ill. Perhaps this is because I can feel an instinctual desire within me. I could want a new car, fast food, mutual funds, and cigarettes if I let myself. It is a battle, one that I fight constantly as if I were an ascetic monk who lacked faith in God. This is the animal within me caged by my ideals. What I want on one very base level is not consistent with what is good for me or the world. This, I suppose, is the human condition and the root of our foolishness. It's hard not to give in, especially when it seems everyone else has. And those are the best reasons I can give you for the pure, unadulterated rage that consumes me on a daily basis.

My eye is critical, my decisions, especially concerning myself, are swift and merciless. When I die my ashes should be scattered. My vision of hell is a simple one. A steel and plastic airtight casket that preserves me in a mummified state and seals my body away from rejoining the natural cycle of life and death is hell. Lenin is in hell where he belongs. The Egyptian Pharaohs are in hell. Sometimes it feels like I am in hell. Trapped in a car, listening to a commercial on the radio, locked in a traffic jam, people all around me, none of whom I can talk to, only the one sided dialogue of the radio mimics my questions and thoughts like a trumpeting parrot.

Right now, I feel an intense desire to stop writing this essay and watch television instead.

I'm back. What was intended as a half-hour break stretched predictably into two hours. A soporific, calm trance held me softly for those one hundred and twenty minutes. With what majesty did I disdainfully hold myself aloft from the simple pleasure of absorbing each program and commercial as if I were a sponge? My comments to my fellow dormies were punctuated with cynical barbs. We watch television in a communal lounge area that smells of stale doritos, old noodles, and burnt ozone. The television, focus of all our attentions, is perched on an old stone hearth and recessed into what used to be the fireplace. This is our community. Most of my happier times in this dorm have been spent in front of this television. This is a fact that I hate, but it is an undeniable fact. Warmth radiates from the off-colored screen in a way that must be reminiscent of the old fires lit in winters past. Sometimes we sit and talk, leaving the television on, while our attention darts back and forth between the screen and what we are saying.

Tonight I had control of the remote and played a favorite game of mine. With the sound turned off I ad libbed my own dialogue into the mouths of the nameless, faceless, pretty people pantomiming to each other with sincere sincerity about him and her, her and him, them and all the others that have no relevance with reality. I made them say the most banal, crude things possible. I made their smiling faces talk about anal sex, shit, blood, cock-

158

sucking, anything that would corrupt the easy mall mentality their image has helped engender.

When I finally turned the sound back on some smiling half-wit on screen suggested, "If we all sit down and talk about it we can work this out!"

Is that a cliche?

Another thought: if I don't turn in this essay I will not graduate. Just a thought.

The house. I started at the base of the main lift around seven o'clock that night. Look in the papers, they'll tell you the exact date. Since I had never done something like this before, I wasn't really sure what I should bring. Eric Osborne, who lives down the hall and is the closest thing I have to a friend, owns a copy of The Anarchist's Cookbook. It tells you how to make pipe bombs and other stuff, but I decided to go with a trusted old formula of gasoline, rags, and as much spare timber as I could find. It took me only twenty minutes to reach the house on my telemarks. Of course they didn't have a guard dog or anything like that.

The way the house loomed above me that night was almost frightening. I snuck around the perimeter, while dodging flapping tarps, in order to scout possible points of conflagration. I moved like I've seen people do in war movies: bent over low to the ground and constantly glancing back over my shoulder. Two window frames mounted up on the second storey glared down at me like the vacant eyes of a skull. The vast infinity of the clouded night sky floated through their empty frames in a silent mass from horizon to black horizon. I moved like a rat beneath their mute gaze, gathering bits of wood and other combustibles, periodically ducking under a tarp to deposit my loads in messy nests at the bases of half completed staircases and ice encrusted doorframes.

I found plenty of scrap bits of particle board and 2 X 4's underneath the tarps and snow. These I gathered into one large pile in the center of the dark house. I was concerned that the ice on the beams would prevent the fire from catching, but when I finished dousing each pile with gasoline and tossed those matches, the flames licked quickly up the frame and spread to the particle board ceiling where they fanned across in a blue wave before joining in the center with a sharp clap and a sudden draft of cold air pulled in from outside. I was down the slope in less than five minutes, stashed my skis in what used to be the shop, then caught the bus back to campus.

No more Mr. New York's house. By now I'm sure you've read what was printed in the town paper. You've probably even read the anonymous letters printed during the months following the fire that suggested the fire department torched the house as a public service for the whole town. I guess everyone was kind of chuckling about it under their breath, because the only person who really minded was Mr. New York. He's started another lawsuit. This one claims malicious conspiracy against him by the town of

Stratton.

It all started with me. And it ended with me too. In a short story or a mystery novel this would make sense. But I got away. Maybe Philip Marlowe, or Miss Marple will show up and nail me. If so, I hope it's Philip Marlowe because he'd probably let me ditch it down to Mexico with some dangerous blond femme fatale who killed her husband. But in the meantime, it's just myself, as I've always felt. Maybe I'll go to college. Hopefully I'll make the U.S. Freestyle Team and tour Europe.

I've decided I'm not going to turn this in to you Ms. Foster. I may be a fool, but I'm not foolish. This means I won't even have a high school diploma. There was a time when I was certain of all the things that I had and that I would have. But something crept in and spoiled it all for me. Imagine a television character that has no life off the set. He believes the father he breakfasts with in the morning is his real father, and that his house and school are real, in a real neighborhood. One day he wanders through a nondescript gray door and finds himself off the set. He sees the directors, the cameras, the people who have been deciding for him all along. He sees the actor who plays his father and he's drunk, with a cigarette dangling out of his mouth, while he harangues somebody over the phone.

Shaken, he goes back through the gray door to the happy house and happy people and finds that he doesn't fit anymore. 'Just smile,' the other actors tell him, 'and let them believe you're the same.'

He leaves. That show is still running today. Same time, same channel every day. It runs without him, chugging along with the foolish energy of a million souls that don't know any better. But that actor returns sometimes, underground, and like a character run amok, he ad libs from the script, disrupts scenes and steals the show. He returns from exile just to remind us, to tell us all how foolish we really are.

And that actor? He's no saint. He struggles with himself, watches television, covets things. He can't help but be human.

Kris Blaze never graduated from Alpine Academy. And it is a historical fact that on February 24, 1981, in Stratton Vermont, the half-completed house of Joseph Swan, a New York bond trader, was consumed by an arsonist's fire. Those are the facts that we have. But as we all know, in real life, one plus one does not always equal two.

The essay? It surfaced years after the facts had all been discussed. Supposedly, it was discovered by students on an old carbon typewriter ribbon. The entire essay was transcribed from a single tape pulled out of the cartridge. Did Kris Blaze actually write it, or is it a fiction created around the legend?

But these are known facts. Back to the mystery. Back to the people who surrounded him during those unconscious days in Vail. No special historical event had taken place. No connection had yet been noticed between those legends of the wild west, Doc Holiday, Billy the Kid, and others who used to frequent the Colorado wilderness, and one crazy arsonist. No one yet saw the bridge between past and present that would allow one man to walk freely between death and life like Elvis, Amelia, Christ, Jim Morrison, or the old Billy the Kid who, legends tell us, continued to wander the New Mexico desert until the middle part of this century. No one, least of all his neglected girlfriend, saw the potential in Kris Blaze.

Two years previous to the events that occurred at the Snowy Mountains Guest Lodge, during late August, a Toyota Camry bearing California plates slowly wound its way east through the construction of the Glenwood Canyon section of Interstate Seventy. Kellie Kay had been in no hurry to reach Vail since leaving her hometown of San Jose a week earlier.

She had driven out through Tahoe, past the roads leading to Heavenly, Kirkwood, and other ski areas in the Sierras where she had cut her teeth during high school and college days at the University of San Francisco. In Tahoe, she had stopped at the MGM for a farewell hand of blackjack. In her mind she had planned this first and last trip to the gaming table as a nostalgic farewell to an area she had known all her life. But she lost the hand and it pissed her off for reasons she did not entirely understand. She was on the move again, and this time she was certain things were going her way. She drove on past the wooded pine forests of Western Nevada, through Reno, and east onto the loneliest road in America across the Nevada desert in a straight line. Desert mountain ranges separated by wide, flat waterless areas of sand and sage rolled underneath the wheels of her car. She was halfway across this desert and on her way into Utah before realizing, as if she were still a college English major, that her five dollar hand of blackjack symbolized the random chances of life that consistently dogged her on her determined path.

It was night. She drove under a sky as clear as she had ever seen and passed a bordello lit with neon signs, surrounded by barbed wire and several mobile homes, honked her horn and raised her middle finger in the air while tears streamed down her cheeks.

Kellie Kay had grown up on the west coast under the most crowded of circumstances. Her parents had divorced when she was seven years old and she had gone to live with her father in the safety of the suburban developments that surround San Jose rather than with her bohemian mother in the Haight district. She had not yet heard of Andy Warhol and his famous prediction of fifteen minutes fame for everyone when she entered a phase of her life that would forever alter her perspective on success.

California is a breeding ground for all kinds of athletes. But the hot

161

sun of the south, and the even, temperate climate of the north lend a certain attraction toward aquatic sports. After two summers of swimming lessons at the community pool it was a natural step for Kellie Kay to join the local age group team and embark upon an athletic career that would mirror the random hand life deals all of us.

At the age of ten she resembled most children her age, neither stronger, faster, nor smarter than the others. Popular and well adjusted at school, she was just beginning to experiment seriously with make-up. But, she worked hard in the pool, and pushed herself more than the other girls. This was her outlet and her creation. She controlled herself in the pool, and pushed herself to where the other girls could not.

By the time of her twelfth birthday everything had changed. Kellie Kay stood five feet six inches tall. Her long arms and legs made her feel awkward and self-conscious in school. She towered over most boys. Only in the pool did her body feel comfortable, supported by the water, she lost her inhibitions and let herself go. It is a strange phenomenon that occurs with younger female swimmers. They blossom like impatient flowers, reaching the top of their respective pyramids at an age when their fathers continue to drive them to practice and don't yet allow them to date.

Kellie Kay swam the hundred and two-hundred meter butterfly. In nineteen eighty, when she was fourteen years old, she finished second only to Mary T. Meagher, in both events, at the U.S. National Championships in Indianapolis, Indiana. That same year she traveled to Berlin and Sydney, Australia as a member of the U.S. National team. With her teddy bears and Judy Blume novels she moved out of her father's house and in with a strange family in Mission Viejo so she could train full time with her eyes set firmly on making the 1984 Olympic team that would compete in the Los Angeles Olympics. Her life revolved around the pool. Practice in the mornings at five a.m.. Weight lifting in the afternoon. Then practice again, two more hours in the pool. Her favorite hobbies were sleeping and eating. Then a strange but predictable event transpired; one over which she had no control. The same month her photograph appeared on the cover of *Swimming World*, Kellie Kay's body began to change.

She could remember it almost to the date. When her breasts and hips grew she was at first pleased. One day she was cruising through practice like always. Two months later her coaches covertly clocked her with stopwatches and shook their heads in unison.

Puberty, for female swimmers, is a risky time. Some retain their skills, keep their muscle tone and speed. But in Kellie Kay's case the change was too radical. Her breasts, formerly slim and efficiently shaped, now dragged through the water like weights attached to her chest. Her hips, the perfect bottom half of her hourglass figure, were no longer the slim, lean flanks of her pre-pubescence. She attempted dieting, and even considered surgery. That more boys asked her out on dates was no consolation.

At the house she lived in with two other swimmers, Kellie Kay examined her naked body in a full length mirror. With an open palm she cupped her breasts, then slapped her thighs in disbelief. She had not asked for this new body. It wasn't fair that her mother was a hippie, nor that she and her dad were on their own. None of it was fair. It was reality and she could not change it.

Reality abruptly clipped her goals. The life of a swimmer, the smell of chlorine on her skin, trips to meets with friends, the pressure: all the familiar and comforting elements of swimming could not be abandoned easily by a young woman who had made them the central focus of her life.

Her new goal was simple. A college scholarship at a major university would justify her time and effort. For two years she struggled with her shattered hopes. Her coaches consoled her. Friends whom she had beaten easily in previous years blossomed and made the trip to Indianapolis and the National Championships without her. But she never complained, she only worked. Every cold winter morning at the outdoor pool, after the warm-up set had been written on the blackboard, the first splash into the cold water was the sharp report of Kellie Kay's determination to persevere despite the odds.

Her coaches consulted and a switch was made. She was converted to a distance swimmer. Her practices consisted of long un-interrupted swims over a thousand yards in length. Three times a week she and the other distance swimmers abandoned the tyranny of the enclosed pool and swam for two hours, out past the surf, in the open ocean. Her comeback, she felt, hinged upon her determination and work ethic. Therefore nothing could stand in her way.

Until the pain came. Razor blades invaded her shoulders, carving her, with each stroke, into hunks of numb flesh. Tendinitis was diagnosed, the result of hours of grinding, repetitive strokes. The advice of her doctor was rest. She returned to San Jose, a town she had left two long years previously with dreams of fame and Olympic gold. A junior in high school, she picked up the remains of vestigial friendships. And on weekends, she began skiing with her father in the Sierras.

She had done all she could only to have what had seemed certain taken away. Kellie Kay finally clipped off her water wings, but like a former spouse who has been divorced she consoled herself that it had been her own choice. Just as she would think in years to come that it was she who had left Kris Blaze, she covered her eyes and imagined she controlled what happened.

In Vail, she had persisted at Beaver Creek Ski School and found the time necessary to earn her full certification as an instructor with the Professional Ski Instructors of America. Her vacation time had been spent at clinics in Taos, Jackson Hole, and other resorts in the Rockies. Contacts at various ski schools knew her name and remembered the stunning blond who was patient with herself as well as her students. At twenty five, talented, with skills in high demand, she could conceivably go anywhere within the large network of the skiing world and earn a decent living. As she gathered Kris Blaze's belongings into an orderly pile in one corner of the room her decision to leave the man who had already left her was made.

It was time to find her own place, her own Telluride or Aspen. She would move somewhere where her career would grow with the ski resort. She wanted to build something constructive, contribute to the growth of a small area somewhere, possibly, in Montana where her input would be instrumental and her work the possible foundation for a whole philosophy of teaching. This is what she told herself. There was an area she had heard of called Snoball. It had two old chairlifts and a single access road frequently buried by avalanches. Tomorrow she would call a friend in Montana and inquire about the possibilities. She was young, without a family, debt, or any other hindrance. Now was the time for her to take a gamble and get in on the ground floor.

When she heard back she would talk to Kris.

Kellie Kay leaned over the carpet as if she were gathering a crop. Her hands moved quickly and smoothly. For the present the situation would continue as it was; she would harvest, without complaint, the varied things Kris Blaze carelessly dropped.

As these thoughts galvanized within Kellie Kay, a long white stretch limousine bearing the distinctive horns of a Texas steer upon the radiator grill glided soundlessly beneath the carriageway of the Snowy Mountains Guest Lodge.

For ten minutes, while the Chauffeur checked himself and his employer in at the front desk, the humanity sheltered by the tinted windows of the passenger compartment remained hidden. The arrangements made, Bennett Beauregard in tow, the Chauffeur returned and opened the door.

A timid foot, gingerly sheltered by loose velvet slippers, appeared first. Purple silk pajama pants followed the foot. And when, at last, the whole person was revealed in his robe and stetson, with an aged face as wrinkled as a prune, and an oxygen mask and tank respectively attached to his nostrils, Bennett Beauregard whispered very gently into the old man's ear, "Welcome to the Snowy Mountains Guest Lodge, Mr. Blazekowski. Welcome."

For through the years after their separation Ike Blazekowski had kept track of the life of his semi-famous son. And now, as he felt death approaching, he craved one last audience with the boy he had raised as his own and to whom, despite it all, he had decided to leave with all of his fortune.

164

Chapter 8:

In which we reach the
inevitable conclusion.

The morning of the Snowflake party dawned clear and blue after a period of almost a week during which the sun had remained tucked behind a thick bank of snow-clouds which had been hung upon the sharper peaks of the continental divide. There these clouds had hung, dropping snow at a rather constant rate of almost a foot a day, until a precocious wind rose from the south and slid the snow clouds north as easily you might slide an ice cube across a slick countertop with your finger. As the sun rose higher above the eastern mountains, snow, regally piled like icing, revealed itself in a thick layer coating houses, cars, trees, telephone lines, road signs, and elk; turning the Vail Valley into a sparkling white jewel of such intensity that without sunglasses a foolish skier would risk blindness.

Through the early morning light, swaying precariously across both lanes on the slick road, a peculiar Volkswagen Van of an even earlier vintage than Kelley Sapp's made its drunken way up the corkscrew road toward the Snowy Mountains Guest Lodge. It paused at the lodge parking lot for a moment. But nobody was yet awake to see the hand painted daisys that decorated the side of the purple bus. The van sagged above its wheels as if a great and mysterious weight were hidden inside. Muffled giggles came from the interior which seemed to cause the van to shift and rock periodically as if elephants and mice were somehow chasing each other within. The van idled in the lot for some time, occasionaly burping, before the front passenger window rolled down and emitted a white cloud of mysterious vapor into the clean Colorado air. A simple gloved hand emerged from the window and pointed the way down the freshly plowed ridge road toward the white tent.

Slowly, the van ground into gear and bounced onto the road, moving across the length of the ridge until it reached the tent. A side door flew open, and from a large cloud of smoke, emerged the tumbling contents of the van. There was a total of six - perfectly graduated in height from near-midget to approximate-giant. Their sex was impossible to decipher since they were dressed androgynously in baggy clothes with their hair completely tucked beneath knit woolen caps. Two, the largest and smallest, held snowboards the way rock stars hold electric guitars.

Magically, cigarettes appeared and were lit. As if some strange drug had rendered all incapable of coherent speech, the pantomime began. There were gestures toward the tent and an expedition inside to explore the white tables and frozen flower displays. A ramp flanked by plastic elves and a plastic banner obscured with fresh snow mutely signaled some unknown signifigance to the visitors, as if they were on Easter Island and walking past statues. Like voyagers from another planet they shuffled through the empty tent with awestruck eyes and slackened jaws until they reached the side of the ridge. Without more than a glance at the slope below, both the tall and short snowboarder stepped into their bindings and pushed off onto the virginal slope. The four remaining watched them disappear. Then, as though the clock had struck midnight, they stood straight and ran for the still idling van. They gunned up the ridge and back onto the road as they headed down to pick up their friends.

By nine that morning, nearly an hour after the snowboarders' van disappeared down the road, preparations for the groundbreaking ceremony were well underway. Within the kitchen Kelley Sapp and his waitstaff were marching like ants, bearing tray-pans and platters of various foodstuffs. They moved in a continuous circle from the refrigerators out to the large trucks idling by the loading dock then back to the refrigerators. They had been doing this for an hour and still had possibly another hour to go. When the trucks were finally loaded they drove them out to the large circus-style tent which had been erected on the top of the ridge. At the tent they began the process anew by hauling food out of the trucks and into the tent - truck-tent, tent-truck, truck-tent, tent-truck. After the food had been loaded into chafing dishes, sternos lit, corks popped, plates and silverware arranged on the buffet, Kelley and his waitstaff would return to the lodge and change into their special sno-flake costumes. At eleven o'clock in the morning the prospects of the day had already made Kelley exhausted, stressed, and somewhat irate.

Round tables covered with white linen had been arranged within the tent. Red banquet chairs circled the tables. All these had been set the day before, along with the namecards and flower arrangements. Five white roses in Limoge vases had been placed in the center of each table. The roses had frozen during the night. When Kelley and his crew arrived with the trucks and turned on the portable heat generators the roses quickly performed a predictable flop.

Earlier in the morning, the entire southern wall of canvas had been lifted away from the ground and tied to the roof posts to provide those within the tent a view of the virginal ski course arranged on the slope beneath them.

At the lip of the ridge a small snow ramp had been constructed. Over this ramp hung a large blue banner which sagged in the middle with a load of snow that hid the message printed upon it. Two life-sized plastic elves, which had been created as mascots for the area, waited on the edge of the ramp with a blue ribbon between them. The elves' names, for unspecified reasons, were Gerald and Betty. They bore happy expressions and gestured with their arms toward the slope beyond the ramp. For it was between these two elves that Kris Blaze was to push off for his inaugural run. With a broomstick Kelley knocked the snow down out of the banner. He leaned backwards and read, "ALL YOU WANT AND MORE OF IT!/ SNOWFLAKE IS IT!"

"Uh, huh," he mumbled skeptically before proceeding to the edge of the ramp, where he brushed the snow off Gerald and Betty, all the time resisting the temptation to push them over into the great drifts piled beneath the ramp.

Pausing for a moment's rest from his labor, Kelley contemplated the arrangement beneath him. The course Kris was to ski had been constructed over a week before and was now greatly obscured by over six feet of dry snow. This snow had drifted and piled into large dunes. The five ramps which the groundscrew had set up were no longer visible. Only the large wooden poles mounted with plastic, blue snowflakes, marked where they lay buried. At the base of the ridge, one thousand feet beneath him, a herd of nearly frozen elk wandered in circles through the drifting snow in frenzied attempts to pack it down and keep from drowning. From the ridge it seemed as if they were playing a strange game. Lured down from the high country by a trail of salt pellets and hay, they had been unwittingly penned beneath the ridge for over a week. The older bull elk eyed the ridge with more fear than one might think necessary. They worked silently, neither bugling, nor wheezing, while encouraging the others in the herd to continue with their lunging attempts to forge a path east and into the aspen groves.

To his right, set upon the western end of the half-moon shaped ridge stood the proud periwinkle walls of the Snowy Mountains Guest Lodge. Her higher parapets and towers obscured by mist rising from her bowels, she melted back and forth between dream and reality. Something so surreal and fairy tale-like, when seen from a distance, carried her with a plastic nobility and saccharine shallowness that had Kelley closing his eyes and imagining her gone. He spun on his heel and returned to the trucks. Z was leaving tomorrow. With Snowflake safely under construction, Bond's work was finished. She would, no doubt, demand his final answer today.

The night before, while sitting in bed, Kelley had composed yet another of his furiously righteous journal entries. *The Snowy Mountains*

Guest Lodge, he had written, *is building a new ski area. Perhaps this may have seemed inevitable to the casual observer. Just as WWII, the Atom Bomb, Punk Rock and Sid Vicious' death all appear, in hindsight, to have been the only possible result of the particular course of history, (be that personal or a larger scale, it does not matter) which had been embarked upon at an earlier, more innocent, stage. What are the next steps in the progression? Will we put a chairlift on Everest along with a road to the top? Who will push the button first? Which young man or woman is willing to be the next martyr for an unspecified cause that we could name angst? These progressions gather speed like avalanches. By the time we see their approach, what started as a silent accumulation of minuscule particles culminates in an overwhelming wave which plateaus at the next level; in our case a new ski area. Another wilderness section of Colorado will be developed. It is simply the continuation of a process begun long ago. As if each piece of the world which has not yet been tilled, cut, or otherwise touched irrevocably is a domino standing in line and waiting for its turn to fall. Until the next progression comes in the form of an even bigger ski area, or a younger dead pop star, or a better bomb, we will continue to dwell beneath the umbrella of our current illusions. When will everything come to a head? No one can stop it, not even the people who started it. Even though I couldn't halt anything this fact still bothers me; a new ski area is under construction at the Snowy Mountains Guest Lodge.*

He had just put down the pen when there was a knock upon his bedroom door. Kris Blaze poked his blond haired blue eyed head in. "Kelley," his eyes surveyed the dirty room and Kelley's nest of a bed; a naked mattress covered with his faded orange sleeping bag, "can you drive me up to the lodge tomorrow for the ceremony?"

"I have to be there at nine in the morning. You don't ski until two o'clock, do you?"

"Yes. Shit, I'll probably just have to hitch it."

"You can take my van. You'll just have to drop me off in the morning."

"That'll have to work. Goodnight." Kris winked at Kelley and disappeared. Neither one slept well. In the morning Kris was too tired to make the drive.

"Kellie," he rolled over on the trampoline and rubbed her shoulder back and forth, "will you do me a huge favor and go with Kelley so you can drive the van back?"

"Ohhh, why don't you go yourself?"

"Because I wouldn't be as companionable as you would. My whole body feels like a punching bag. I skied all day yesterday."

"Can't stand to hear you whine like that. Only if I get to drive up with you this afternoon and watch."

"Absolutely," Kris mumbled before rolling over and resuming his snores.

On the drive up to the lodge Kellie Kay rested her head against the passenger window and slept all the way into the parking lot. Kelley poked her awake.

"Come inside and get some coffee before you drive down," he had suggested.

"No, I'll be fine." Kellie hopped out of the van and walked around to the driver's side. She'd shut the door and was about to toss the stick into reverse when Kelley, who hadn't moved since stepping out, tapped on the glass and motioned her to roll down the window.

"I haven't seen you in a while and I thought I should let you know something." Kellie Kay's drowsy face perked up. The mist cleared from her eyes and her nose twitched.

"I might be leaving soon. I still haven't made up my mind about it, but it is a possibility. We can work out an arrangement with the rent, I suppose."

"Where will you be going?"

"I don't know. I'd be with somebody, but I can't decide if I want to live with her."

"I'm leaving Kris," Kelley was the first person she had told.

"That's understandable. Where will you go?"

"I'm moving to Sno Ball, Montana. I've already been hired as a ski instructor for the remainder of the winter. I've got a cabin with a woodstove and a pet porcupine out back."

"Have you told Kris?"

"Today I will."

"That's good."

They watched each other curiously until Kelley was reminded of the first day they had met. That obligatory curiosity with which they had viewed each other was still present. Perhaps, he felt, they were in some ways right for each other. He was about to suggest something crazy when Kellie shook her head.

"No," she said.

"No?"

In later years Kelley would look back upon that moment and come to understand what Kellie had already known. They never knew each other and had never taken time to probe beneath the skin. Their curiosity was the same as a child's at Christmas when faced with the bright mystery of a large package covered in gift wrap. That they had slept with each other and lived with each other for a period in no way diminished this truth. There had been people he had met before and after her, people who within five minutes' conversation with him were no longer strangers. But Kellie Kay, Friday, Kris Blaze, and all the others who could possibly have been termed his friends had in actuality been something less than that. They were acquaintances. Strangers, they had met in Vail and then drifted away from each other. Perhaps, if he had lasted at least a full winter, his life there could have been different. Like characters in a movie who walk and talk only to themselves, Kelley's memories of the people he knew in Vail were oddly sterile. Was it just him? He didn't know.

Kellie rolled the window up and roared out of the parking lot leaving Kelley alone. He trudged up the driveway while dwelling upon memories of that first morning when there it was. Standing next to the carriageway, as if in warning, was a peculiarly normal snowman. A proper carrot nose pointed out. Charcoal eyes peeked from underneath the brim of his top-hat. Mawkish stick arms jutted at odd angles from the rounded torso. Completed late last evening by a young child staying at the lodge, the snowman was an approximate replica of the one Kelley had destroyed months earlier. Today, for reasons of maturity, Kelley was in a much better mood. Even though he was going to work at the Snowy Mountains Guest Lodge, he no longer felt the need to vent his frustration.

He softly patted Frosty's hat and made his way into the kitchen with the food, the trucks, the chaos, and the clamor; all that one would expect from a day weighted with the heady, sweet aroma of fruit finally ripened and ready for consumption.

It was hours later before he ran into Z. The food had been unloaded into the tent and the trucks were idling in the makeshift parking area, the chains on their tires gripping the packed snow, while Kelley and his crew of waiters relaxed for a moment before returning to the lodge.

The black Range Rover wound along the road from the lodge bouncing over each knoll and then disappeared into little troughs as it climbed the ridge line toward the tent.

In a buttoned London Fog raincoat that extended to her knees, Z stepped out of the Range Rover and made her way gingerly across the snow in her red cowboy boots.

"Let the others meet you back at the lodge," she said to Kelley. "I've a man who wants to speak with you."

Halfway back and behind one of the knolls she tossed the transmission into park and looked at Kelley.

"I don't know what to tell you yet, but I'll decide by the end of the day." Kelley blew his nose, then added, "I'll tell you right after the party."

"You'd better," Z tossed the stick back into drive and pushed the pedal. They were moving again when she added, "Bond wants me to stay in bed with him all day today. He hates parties, especially this kind. He has two magnums of Cristal on ice and he's opened the balcony doors wide open. We're going to stay in bed, under the covers, and watch from the room. Oh, by the way, there really is someone who wants to talk to you."

"Who's that?"

"Some old man with an oxygen tank. I think it's about your roommate."

"Kellie?"

"No, Kris."

Ike Blazekowski was seated on one of the great leather couches near the stuffed polar bear. In his silk robe and velvet slippers he resembled a decrepit playboy more than an oil mogul whose interests totaled over one billion dollars. He was sucking oxygen when Kelley approached, trying to gather enough strength to speak. In the years since his son had left him, and during the time he had covertly tracked his skiing career, Ike Blazekowski had been hard at work with various ventures which he unconsciously hoped would redeem himself in the eyes of his last child.

When children in Borneo had needed measles shots, Ike Blazekowski's money was there. The earlier goals of his philanthropy had been brassy publication of his own name. But with Kris' disappearance he had stopped wishing for public bridges and buildings to be named for him and had instead been donating anonymously to various institutions in varied ways. At Harvard, the Harriet Tubman Center for Black Womens' Studies had been created with his gift. He had endowed chairs in the petroleum engineering department of the University of Texas that honored Cesar Chavez, Sacco and Vanzetti, and even more perplexing, Teddy Roosevelt. He tried to cover all the bases wanting to seem something other than the dinosaur he was. Throughout it all he seemed to be acting under the influence of something beside his own inclinations. Like a ghost whose presence guides the actions of the living, the spirit of Kris Blaze lived within Ike Blazekowski and goaded him to ridiculous extremes.

It was Ike's last wish that he be reunited with the son he had stolen from a crib some twenty eight years earlier. Now that there was cancer and the end was near, he had come back to Vail for the first time since that Christmas ski trip long ago in one last attempt to stave off the dire prophecies that Tommy Bird had cast upon him and his life like a curse.

"Mr. Blazekowski," Kelley and he shook hands, "I'm Kelley Sapp, Kris' roommate. What can I do for you."

Ike motioned Kelley onto the sofa next to him. If they could have realized the proximity of their lives to one another, they would have been amazed. That Kris and Kelley were natural brothers mattered only to Kris. It had proven the old Biblical tenets correct. *Love thy neighbor as thy brother* had been true in more ways than one. We don't know just how much we all have in common, Kris felt. It sounded like a cliche, but the shock of discovering who his roommate was made it seem profound and undeniable.

Kelley and Ike sat on a couch in the lobby of the Snowy Mountains Guest Lodge blithely ignorant of the fact that they both played central roles

171

in the same great drama. The younger of the two symbolized what small bit of compassion Kris Blaze found within his heart for his fellow human beings. The other had long ago sparked the rage within Kris that went on to catch the dry timber of certain houses. It was the strange dichotomy within Kris Blaze that Ike Blazekowski and Kelley Sapp represented. They composed the psychological ingredients needed by a man who fervently believed his destructive acts were, in actuality, for the general good.

In any case, their meeting, although dynamic in some senses of the word, perhaps even pre-ordained within some celestial outline Tommy Bird witnessed in those stars long ago, was quite uneventful.

"KRIS WILL BE SKIING AT TWO O'CLOCK," Kelley repeated for the third time.

Ike's face lit up. He held two fingers in the air as if he were a simpleton.

"YES. TWO O'CLOCK."

"Will you bring him to me?" Ike croaked.

"I will introduce you when I get the chance," Kelley nodded his head. Only then did Ike let go of the hand he had grasped so tightly.

"Thank you," he whispered, but Kelley was already on his way back to the kitchen. "Thank you."

It was the initial arrival of the media that caused Bennett Beauregard's first flash of concern. The two white vans pulled into the small parking area beside the tent and came to rest with a businesslike air that combined the self-importance and ignorance found only within the small coterie of broadcast journalists. That the two vans now occupied over half of the available parking was obviously no concern of theirs. The side panel door swung open on one van spilling an overweight man who carried yards of black cable wound about his shoulders like rope. These cables he began to attach together and string in long lines across the snow toward metal boxes which jutted with control switches. From the other van came a whirring purr, followed by the emergence of a small satellite dish from the roof. As if it were a butterfly emerging from a chrysalis, the wings of the dish folded slowly down until they extended into a sharp click. After this, the dish began to rotate slowly until it locked online with whichever broadcast satellite among the many floating invisibly beyond the blue sky connected this small van to the international web of news and information encircling our globe.

Three more vans entered the parking lot, and soon the snowfields around the tent began to resemble a forest thick with black vines and the spinning metal superstructures of miniature broadcast stations. Like rival tribes within some jungle, the various crews of journalists jockeyed one another for positions in and around the tent. Reporters applied blush and

172

make-up, religiously preening themselves before stepping in front of the cameras for their practice takes. It all happened within the space of a half an hour. It all happened so fast that Bennett Beauregard had not been given a chance to inspect the area before their arrival.

Followed by two vans filled with tardy newscrews, Bennett Beauregard parked his Ford Explorer at the neck of the driveway and dashed quickly into the tent. He ignored the desperate honking of those TV crews he had left stranded behind his car and frantically began his cast iron inspection of the tent and its surrounding area.

At the starting ramp where Kris Blaze was to launch himself down the ridge, between the two plastic elves, he watched the elk far below him continue their silent assault against the drifts that penned them from the trees. He noted their frenzied leaps, and slow progress with the calculating eye of concern. Conceived within his mind had been a plan which included the scenic presence of elk. Elk were essential. If they were trying to thwart his plans by escaping, then he would stop them.

A cold sense of purpose descended upon Bennett Beauregard like a shroud. A slight shiver took hold of his shoulders and head, as if the cold had bitten through his double breasted wool jacket. At the corner of his mouth, just to the inside of the intersection joining both lips, a small well of white spittle bubbled into the air. With an unconscious hand he wiped the offending foam away, then turned and marched into the tent. His eyes, if anyone had cared to notice, were as black and impenetrable as those of a rat.

The roses, the white roses! A cameraman focused on the drooping centerpiece of one table, unaware of the cold loathing that filled Bennett Beauregard as he watched him pan away.

The tackle was a neat one, down around the knees. When the cameraman fell he landed with his head on the side of a chair. Though it had not been his intention to do so, Bennett Beauregard found it quite irresistible. He clamped his teeth onto the exposed wrist of the unconscious cameraman, just enough to break the skin. With the taste of blood in his mouth, Bennett Beauregard felt such intense pleasure that he almost fainted. He bounded to his feet and walked out of the tent toward a crew of newsmen gathered near one of the vans.

"One of your cameramen's slipped and hurt himself," he said. They followed him inside and circled about the cameraman. Someone left to call an ambulance as Bennett Beauregard cheerfully swept around the tent, gathering the dead roses from their vases. He would head back to the lodge and get more. Then he would figure what to do with the elk. The wheels of his Ford Explorer cut through the snow as he swung around in a crazy arc and clipped the side mirror off on a scrub aspen.

He barrelled down the road toward the looming walls and towers of the lodge like Dracula returning home. His car driven by the same insane ghost which centuries before would have possessed the black coach horses, he disappeared beneath the periwinkle shadow stretched forth from the mist which spewed gaseously, like poison, from the lodge vents. Their wispy tendrils reached out to him, and as he drove he laughed and laughed and laughed as if he were about to die.

The Explorer spun carelessly into the loading area just as everyone else was departing for the tent. There was Kelley Sapp and his waitstaff. Garbed now in their styrofoam snowflake outfits, they piled into trucks and cars and waved to him with pained expressions as they drove off.

Guests filed out to their rental cars or embarked in pairs upon the road for the two mile hike up to the tent. Friday switched the answering machine on at the Front Desk, then stepped out through the foyer. The door closed silently behind him.

When Bennett Beauregard stepped into the kitchen to look for more roses, he was very nearly the only person left in the lodge. He breezed through the kitchen and into the restaurant, past the black table of Lumsden of Strathdrummond, all the time unaware of the fact that someone was following him.

During the two weeks previous to the Snowflake party, Chef Christian LeForrestier had been deeply engrossed in two separate plans of entirely different natures. Sabotage had never really been his style before, but he had done his best with the food. The chocolate crab cakes were laced with a small amount of powerful laxative, as was the game pate. The salmon had been cured in a suspect mixture of vinegar and Chef Christian's own urine. Mixed in with the bread dough was over two ounces of cocaine. He had laced the chocolate mousse with even more Peruvian snow, and had nearly laughed himself to death with visions of the entire party running about in circles, like oversexed hamsters, before they were compelled to squat in the snow with their bare asses and shit like machine guns.

For his other plan he had concocted an elaborate scheme. The mechanics involved with it were very simple. One night he took dental floss and tied it around his wife's leg when she was asleep. Next, he stole into the kitchen clutching the plastic floss box, until he reached the dining room table. On the table was an elaborate gizmo he had created without the help of any technical expertise. A Coleman gas camping stove sat on the table. Attached to it with duct tape was a lighter, the sort that used a trigger rather than a flint wheel. The base of the stove was weighted with bricks. Taped above the circular burner of gas jets was a single cigarette, its tip poised directly above the edge of the jets. Chef Christian tied the floss through a tiny hole he had drilled in the trigger of the lighter. He tied the floss securely, making sure he left enough play for his wife to roll over in her sleep. Next, he opened the gas valve on the stove, then crept to the stereo, put the volume on ten, and blasted Parliament Funkadelic for about two seconds.

The floss went taut. The trigger clicked. A flame came from the lighter, and the stove ignited into a ring of blue flame. With the air of a sophisticated secret agent, Chef Christian plucked the smoking cigarette from the edge of the burner and took a deep drag. When his haggard wife appeared in the doorway and bore down upon him with angry questions, he simply passed her the cigarette and said the one thing she had been waiting two years for him to suggest.

"Why don't we go back to New York? I think I'm going crazy here."

He had waited until nearly everyone had left for the party before stealing into his office and beginning. That Bennett Beauregard would return to the lodge on the heels of a crisis was an act of *fait accompli* so firmly predictable that Chef Christian hardly gave it more than a passing thought. From the window in his office he saw the Ford Explorer skid wildly into the parking lot. Bennett Beauregard's shoulders hunched forward as he ran into the kitchen. Chuckling happily to himself, he turned away from the window and fingered the dull edge of his cleaver before slowly stepping down into the kitchen for the chase. Around one shoulder was a length of nylon cord. In his pocket was a bandanna. He held the dental floss, cinnamon flavored and over two-hundred yards in length, in his right hand. Clenched in his teeth, as if it were a knife, was the cleaver.

Bennett Beauregard wheeled and spun for no apparent reason. *Roses!* Where could they be? Where should he look, he wondered? His heart raced like an engine stuck in neutral. *Roses!*

A deep growl rose from the center of his stomach. White flecks of foam churned on the edges of his lips. Bennett Beauregard sprinted through the tilting hallways in no clear direction, and with no clear plan. The roses were back in the kitchen, where they always were, in the refrigerator. He spun through the halls, stepped out onto balconies and shouted insane gibberish toward the receding couples, neatly dressed in their walking shoes and heavy tweeds, who were disappearing over the first knoll on their way to the tent. He waved and yelled, imploring these couples to do something about the elk, which had managed to move closer to the trees and were madly lunging through the drifts in a slow churn that had them nearly exhausted. Only fear kept them silent and moving away from the ridge.

"Look at those elk jump. You'd think something was chasing them." In his pajamas, Bond stood at the edge of the open balcony. South of him, at the end of the ridge, the three peaks of the white circus tent rose out of the snow white landscape.

"Did you hear someone scream?" Z asked from the bed. She leaned over and pulled the champagne bottle from the ice bucket and refilled her glass. "I could have sworn I heard something."

They were both silent. Out at the tent, Bond could see the tiny figures of well-dressed people doing what could only be described as a cross between jogging and dancing. "Honey, I think they're dancing over at the tent. How funny."

"Shush! Listen!"

Bond was in no mood to be quiet. He had just succeeded in opening the way for Ricky Rico to launder millions of dollars through his new ski area. The potential headaches and losses were enormous, and Ricky Rico had him to thank. In less than two weeks he would be flying into Zurich to meet with the man himself. He was already a rich man, and he was about to get richer.

"Is Pudding frozen?" He petted the dog, which showed no sign of response.

"I doubt it. She just stiffens up in the cold. Joey's wrapped around my feet."

"I think I heard something. Listen, down by one of the balconies."

They both cocked their ears while a stream of obscenities and nonsensical rants floated up to them on a white ribbon of sulfurous mist.

"Hmm," Bond sipped his champagne. "Sounds like someone is in trouble."

"Better go investigate, honey," Z smiled at him from the bed.

"I suppose you're right. Someone could be hurt."

He put on his slippers and stepped out the door.

Bennett Beauregard skidded into the lobby. There it was, the only thing capable of controlling the elk. All thoughts of roses had disappeared from his short circuiting mind. There was only the elk now.

"Do something!" he screamed at the top of his lungs. "Don't just stand there!" He lunged into the arms of the polar bear, the same stuffed polar bear that had fascinated Kelley Sapp those long months ago. Bennett Beauregard wrapped his arms around the Bear's waist and heaved in repeated attempts to move it somehow. If he could just get it out onto the balcony, it might see the elk and go chase them. Only the bear could round them up again. *Only the bear. Only the bear.*

Slowly, stiffly, the bear moved. Bennett Beauregard's grunts were punctuated by involuntary spasms, during which he retched his foaming spittle into the rosy light that spun through the nave of the lobby. He paused for a moment and stared blankly as the blue walls convulsed. A flurry of soft blue stucco floated down from the ceiling. A thin blue laugh echoed along with a voice that intoned gravely, *you are mine.*

The Snowy Mountains Guest Lodge was a decaying and consump-

tive body. A place of cancerous growth, constant depression, and clairvoyant terror. That Bennett Beauregard had always regarded the lodge with a certain degree of possessiveness seemed natural to him. He had never dreamed that it could return the favor with a similar degree of passion.

He made one last lunge with the bear. It toppled out onto the balcony and fell on top of him. Just before he lost consciousness, Bennett Beauregard smiled as the bear leapt the railing like a ghost and sprinted for the elk. He closed his eyes and slipped into unconsciousness.

The clock struck one as both Bond and Chef Christian LeForrestier approached the lobby.

Champagne glass in hand, Bond reached the tragic scene first.

"There's got to be some strange explanation for all this," he mumbled. There was no way in hell he was going to touch any of it. Bennett Beauregard's mouth oozed a clear liquid. He would call the ambulance. It was just as he was about to turn that the cleaver whistled down onto his skull and split it like a nut. Trailing a stream of blood, Chef Christian LeForrestier dragged the body into *Au Naturel*, and disposed of it beneath the black table of Lumsden of Strathdrummond, where it disappeared with an audible plop. To this day the bones have not been found.

With a strength born of Gallic ancestors who regularly slaughtered Romans with abandon, Chef Christian rolled the stuffed body of the polar bear off Bennett Beauregard. He was feeling for a pulse on the neck when Bennett bit him. The movement of the polar bear had stirred Bennett deep within his rabid soul. His first instinct was to bite, and bite he did, down onto the two fingers that palpitated his neck.

Chef Christian responded with a resounding swat to Bennett's head with the flat of his cleaver.

"Fuck!" he screamed, then stuck his bloody fingers in his mouth and sucked until they were clean. After binding them with his shirt tail he began the execution of his plan. He tied the dental floss securely about Bennett's limp ankle before securing his arms with the rope and binding his mouth with the bandanna. Then he abandoned him forever on the balcony and proceeded back to the kitchen, the dental floss unwinding behind him. In the depths of the medieval kitchen Chef Christian arranged his Coleman stove. He tied the dental floss to the lighter's trigger and turned on the gas. He then went to the large kitchen stoves behind him. After snuffing out each pilot light, he carefully twisted the valves for each stove and burner wide open. Gas hissed into the air, the smell of rotten eggs quickly filled the kitchen. His hand over his mouth, he was out the back door before it could overcome him.

Two miles away, over at the tent, no one noticed as a red Ferrari sped down the windy road away from the lodge. Perhaps this was due to the fact that most people were collectively losing their bowels in moaning unison about the surrounding snowfields. Of the few people who had wisely refrained from eating, most were waitstaff and newscrew. Kelley and Friday hurried about, assisting as much as possible, though, in truth, not much practical assistance could be offered during the course of such a personal dilemma.

"Why don't they at least stand still?" Friday wondered.

"Maybe it's the cameras," Kelley said. For camera-people were everywhere, filming the event for posterity. Various people had resorted to scooping the plentiful feces off the snow and hurling it at the camera-people in ironic last ditch efforts to preserve their dignity.

Late comers, who had been warned about the food, mingled at the front of the tent in a valiant attempt to keep the party going. Frank Posthelwait's proud figure churned among them, as did Ike Blazekowski's wheelchair. They drank the wine, which was safe, and blithely chatted away despite the awful smells.

"Look at those elk, they seem close to the forest," Frank Posthelwait said to no one in particular. It was then that Kelley Sapp's Volkswagen Van spun noisily into the parking lot. When Kris Blaze stepped from the van all eyes turned to him. Kellie Kay held his hand as they strode through the newscrews toward the tent. She looked radiant, and he, for some inexplicable reason, carried his skis over his shoulder like a hero.

"Jesus Christ," Kris sniffed the air, "this place smells like a septic tank. Where do I ski?"

A natural gravity pulled all eyes toward him. And as he made his way through the various groups of people filtering about the tent he reminded some of Patton, or Elvis, Paul Bunyan even. Kellie Kay walked proudly by his side. And if there had ever been any justice in this world, then rose petals would have been scattered on the snow before him. All cleared the way for Kris Blaze. All let him pass as he made his way toward the stage which had been set for him. The cameras turned from the wretched scene in the snowfield and focused rightfully upon his broad shoulders and smiling face. Unaware of who sat in the wheelchair watching him, tears streaming down his cheek, Kris marched past Ike and up onto the ramp where he shook his skis in the air and magnificently stretched his body. The Public Address crackled with static as Frank Posthelwait mounted the ramp beside Kris.

"Ladies and gentlemen," Mr. Posthelwait began in the traditional manner, "I would like to thank you all for coming today. Today is the first day in a new era of Colorado skiing. Today is the first day of what I believe will be the finest ski resort in the entire world. This, ladies and gentlemen, is the first day of Snowflake!"

Two miles away, back at the lodge, scattered applause drifted through the open balcony of Z's room like fall's dead leaves. Bond had been gone for at least a half an hour. She finished her champagne with a quick tilt of her head then hopped out of bed. She donned her robe and was about to step through the door and out into the hallway to begin her own search when she smelled the gas. It seeped in through the base of the door with the unmistakable odor of sulfur.

"Oh, Christ!" Z jumped back from the door. The open balcony loomed behind her like a mouth. There was only one way she could leave now. Quickly, she began tying the bedsheets together until she had a long, white rope of dubious strength. One end she fastened to the balcony railing before dropping the remainder over the edge. She watched it tumble and unravel, until the end appeared, dangling at a stop some twenty feet above the snow. Nothing she could do about it, she must move, quickly.

"Come on Pudding," she shook the dog. It did seem stiffer than usual. She put her hand underneath the dog's nose. No breath, nothing, the nose was dry. "Oh, you're dead! How convenient." She gathered Joey from under the sheets and wrapped him around her neck. Just as she was about to put one foot over the railing she remembered the suitcase. Over two million dollars in cash resided in Bond's aluminum suitcase. After checking the locks to make sure they were secure, she tossed the suitcase over the edge and into the snow. Then she began her descent, lowering herself slowly, until she reached the end of the rope and dangled precariously in the air.

She took a deep breath and let go.

At the top of the ramp, poised like a diamond on a mountain of sugar, Kris Blaze waved his pole through the fragrant air one last time.

"Ladies and Gentlemen," Mr. Posthelwait continued his address, "The world famous mogul skier, Kris Blaze, will now perform an inaugural run in honor of this first day in Snowflake history. Kris, take it away!"

He pushed off and swept down. Newscrews rushed to the edge of the ridge, trampling sick people into the snow and kicking others in their attempts to film his descent. The snow was perfect Colorado champagne powder, and Kris carved his way through with the precise symmetry of a pro.

His turns formed long chains of the letter S as he carved through the waist deep crystals that flowed like water around him. He spun and pirouetted into a helicopter at the first ramp, before catching his rhythm down on the snow. A wind kicked across the valley, sweeping up snow devils that vaporized in the sun. He skied, and skied, and that's all that can be said about what he did, about what magic was in the air that day. It was Colorado magic

179

- Colorado snow, sky, air, sun, mountains. It was all beautiful, no one could deny that, least of all those who would try to sell it.

The elk could feel it coming. It raced toward them, swept down from the top of the ridge with a stiff wind, it swiftly roared in among them, a great white bear, its teeth bared and nostrils flaring. Then it was gone. The entire herd reared in panic and broke for the woods.

On the balcony, in the fresh air, a breeze stirred and the prostrate body of Bennett Beauregard began to shudder. Slowly, his cadaverous eyelids lifted, and between the iron railings, far below him at the bottom of the ridge, he saw the elk breaking clear into the aspens.

"No!" he screamed. "No one shall disobey me! Come back here!" he shouted as he rose to his knees. The froth was boiling at the back of his throat, getting ready to jump, when he jerked his leg just a little too hard...

Boom!

The avalanche began only seconds later, with a boom almost as loud as the one that destroyed the lodge. A fracture line appeared in the snow near the top of the ridge. The snow beneath it crumbled away in a runaway slide that sent billowing clouds of fine white snow high up into the air, obscuring the sun and Kris Blaze from sight. There were anxious moments of silence above the low rumble of the cascading snow. Silence that reigned supreme until a high pitched cry, like that of a wolf, echoed out from the billowing depths and spread across the ridge with a volume so terrifying that in the future some would deny that they had heard any such thing. No mortal being could have sent a cry that loud into the Colorado air. Some say it was something else that made that cry of the wolf, a cry so loud and real it froze two of the last elk in their tracks. Their hooves halted by the vestigial remembrance of cries heard by ancestors centuries ago, they succumbed to the wolf and were swallowed by the avalanche mere yards from the safety of the aspens.

The phone call went into the police station only an hour later. *My name is Lone Wolf. I strike for those who have no voice. As long as there are mountains without ski runs I will fight to keep them that way. How can we keep killing ourselves with our own stupidity? I know, what a dumb question. Next on my list are the cows of the world! Ha ha, ha ha! The whole world is becoming warm because of the farts of cows! What is the life of a cow? These questions and more I will answer next time. Ciao!*

And though experts almost certainly confirmed that the voice recorded after the Snowy Mountains disaster did not match those recorded at Killington or Beaver Creek, no one would rule out the possibility that Kris

Blaze was still alive. For days, weeks, months, and years later, after Snowflake was fully operational, they had yet to find his body.

The news crews began their interviews only minutes after the dust had settled. Friday started it all with his mere speculation.

"I was there the night Lone Wolf torched that house up in Beaver Creek," Friday told his story, spinning it out like a yarn, like the old Friday in Robinson Crusoe could never have done because he didn't have the white man's words. Our man Friday made it up for the old one by launching the greatest legend of our century with his voice, "I was there that night. Up in Gerald Ford's house. My friend and I were hanging out. I shouldn't tell you that, but I have to because what I'm going to say next scares the hell out of me." A fine blue dust began to settle through the air, lending a hazy aura to the spectral scene. Neither in nor out of time, the events of that afternoon sparkled with the opaque glitter of immortality, as if frozen in crystal. "We saw Lone Wolf torch that house. We heard him give his cry. Only one man could cry like that. It had to be Lone Wolf. Kris Blaze was Lone Wolf! You can go ask my friend, Kelley Sapp, he was there that night. He'll tell you they're the same!"

But Kelley was gone already. The Snowy Mountains Guest Lodge had been reduced to a smoldering heap of blackened stucco and the charred uprights of Douglas Fir beams that stood like a skeleton framed against the blue sky. As he ran toward the lodge in his styrofoam snowflake outfit tears were streaming down his cheeks.

At the other end of the tent from Friday, Ike Blazekowski began his now famous confessional with a crew from CNN news. "I'm so sorry," he began, then proceeded to spill his guts.

Frank Posthelwait radiantly surveyed the ruins of his lodge. Silently, in his soul, he thanked God that his prayers had been answered.

Kelley found Z stumbling drunkenly down the road toward the tent. Clutched in her hand was the aluminum suitcase. Soot blackened one side of her face and her robe was in charred tatters. He realized she was limping horribly as they ran toward each other.

"Oh, Z!" Kelley hugged her, "You looked positively drunk from far away. I thought you were dead. What did you do to your leg?"

"I am drunk. And I fell out the window. That's what saved my life. Good thing I had this in my hands." She opened the suitcase for Kelley's benefit before asking in a shy voice, "Rio, Darling?"

That night, on a plane flying south, Kelley Sapp gazed out the window at the lights of Colorado and New Mexico as they slid beneath the wings. Down there, unbeknownst to him, the seeds had been sown. Already the story of Kris Blaze was spreading from town to town, his place among the immortals like Jim Morrison, Billy the Kid, and Paul Bunyan growing more secure with every second. He straddled both worlds, both alive and dead, so that whenever some zealous kid sparked a house, or blew a dam, the name invoked would be that of Kris Blaze. His story is known by all but a few. Kris Blaze. He rode that avalanche, pure and white, and lives to this day in the mountains he loves. Kris Blaze could not die! Kris Blaze lives. He lives and will keep on living with those few who managed to pass muster and graduate into the realm of legend.

But you know all this, of course. Life goes on in its mundane way. There is still the story around the story, as there always is ...

At the Silver Aspen Condominiums Kellie Kay packed. A cabin and a new life were waiting for her. She would leave Vail in the morning. Already the future seemed benevolently wide open to her. In her heart, tucked away from the rest of the world, was a small section that would always belong to Kris. Not that she was nostalgic for him or pining. It's just that with age we always leave a little of ourselves in the past. She hummed and went about her work.

Heading toward the equator, Kris Blaze's brother, Kelley Sapp, rocketed away from Vail for what he imagined could be forever on that day in March of nineteen ninety two. A million mundane details, a thousand mundane lies stretched before himself and Kellie Kay and all the rest of us who, unlike Kris Blaze, live lives of relative obscurity for our own purposes.

Kelley had spent less than half a year in the mountains of Colorado. And as he flew south toward a new life with new people and an old girl-friend, he had the presence of mind to realize that he still didn't have a clue, not one single clue, in the whole entire world. That he ever would was something he had seriously begun to doubt.

The End.